ce

...argaret Barnes

Margaret Barnes.

New Generation **Publishing**

Acknowledgements

This novel began life as part of my dissertation for the MA in Creative Writing at the University of Exeter, and I would like to thank my tutors, Philip Hensher and Sam North, who encouraged me to write this story drawing on my experiences at the English Bar. I would also thank fellow students Sue Tong, Ann Castell, Judy Birkbeck and Fenella Montgomery for their advice.

Since I finished the MA, others have added their comments which have been of assistance in producing the novel as it now reads. Amongst them are Sally Flint, Ray Tarleton, Alison Napier, Nuala Butler and Maggie Harkness, and I am grateful for the time they took to read and consider the rough drafts.

Finally there are two people who deserve my special thanks, Kate McCormick who was my writing 'buddy' as we edited each other's books, and my husband Alan who gave me the space to write in the first place.

Margaret Barnes

Chapter 1

Cassie opened the brown covered album of photographs, marked 'Exhibit 1', and found herself looking at the face of a young woman; the blonde hair had been pulled back from the forehead, the eyelids closed, long lashes curled on the high cheekbones, the skin was pale but the lips still bore a trace of raspberry pink lipstick. There was no hint of the violence that had ended the woman's life. Cassie studied the face, compelling in its calm beauty. She traced the outline of the lips with her finger; she felt a sense of loss at this life cut short, then she turned the pages to the photographs of the woman's body, which revealed how she had met her death. Blood from a single stab wound below her left breast had dried into strange shapes across the skin of her torso, defiling her model girl figure. Cassie closed the album quickly; she had seen enough.

She picked up another set of pictures; these showed the scene of the murder, taken some weeks later, in daylight, and after the leaves had fallen from the trees. Holland Walk looked like a country lane, tree-lined on one side and a high brick wall on the other, rather than a pedestrian thoroughfare in the middle of London. Cassie knew Holland Park was closed after dark, but the Walk was not; she had taken that way home often since she had moved to her flat in Notting Hill, but never alone. The path was poorly lit, the overhanging trees created areas of deep shade; just the sort of place for a murder.

She pushed the photograph albums back across the large oak desk, made for her by her grandfather, and

1

because of that, her most treasured possession, and leant back pushing her hands through her short brown hair. The light had faded, and from the windows of her flat, on the top floor of a white-stuccoed house, she let her eyes follow the lights of aircraft heading towards Heathrow, winking across the night sky, then she stood up and leant across the desk to close the curtains, before heading for the kitchen to make her evening meal.

She liked cooking; she had no time for hobbies, but she had to eat, and rather than snack she cooked herself a meal most evenings. Her mother had worked at a bakery until Cassie was born, and while she stayed at home to look after her children – Cassie had a younger sister, Amanda – she had started making cakes for birthdays and weddings to supplement the family income. Cassie had spent her early years in her mother's kitchen, standing on a stool, helping to stir the treacle into gingerbread mixes and the dried fruit into cake batter. Her mother was convinced Cassie would become a chef, and had been shocked at a parents' evening, when in response to her comment that she hoped Cassie would go to the catering college in Blackpool, the headmistress had said she hoped for better things for Cassie. That hope, kindled seventeen years ago, had given life to her ambition, taking her from Lancaster to 3 Burke Court, a set of barristers' Chambers in the Temple.

She continued to cook, experimenting with different recipes, making simple but tasty dishes to enjoy with a glass of wine. It had become her way of winding down and doing something creative for a short while; an interlude between finishing in court and the preparation for the next day, or the next trial. Now she wilted some young spinach with salt, pepper and nutmeg, seared a piece of salmon and ate it slowly, with bread from a local French bakery, and a glass of Chablis. When she had finished she went back to her desk and turned on the reading lamp, before picking up one of the two black lever-arch files containing the trial papers.

The name of the dead woman was Shelley Paulson. Her mother, who had identified the body, believed her daughter was a director of a successful employment agency providing PAs for overseas businessmen. The reality was she worked as an escort, accompanying lone men to dinner and providing more intimate services for which she had been well paid. She had been able to buy and furnish a luxurious flat in one of the garden squares in Notting Hill. Amongst the items taken by the police from her home were the paraphernalia of a drug user – a broken mirror, squares of aluminium foil and a few small packets of a white powder; something else of which her mother was unaware. Cassie tried to imagine what Mrs Paulson might have felt; the shock when the policemen came to the door, the nightmare of the journey to the mortuary, hoping they were wrong and it wasn't her child, and then, looking at the beautiful face, realising it was true, and in that single moment the axis of her world shifting.

How Shelley had died was not the issue for Cassie, it was who was responsible. Her client, Lenny Barker, had been charged with the murder and he was pleading not guilty; she had to prepare his defence. She was meeting him the next day to discuss the evidence, and even though she wouldn't be the one to decide what questions to ask the witnesses, or be making a speech to the jury, some senior barrister, probably a silk,

3

someone with the magic initials QC behind his name, would be doing that; never the less she needed to have all the facts at her fingertips. She wanted to impress with her understanding of the case and the issue of identification on which the trial would turn.

Cassie moved on to the second file, which contained the witness statements, reports and police logs that were thought unnecessary for the prosecution case. Although none of them would be used in the course of the trial, sometimes they provided information that would assist the defence, or give the lawyers a better understanding of the police investigation. She flicked through them, in case there was anything she needed to ask Barker about. Most of them were the evidence of friends and clients of the dead woman, but then she found a report from a fingerprint expert who had compared prints taken from a silver bracelet worn by Shelley Paulson at the time of her death and the fingerprints taken from Lenny Barker on his arrest. The expert had come to the conclusion that there were insufficient ridge characteristics for her to say, with any certainty, that any of the fingerprints on the bracelet were made by Barker. Cassie picked up the copy prints, held them close to the light, and examined them carefully. The first sheets showed clear prints of all eight of Lenny Barker's fingertips and both thumbs; they were clear, the lines well defined. The print from the middle finger had six tiny paper arrows pointing to ridges and whorls, the identifying marks of the print. On the sheet which showed the prints found on the bracelet a number of prints were smudged where the hand making them had dragged across the surface of the exhibit, and others were overlaid as if one hand had been placed where another had already been. That too had arrows pointing to significant marks. She compared them and, although she was not the expert, came to the conclusion they were probably identical. Certainly she would not want a jury to see them; she felt sure they, like her, would come to the conclusion the prints on the bracelet were Barker's, despite the expert's report

She closed the file and tied the papers together before putting them in her holdall, and then went to the kitchen to clear up after her evening meal. The sense of wellbeing she had been given by the food and wine had vanished, dispelled by the discovery of the fingerprint report. Now the conference would be a formality; Lenny Barker was just another defendant trying to escape responsibility for his crime.

Chapter 2

The offices of Durrant and Smythe, Solicitors, were in a converted shop on the Uxbridge Road. A bell rang as Cassie opened the door and the receptionist, a dark-haired woman in her late fifties, looked up from the computer screen.

'Cassie Hardman, to see Mr Durrant.'

'Take a seat and I'll let him know you're here.'

Cassie sat down on one of the well-used chairs. She suppressed the feeling of anxiety, not wanting to betray her feelings. Meeting a client for the first time was like a blind date, each person having their own expectations, and each hoping to avoid any embarrassment. Lenny Barker was an unknown quantity to her. Of course she knew the formal details, his age, where he lived, which school he had attended and where he now worked, but that was just the framework. The people and places he cared about, the prejudices that drove him were still a mystery to her. She had no idea what he would expect of her, would he be worried she might be forbidding, or think she was too young, even though she had been qualified for eleven years; most importantly, would he be disappointed his barrister was a woman?

Her thoughts were interrupted by the receptionist directing her along the corridor to Tim Durrant's office. His room was, like him, a little frayed at the edges. When Cassie walked into the room, he was moving files from his desk to the floor, the only available space. He turned his computer screen off and waved at the chair behind the desk, saying he would sit to one side and take notes. Barker arrived shortly after she had got her papers out, and was ushered into the room by the same dark-haired woman. Tim introduced her to him, but before she could say anything, he said, 'I didn't kill her.' He spat out his denial with such force that Cassie felt as if a door had been slammed in her face, closed to prevent her from probing his account.

'That's why we're here, Lenny. Is it all right if I call you Lenny rather than Mr Barker?' she asked.

He nodded at her, hostility in his dark brown eyes.

'I am here to help you, you know,' she said to him.

His expression didn't change, but he told her he knew that, and then looked at Tim Durrant, seeking reassurance. Cassie felt the resentment, she needed to win his trust; when the time came to advise him how he should plead he must have confidence in her. Start softly, she thought.

'Tell me a bit about yourself first, before we discuss the case against you. How old are you, where do you live? Things like that.'

'I've already told Mr Durrant, Miss.'

'I know, but I'd like you to tell me.' However difficult he was, and even though she believed him to be a murderer, she had to appear sympathetic to him. She smiled at him hoping to encourage his faith in her.

'I'm twenty-two and I live at twenty-six Lancaster Close with my mum and sister, Jane.' He kept his eyes averted and his voice was a monotone, revealing nothing.

As she questioned him and listened to his answers Cassie took the opportunity to observe him. Although it was pointless, at this stage, thinking about a jury, she looked at him as she believed a juror would, and asked herself if he would make a good first impression. He was a well-built young man, wearing a battered leather bomber jacket and a red-checked shirt, which had the appearance of being hastily tucked into his trousers. He was sitting stiffly on an upright chair, his face tipped downwards. His denim jeans were clean and didn't have any fashionable rips in the knees. She couldn't see what sort of shoes he was wearing. His dark hair was closely cut round the sides, curly where it was longer. She pushed the thought of a trial out of her mind, sure that when the trial was about to begin and he was faced with the enormity of lying throughout the proceedings, he would plead guilty and a jury would be unnecessary.

He told her he worked in a hardware store just off the Portobello Road for a Mr Boxall, but he still didn't look at her as he spoke; instead he turned away and concentrated on Tim. The two men were sat on the other side of the desk from her, Tim a little to one side, but closer to Barker than she was; perhaps he found the desk a barrier and the distance between them intimidating.

Cassie knew the store, it wasn't far from her home, and she shopped on the Portobello Market frequently; this was an opportunity to show him they had a shared experience.

'I think I know it, lots of door handles in the window. Is that it?' she said.

'Yes, Miss.' He managed to smile at her but his hands were making fists and he had a twitch in his left cheek.

'What about your father? Does he live with you?' Cassie asked.

'No. He's in Australia.'

She thought he had tensed at the mention of his father; she pondered briefly whether to ask him any more questions about his parents, she was wary of antagonising him, but decided she needed to know more about his family, and asked, 'How long has he lived there?'

'Not sure. I think I was about eleven or twelve when he and mum split up and he met someone else. She wanted to go home, to Australia, you know, and after a bit they did.'

'So you were still at school when he left. Which school did you go to?'

'Holland Park,' Lenny replied. Cassie already knew that from the written statement, his proof, as lawyers called it, and they both knew the murder had taken place near the school. He would be very familiar with the school grounds, and the location of the bridge that joined two of the buildings, under which was a walkway into Campden Hill Road. The knowledge of that escape route would give him the ability to vanish just as the murderer had succeeded in doing.

'Let's go back to your job. Do you have to do paperwork at the shop?' she enquired. It was a polite way of asking if he could read and write; it was such an embarrassing question, but she needed to know, and too many of her clients were only semi-literate.

'Yes, but we use the computer for the stockroom. Reordering and things like that.' As he talked about his job, he became more animated, more alert, he lifted his head, and his eyes lit up. There was something rather appealing about him, and despite his wariness, she felt he was beginning to relate to her, and now she could begin to question him about his interviews with the police.

'You told the police you went to Holland Walk on the night of the murder. Was that right?'

'Not sure. Couldn't remember where I was. It was weeks before.' He began to stutter and his left cheek twitched.

'But you had been in the Walk about that time?'

'I think so. There's a sports pitch there and, well, sometimes I go and watch the football.'

'Can you remember who was playing that night?'

'No.'

Lenny looked away from her, avoiding any eye contact, but his voice was firm and sounded defiant. He wasn't going to volunteer any more information, whether true or not.

'It was mid-September, it would have been dusk soon after eight. They don't play after dark, do they?'

'There's the shop windows; the sports shops, on the High Street. You know, I like looking at them before going home.'

'Gets a bit much at home, with Mum and Jane?' Tim chipped in. He sounded sympathetic, as if he too felt hemmed in by the women in his life. Lenny just nodded in response.

Cassie found his account, she never used the word story, unbelievable. She wanted to question him forcefully, but concluded he would just clam up; she would learn nothing and destroy what little confidence he had in her.

'Lenny,' she continued, 'do you have any clear recollection of being in Holland Walk on the night Miss Paulson was murdered?'

He gulped and began to pull at the zip of his jacket, 'I didn't see her. Miss. I thought I was there, but, you know, I didn't see her. ' His voice rose with anxiety.

10

'You did know her?'

'I've not spoken to her. You know, lots of people knew who she was.' He looked away from her and when he faced her again, the hostility had returned to his eyes.

'Why, if you were not sure where you were, did you tell the police you were in the Walk?'

'They said there was a video. You know, you know, I thought I must be on it.'

Tim interrupted, 'They must have suggested it to him before I saw him. He was fairly disorientated when I turned up, and he kept going on about this video. From what I was told by the police it seemed unlikely Lenny was on it.'

'Miss, they dragged me out of bed real early.' Lenny had become very agitated, his hands gripping the sides of his chair and turning to look first at Tim and then back at her.

'Wouldn't let me get dressed. You know, made me stand there, with nothing on. Made me wait while they got one of those white overall things.' He was struggling to get the words out. 'Stuffed all my clothes in plastic bags. Everything. I'd no idea what was going on.' When he faced Cassie, his arms were folded across his chest.

'Didn't they tell you, you were being arrested for the murder of Shelley Paulson?' asked Cassie rather gently, trying again to reassure him, hoping she hadn't lost his confidence completely. Lenny looked at her, his eyes glistened.

'Don't remember, Miss, I've not been nicked before. You know, it were so fast.' Cassie could hear the stress in his voice so she turned to a less confrontational topic.

11

'Let's go back to Shelley. You've just said everyone knew her. Can you tell me who you mean?'

Lenny stifled a sob, 'She came to the market a lot. You know, shopped there. The traders all knew her. She was very beautiful.' He paused and then added 'I didn't kill her, Miss. Why would I?'

'The prosecution will say you tried to chat her up, made advances towards her and when she refused, you killed her.'

'No, no. Didn't. I didn't.' His voice trailed off, he pulled a grubby paper tissue from his pocket and blew his nose. 'I didn't kill her.'

Cassie waited until he composed himself, before asking whether he had any girlfriends. He put his head down and played with his fingers.

'The police asked me that. I told them not for a while.'

He's a bit immature, she thought as a faint blush crossed his cheeks.

'Any reason? Let down by someone?' As she waited for his reply, an image of her ex-husband flashed into her own memory, an image she hastily suppressed. This was not the time to dwell on her own past.

'No, not really. Thought I would be going to Australia, join my Dad, so I didn't want to start anything.'

'OK, but you're not leaving now?'

'No, not now. Dad's gone all quiet about it. So, no.' His voice had softened as if tinged with regret.

There was silence for a few moments before Tim said, 'Is there anything else, Miss Hardman?'

'I don't think so for now. I assume we'll have another conference before the trial.'

12

Tim stood up, 'OK Lenny. I'll be in touch. If there is anything you want to know just give me a bell. And don't forget the curfew times. They'll have you in Brixton before you can sneeze if they catch you out after seven.'

'Well, he's not being very cooperative is he?' Cassie said to Tim after the door had closed behind their client. The effort of hiding her belief of Barker's guilt had left her feeling frustrated and angry, and she just needed to go home, but she wanted to check that Tim had made the same deductions from the evidence as she had.

'He's covering up. He knows what he's done and is just lying to cover his tracks. Then there is the admission he was in the park that night. I really don't understand why he said he was in Holland Walk if he wasn't. I told him quite clearly they didn't have a video of him. That's just an excuse. He must have been there,' Tim said.

'I thought he was rather shy. He seems an unlikely killer.'

'He's a bit of a loner, and it's often the ones who struggle to make any relationships who kill.'

He paused and then said, 'I can't stop thinking about the expert's report. I know there are only six points of similarity, but they look the same to me. If I was prosecuting I'd want to get them in front of the jury.

'It's difficult to say the jury can rely on it when the expert isn't sure. But, presumably the prosecution think it's not a very strong case or you wouldn't have got bail?' she asked.

'There was some sort of a row between the CPS lawyer and O'Connor; he's the Detective Chief Superintendent. I think the lawyer was worried about the ID parade, and he wanted to defer charging Lenny until they had the results of the various forensics. I'd discussed him being bailed from the police station after he was interviewed, and the CPS said they had no objection. O'Connor then went against the CPS advice and wouldn't wait. If they were prepared to release him on bail pending the result of the scientific examination of his clothing, it was a bit difficult to object in court.'

'What happened at the identification parade?'

'The eyewitness, Compton, walked up and down the viewing gallery quite slowly. He was told the man might not be there. He didn't seem to stop and look at anyone in particular. When he was asked if he could make an identification he shook his head. He was leaving the room when he kind of turned, and said he thought it was number three, Lenny's position. By that time Colin Dean, he's the sergeant in charge, had come to the door, but I'm fairly sure he said nothing to Compton. You can see for yourself, there's a video. He's straight anyway. Although I'm not so confident about O'Connor, he's a bastard.' Tim paused, pulling on the corners of his notebook. 'I've seen more convincing IDs.'

'How tall is Lenny? He's not much taller than me, I would have thought.' Although she was sure the fingerprints on the deceased's bracelet were Barker's, while he protested his innocence she would still prepare the case as if she believed he was.

Tim flicked through one of his files until he found the custody record. 'You're right. He's five foot nine.'

'The witness said the man was taller than Shelley. We must check her height and what about her shoes? We'll ask about the exhibits at the Pleas and Directions hearing, and see if we can see them before trial. I bet she was wearing high-heels.' She shook her head, 'It's a waste of time really, but we have to go through the motions. Have you decided who will be leading me?' If Tim hadn't already instructed somebody, she might get the opportunity to choose the silk.

'Marcus Pike. Do you know him?'

'By reputation. I'm surprised he's available. When are we having a conference with him?'

Tim said he thought it would probably be the week before the trial, and added he would keep her posted if anything new turned up.

As she walked in the direction of home with her head bent against the rain, she imagined Lenny Barker in Holland Walk, approaching Shelley Paulson, trying to talk to her, touching her tenderly at first, being pushed away, then grabbing hold of her, pressing her against his body, reaching for his knife and pushing it into her side before she fell at his feet. She liked him, and because she did, she wanted him to be innocent, but the evidence pointed to another verdict, and it was the evidence a jury would hear and on which they would decide whether he was guilty or not.

Chapter 3

Cassie's chambers at 3 Burke Court were in part of that area of London inhabited by lawyers for centuries and known as the Temple. Walking through the arch bearing the Pascal Lamb was like time travelling; each time, she stepped out of the tumult of the twenty-first century into the ordered calm of the eighteenth. She was reminded of her home town, Lancaster, where similar Georgian buildings surrounded the castle, built by John O'Gaunt, which remained a centre of law and punishment, judges and offenders at its heart. So unlike the Temple, which turned its back on the bulk of the Royal Courts of Justice across the Strand, a row of banks and sandwich shops providing a barricade to the noise of traffic and the bustle of pedestrians, and creating a sanctuary of narrow lanes and courtyards for the lawyers who worked and lived there.

She came here most days, to collect her papers, have conferences and run her legal practice. If the Temple was a tranquil oasis, then the clerks' room was manic, particularly in the early evening with telephones ringing and computers burping. Three young men and one similar-aged woman took calls from solicitors wanting to instruct their barristers, made the bookings and maintained the diaries, sorted the post, kept track of fees and checked every day for cases in which members of Chambers were working. Sometimes Cassie wondered who worked for whom; the clerks had so much control over her life.

Her arrival in Chambers was usually met with a certain amount of indifference but on this occasion, Hamish, one of the junior clerks, told her Tim Durrant

had sent her some †
She was there to coll
she found it together
from Tim in her pigeo⌐

The brief was quite
tape that held it togethe
like a bracelet. She ⌐
defendant was a female
was the sort of brief she ⌐
a woman on a minor cha⌐
important to the defenda⌐
didn't get sent these cases   ⌐ one felt like
an actor must when they get typecast in particular
roles. She wanted to be instructed in frauds, armed
robberies, drug importations and serious assaults, but
still it was better to be in court on any sort of case than
not, and she did have a murder.

She opened the slim set of papers in the Barker
case. Her instructions from Tim were simple, 'Another
nail in the coffin!!' There was a two page witness
statement from Simon Jolly, a forensic scientist. He
had examined Shelley Paulson's clothing, and taken
from them several different types of fibres. Some of
those fibres matched a sweatshirt seized during a
search of Lenny Barker's home. Cassie pulled a face as
she pushed the two briefs into her briefcase. 'Is there
anything else? I'm going home,' she said to Hamish.

'There's those tenancy interviews.' He searched
through the bundles on his desk until he found some
large brown envelopes. He looked through them and
found one with her name on it and handed it to her.
Inwardly she groaned, more reading and the impossible
task of separating the brilliant from the very good.

at Chancery Lane tube station, she
ring. It was a text from Ben. She was
when the train arrived, stuffed with
om the City. She didn't want to struggle with
bile as well as hanging onto the overhead rails,
ng pushed and jostled as more passengers got into
the carriage. She would wait until she got home. She
was pleased he had contacted her. Since her divorce no
relationship had lasted very long, most men found it
difficult to cope with her lifestyle; the last minute
changes to plans and the almost daily deadlines that
kept her working nearly every evening and part of the
weekend. Nor was she sure that she wanted another
man in her life yet, her marriage had ended badly, and
although she thought her ex-husband, Tony Cranston,
had been in the wrong when he began a relationship
with a fellow student, she was partly to blame. They
were totally incompatible, she wanted a career and he
was a party animal. Now she was more determined
than ever to make a success of her work.

Ben was ambitious too, a junior lectureship at
Imperial College had come early, but his teaching
schedule and his research work gave him a more
structured life. If he minded about the cancelled dates,
he didn't let it show.

Once in her apartment, she dropped her bags to the
floor; her hands ached with the effort of carrying her
holdall and briefcase. The message from Ben read
'back from US. can we meet? in need of tlc'

From the windows she looked down onto the
pedestrians far below; she enjoyed observing the street
life from her vantage point, the sense of being apart
from the scuttling pedestrians and anxious traffic. She
tried to call Ben back, but he didn't answer so she sent

18

a text, 'Friday 7pm here.' She would need to do some shopping if she was to cook a meal for the two of them; a few recipes came to mind before she dismissed the thought, reminding herself she had more important things to do before Friday.

She took the next day's brief and the folder of tenancy applications out of her bag, putting them on her desk. Her ex-husband had wanted to keep it, saying she had given it to him as a wedding present, but she had insisted it was hers, allowing him to take the remainder of their possessions rather than sacrifice this one item. She couldn't bear the thought of Tony using the desk; she had loved her grandfather and the gift of his time and workmanship made it very precious.

She spent an hour reading the brief for the next day. The case against the young woman was overwhelming, and her solicitors thought that with some strong advice she would plead guilty. She turned then to the applications for a tenancy in her Chambers. There had been about seventy, and the difference between the individuals was marginal, but in the end they had decided to invite ten newly qualified barristers for interview. She read again each of the applicants' submissions trying to find something that would indicate a fresh approach, or something unique that would distinguish the individual from all the others. She had struggled writing her own CV, trying to make the short period of work experience with a firm of solicitors in Lancaster sound important, when all she had done was sit in an office with a legal executive who did nothing but complain; and that her time working at Boots as a shop assistant had really taught her how to deal with difficult customers, rather than just be a financial necessity. She had never had enough money to take a gap year and travel, or do unpaid work in order to boost her credentials.

Her initial view of this group of newly qualified barristers was that the former pupil was probably the frontrunner, but they had not offered a tenancy to a woman for some years, and Chambers were gaining a reputation for being sexist. Cassie looked again at the applications from the two women they had shortlisted, one of them, Mitzie Baldwin, was in her mid-thirties, older than normal, just a little older than she was now and she had been at the bar for eleven years. Mitzie had worked in the Foreign Office before taking Bar Finals and had been employed in the prosecuting attorney's office in New York, which suggested she might have a different perspective on the legal process. Perhaps, if she was impressive enough in the interviews, Cassie's colleagues might be ready to consider taking her on, but it was unlikely. As she put the papers back in the folder, her mobile rang. She picked it up without looking at it, and said, 'Ben.'

'Sorry to disappoint you. It's Tim. Have you got the evidence of Jolly?'

'Yes. It's not good, is it?'

'We know he's the killer. I think we should have a conference soon with Marcus. Immediately after Christmas, is that OK with you? Lenny needs to face up to it and plead. Marcus will get him to see sense.'

'That's fine. I'm going home for the holidays, but I'll be back the first week in January.'

'Great. I'll get back to your clerk and fix a date and time in the New Year. Have a great time.'

She didn't get a chance to wish him a Happy Christmas, although on reflection she thought he wouldn't enjoy the break.

20

Cassie went back home for the Christmas holiday to the small terraced house where her parents lived; even though she had left over seventeen years ago it was still the place she called home. Here she could relax, she was a beloved daughter and sister, accepted as she was, and she valued the respite from her professional life. She helped her mother prepare lunch on Christmas Day for all the family, her sister, Amanda, brother in law Colin, her two nephews and an elderly relative of her mother's; the two of them laughing in the kitchen as they worked together. As she mixed the ingredients of a chestnut stuffing, she thought how easily her sister had settled into marriage, despite her teenage dreams of working in television, enjoying the roles of wife, mother and teacher, whilst she, the domesticated one, was a single career girl. She wasn't sure what had triggered her ambition to be a barrister, it had appealed to some part of her that believed in being fair, rather than deciding what was good or evil; that was easy, being just was more difficult and that she liked.

She returned to London a day later, refreshed and with a north-country burr back in her speech, so that she and Ben could celebrate New Year's Eve together, with a bottle of champagne and a carefully prepared meal of duck breasts with plum sauce. Ben was always appreciative of her cooking; unlike her ex-husband, for whom food was almost a distraction. She wanted to impress Ben and enjoyed the time they spent together as long as it didn't interfere with her work; she wasn't ready to make compromises yet, but she didn't want him to walk away from their relationship either. She tried not to think about it too much, and just enjoy the moment.

Once the holiday was over she soon settled back into work, preparing her cases and going to court. Lenny Barker's case wasn't at the forefront of her mind, until another file appeared. Tim Durrant, her instructing solicitor, was always in a hurry, and in consequence, his instructions were brief. 'No time to read these.'

The file contained transcripts of meetings between Lenny and a young woman using the name Rose Cummings, who, Cassie deduced, was an undercover policewoman. She was astonished the investigation had taken that route, there was sufficient evidence without trying underhand tactics. The last time the police had tried such a subterfuge, they had been strongly criticised by the judge; but Rose had met Lenny Barker at a public house on the Portobello Road in late November, about six weeks after his arrest. The police officer had struggled to find any common ground between them and they had spent some time playing pool. He talked about football and his favourite team, Chelsea, and amongst other details about the team, told Rose he had been to watch them play Everton a few weeks before, with a friend called Hinds. If Rose had hoped to get admissions or information from him that would assist the prosecution case, she had failed. It was a pity Barker hadn't gone to a football match instead of hanging around in Holland Park, then he would not have met Shelley Paulson and killed her.

Chapter 4

'Is that Detective Constable Seymour?' said a voice Alexis thought was vaguely familiar.

'Yes, who is it?'

'It's Mr Collins, Cotburn Square. We met last September when you came to the garden.'

'Sure, I remember.' She had gone to meet him when a pizza box containing drugs had been found under a garden shed by a Community Support Officer. Mr Collins and a Mr Meredith had reported seeing a stranger in the communal gardens and called the police. When she went to Cotburn Square, Mr Collins, who had seen the intruder, had told her that the man was white, tall, probably over six foot and had a birthmark on his left cheek.

The garden square wasn't actually square, but an oblong, surrounded by iron railings with gates on two sides. They were private; the spiked iron railings surrounding them were too high to jump, so whoever was using the garden must have a key. She had quizzed Robert Meredith, who was the secretary to the Garden Committee, and he had told her he knew of a hundred and forty keys but he thought there were many more. Over the years the number of keys had multiplied as the large houses were divided into flats, some owner occupied and some tenanted. Then they got copied, and when people moved they forgot to hand them back, so new ones had to be made. The Garden Committee levied a rate, and the local authority collected it along with the council tax. As long as the property owner or tenant paid the garden rate, and could prove they lived in the square, the Committee let them have a key. She realised straightaway the impossibility of tracing all the keys and thereby the identity of the person who had left the drugs.

'How can I help?' she asked, 'Has the man been back again?'

'I haven't seen him since. No, it's just that Tom, the gardener, was sorting out one of the compost heaps and found this knife.'

'A knife, what sort of knife?'

'I'm fairly sure it's a flick knife and Tom is adamant that it's been there quite a while, possibly since autumn last year. I thought it might help you trace the man who left those drugs under the shed.'

Alex thought for a moment, if he was right and it was a flick knife, then it was an offensive weapon, and it seemed unlikely that more than one person was using the garden to hide things. 'Right I'll come and get it.'

'I've been very careful not to touch the knife and I think Tom was as well. I thought there might be fingerprints on it.'

Trying to play the detective she thought, but said, 'I'll be with you in about twenty minutes.' It was a good excuse not to stay at her desk and do paperwork.

'Do you want to meet me at the gate to the garden, and then I can show you where it was found.'

'I'll see you there in ten minutes, Mr Collins. Bye.'

Since her last visit to the garden the leaves had blown off the trees and the flowers had all been touched by frost. The gardener had been busy, removing dead plants so that the soil was exposed, and Alex could see that mulch had been spread over the bare earth. She wasn't a gardener herself, but over the years, she had learnt a bit from her mother. Mr Collins took her round

24

to the rear of the garden shed under which the drugs had been found, where a number of compost heaps had been created out of wood and corrugated iron. One of the piles of fallen leaves and grass cuttings had been pulled apart to reveal a thin layer of rotted material that smelt of over-ripe fruit and bad eggs.

'That's where Tom found the knife,' said Mr Collins pointing towards the compost heap, 'and it's in here.' He ushered her into the garden shed, where, despite the gloomy light and the clutter, she could see, on a wooden bench, a flick knife with an ivory coloured handle lying on a plastic supermarket bag. The blade was shut and the catch was covered in a black slimy material.

Alex put a plastic glove on her right hand, picked up the knife, and examined it briefly before putting it into a clear exhibit bag.

'I'll take it back and get the fingerprint guy to have a look at it; it takes a little while before we get any result though.' She continued to turn the knife over in her hand. 'Do you know why the gardener, Tom is it, thought it must have been put there in the autumn?'

'I'm not sure,' said Mr Meredith, 'something to do with the type of plants in the layer immediately above where he found it.'

The drug squad office was unusually quiet, but as she entered the room she saw Mel Haskins sitting at a computer terminal with his back to her. He seemed to be unaware she was there. 'Excuse me,' Alex said. He swung round to face her. Most of the drug squad officers were young and wore jeans with leather jackets, in the forlorn hope they would not be identified as police officers, but he wore a suit and tie.

'Yes? Didn't realize you were there.' He eyed her up and down. 'Mm, the glamorous Detective Constable from the robbery squad, back again. I know I'm irresistible, you just can't keep away.'

Of course he was teasing her, but she wasn't prepared to indulge him by flirting with him. 'Not sure about that, it's been months,' she said and without giving him time to respond, carried on, 'That pizza box with drugs in it, have you been able to identify who left it in Cotburn Square?'

'No, we haven't.' He shrugged his shoulders. 'The fingerprints on the plastic covering and on the drug packets are not in our records.'

'So there isn't a lot of point sending this for dusting?' she held up the knife in the exhibit bag.

'Probably not, but you could try. Not that the SOCO will be pleased, they have a lot on, and if there's no crime worth speaking of, then it's not going to have much priority.'

'I thought it might help with identifying the drug dealer.' She was disappointed at wasting her time on what it seemed was a dead end.

'We do have something, not much but,' he stopped and began to search through the information collected and filed by the officers he worked with. 'Something about that garden square. Can't say it's the same man. Yes.' He began to read from the screen, 'Sixth June, Twenty-two hundred hours. Man IC1, six foot three, birthmark to left side of face, emerged from garden of Cotburn Square. Went to cycle and rode off in direction of flyover. Followed to Nightjar Club, where he dismounted and went inside. Followed him into toilets, where he went into a compartment.

Checked cistern after he left. Small packet seized, query Ecstasy.'

'When was that?'

'June last year. We discussed him at the next briefing, keeping the gardens under surveillance, in the hope he'd turn up again, but there was so little to go on we decided to take a passive position on him. The drugs were one of the legal highs, not Ecstasy, anyway.'

'And there haven't been any sightings since?'

'No.'

'At least not until he was spotted by our Mr Collins in the gardens in September. Not that I'd want to rely on him.' She told Mel about going to see Mr Collins in his flat, where she caught the faint scent of malt whisky on his breath, and he had confided in her that he went into the garden at night, taking with him a hip flask so he could have a drink without his wife knowing.

'But it is the same description. There can't be that many men around with birthmarks on their left jaw,' Alex said.

'No, I suppose not, but how does he keep below the radar if he's a dealer?' Mel sounded very confident the man could not escape notice if he was supplying drugs on their manor; Alex wasn't so sure. Back at her desk, she pushed the plastic wrapped knife into a drawer and went back to the paperwork in front of her.

Chapter 5

When Cassie arrived for the conference with Marcus Pike QC, the silk who would be leading her, at his chambers in Middle Temple Lane, the same frenzied activity was taking place in the clerks' room as in the one she had just left, so it was several minutes before she was directed to the waiting room. Tim was reading a newspaper, his scuffed black shoes firmly planted in front of him, and next to him the documents for the conference in plastic shopping bags. Sitting next to him was Lenny Barker, head bowed, staring at the swirly patterned carpet. She said, 'Hello, sorry I'm late,' to them both. Lenny didn't reply but Tim said, 'It's OK, Mr Pike has just got back from court.'

Cassie put her papers on the chair next to her and looked round the room, which was almost identical to the one in her own chambers, well-used chairs and prints from a nineteenth century magazine depicting caricatures of legal figures on the walls. She picked up one of the dog-eared magazines on the low table in front of her, and opened it, but instead of reading, she began watching Lenny. She noticed the twitch in his left cheek, his arms folded across his chest and his hands clenched. If he appeared so defensive in court, a jury might interpret it as hiding his guilt; but he was, wasn't he? She went back to the magazine, and had just turned over the page, when one of the office juniors came in and asked them to accompany him to Marcus Pike's room.

Tim bent over to pick up the two carrier bags; as he lifted them up the contents of one of them fell to the floor, and scattered around his feet. He swore softly and started to push the papers back. Cassie went over to help him, gathering together the copy documents. Under the chair on which he had been sat, she saw a copy of the Evening Standard, with an action photograph of a football player dressed in blue and white on the back page.

'Is this yours as well?' she asked.

'Yes, it's the copy the police referred to in interview. It has the report of the murder inside.'

'Do you mind if I take it? I'd like to have a look at it,' Cassie said.

'No, I don't think it adds anything and I don't need it.' Tim replied as they were led to Marcus Pike's room.

The silk was sitting behind a large leather-topped desk; behind him the shelves were filled with books, briefs tied with pink tape and several lever-arch files. To one side of the room the windows overlooked the gardens of Inner Temple and beyond the silvery band of the River Thames. Cassie shared a room with three others that overlooked a sunless cobbled square, but one day she was sure she would have an office to herself, and it would be just as splendid as this one.

She knew Marcus by sight, but they had never worked together. There was a story about him, most certainly exaggerated, defending, in a multi-defendant assault case, a man of a singular description; a difficulty when the issue was the identity of the assailants. Marcus Pike had described him to the jury as a chimpanzee, which made the jury laugh and the judge annoyed, but pleased the defendant despite his inevitable conviction.

He got up when they came in and she could see he was quite small, about the same height as her; well groomed, dressed in a black jacket and pin-striped trousers, a head waiter's uniform only better cut. He motioned them to sit at the three chairs in front of the desk, introduced himself to Lenny and then sat down again.

'I've read all the papers, Mr Barker, but there are a few questions I want to ask you and then we'll discuss what we are going to do. I understand you can read and write?'

'Yes.' Lenny didn't look up and shifted uneasily in his seat. Cassie sat poised with pen and notebook to take notes of the conference. Marcus would advise him to plead guilty, but Lenny was so uncooperative she doubted he would accept the advice. He would continue to deny the offence, and they would have to do their best to defend him, whatever they thought.

'Have you read the transcript of your interviews?' Marcus asked. Lenny nodded.

'Can you remember where you were the night Shelley Paulson was killed?'

'No, Sir. I didn't see her in Holland Walk.'

Marcus was being very brusque with Lenny, where she would have been less abrasive; it was too early in the conference and Lenny was likely to become antagonistic towards them. Of course he had to point out the difficulties in the case, but a gentler approach would have more chance of success.

'Have you ever seen her in the park?'

'No, only on the market.'

'Portobello Market?' Lenny didn't reply so Marcus continued, 'You told the police you were in Holland Park that evening, didn't you?'

'Yes, Sir.' Lenny didn't look at Marcus when he spoke, but looked over the silk's left shoulder towards the gardens of Inner Temple.

'Was that true?'

Marcus sounded very sceptical, as she knew he was, but disguising one's feelings was part of the job.

'I don't know,' he stumbled over his words, 'I know I'd been to the park, quite a few times before they arrested me. Watching the football. The park closes just before dark, so I don't go then, when it gets dark early, you know.'

'When the park closed, what did you usually do?'

'Not sure,' he replied. Cassie hesitated, her pen hovering over her notebook, at the change of account.

Marcus had seen the notes she had made of the earlier conference, 'You told Miss Hardman you sometimes went to look at the shops in Kensington High Street. Is that right?'

'Yes, or if some of my mates from school were hanging around in the Walk, I might join them.'

'Did you hang around, as you put it, near the school?'

'Usually, yes.' Cassie wanted to intervene. She knew there was a history of assaults on gay men in the Walk and she was about to ask Lenny if he had been involved in them, but she stopped herself, and left the questioning to Marcus.

'Miss Paulson was killed at about ten past ten, it would have been dark and the park closed. So if you had gone to the park that evening you would have left by that time?'

'I think so.' The words were slow as Lenny confirmed the information to himself.

31

'You must have either gone home or been in Kensington High Street when she was killed.'

'Yes, I suppose so.' Lenny dragged out the words, sounding as if he really wasn't certain.

'Why did you not tell the police you had left the park by ten?'

Lenny hung his head and whispered, 'They didn't ask me.'

Marcus Picked up a set of papers from his desk and turned over a few pages to where a yellow Post-it note was sticking out of the file. 'I'm looking at page six of the second interview, Miss Hardman.' Cassie found the page in her files.

'Can you let Mr Barker see that?' Before she could hand Lenny the papers, Tim had moved forward from his seat behind her and placed a copy in his hands. Lenny was being evasive; the police officer had asked him what time he left the park, as Marcus was about to demonstrate.

'Now about half way down, Sergeant Dean asks you if you had gone to the park the evening of the murder and you say "Yes". He then asks you what time you left and you replied you didn't know. Have you got that? It's about half way down the page.'

Marcus was jabbing with his finger at his copy, but Lenny hadn't been looking at the transcript. Cassie leant over and pointed at the part Marcus wanted him to look at, and Lenny let his eyes drop to the page. 'Yes, Sir.'

'Right, then the Sergeant asks you "Was it still light?" and you said, "No, I think it was dark." Then, "Did you go into Holland Walk?" and you say, "I must have done."'

'"Did you go straight home?" You said, "I don't know." So you were asked what time you left, and given every opportunity to think about it.'

Lenny looked defiantly at Marcus, 'I didn't kill her.'

'Mr Barker, in addition to the witness identifying you, and now these fibres from the girl's clothing matching one of your sweatshirts, you have admitted being in the vicinity about the time of the murder.'

'But, I couldn't have been. I would have seen her.' Lenny said. His voice was firm.

'Exactly, if you were there you would have seen her. The prosecution will say you are denying seeing her because you were responsible for her death.' Marcus threw the words forcefully at Lenny, whose eyes were beginning to glisten with tears; Lenny was so inconsistent, challenging one minute and then in tears the next. He puzzled her, was he really innocent or just very afraid?

Marcus looked up at the ceiling, putting his hands together as if praying, before continuing, 'I have given considerable thought to your case and I am not optimistic about the outcome. I would advise you to think carefully about what happened that night. It may be that, if the circumstances were right, we could persuade the prosecution to accept a plea to manslaughter. Single knife wound, intended to frighten rather than cause serious harm, in the struggle she fell on the knife. It's a bit implausible but you never know your luck, and then the judge would have the option of giving you a determinate sentence rather than life imprisonment.'

He really was putting the pressure on; most defendants were terrified of getting a life sentence.

For a moment there was complete silence. Lenny had gone pale and his left cheek was twitching. He stared at Marcus, and said, 'I didn't kill her.'

'Think about what I've said. I'm sure Mr Durrant will be ready to talk it over with you, in the next day or so.'

Cassie found it difficult to come to any conclusion about Lenny; he was so insistent on his innocence, but then so many defendants were, particularly when charged with the most serious offences. She found him likeable, but that was not a defence, and, certainly, there was sufficient evidence on which a jury could convict. Whatever had happened in the park a young woman had been killed, and there was the smudged fingerprint which looked as if it was his.

Marcus stood and pushed his papers together, 'My clerk is trying to fix the case for March, when I have a week free. I hope that's OK for everyone?' He wasn't expecting an answer, but waved them towards the door.

It took Cassie a little longer to put her papers together and push them into the large canvas bag she used to carry her documents and barrister's robes. As she made her way round the chairs on which they had been sitting, Marcus called her back and asked her to shut the door.

'You think I was being hard on him, but there's that report from the fingerprint expert, Alison Pretty. I know the prosecution are not using it, can't really, they'd be asking the jury to substitute their opinion for an expert's, but it clearly points to him being the murderer, and he needs to face up to what he's done. He's bound to be convicted.'

34

'Do you know why they aren't relying on it, if only to support the identification? ' Cassie asked.

'No, I asked Howard about it, but he wasn't prepared to say. I assume there's a further report, or something, that confirms the conclusion she made originally. She's obviously reluctant to say they're his.'

'Should we ask about it?'

'No, we might risk opening Pandora's Box. Unless the issue of fingerprints is raised again, we'll accept the Crown's decision. The case would be hopeless if the evidence went in front of the jury.'

'But, without that, I don't think it's such a strong case. The identification is weak. The witness appeared unsure at the parade. There are material discrepancies between his initial description and Lenny Barker.'

'You mean the beard and the height. I'm not so sure the height is such a significant difference. My recollection is Holland Walk slopes uphill towards the school, so the witness would be looking up towards them. That could make him think the man was taller than he really was, and the girl was slipping down, reducing her height. Getting round his admission he was in the park that night will be very difficult.'

'The police humiliated him when they arrested him. Then he was misled into thinking he was in the park by this talk about the camera on the walls of Aubrey House.' She clutched her files to her. Marcus was being very prosecution minded; Barker was pleading not guilty, they had to defend him and forget the fingerprint.

'Yes, yes, he has an explanation, but Tim says it was made very clear to Barker that the video did not show him in the walk. It just doesn't stand up, when he knows he's being interviewed about the murder of somebody he knew. There are just too many coincidences.'

'There is no real motive either. No evidence of a struggle, torn clothes anything to indicate he'd tried to sexually assault her. Nor is there any DNA to link him with the murder, rather the opposite with the scrapings from Shelley's fingernails. The only forensic is the few, very few fibres, and I bet there are thousands of similar sweatshirts.' Cassie retorted.

'No, but the lack of her DNA on his clothes can be explained by the time between the murder and his arrest, and the DNA from under Shelley's fingernails the Crown will say has nothing to do with the murder. There's not much evidence of a struggle for that to be the killer's. It could have come from sexual activity. And as far as motive is concerned, the Crown don't have to prove one. They will say he tried to force himself on her, and when she rejected him he killed her. They don't even have to prove that happened, just suggest it. Cassie, he's guilty, and if he has any sense he'll admit it. We might just get away with manslaughter, if Howard Alsopp has a better case to go to.'

Chapter 6

The next evening, when Cassie entered Richard Jago QC's room for the meeting of the Tenancy Committee, she found her head of Chambers conversing with the only female silk, Eleanor Hesketh. The room, all mahogany and green leather like a gentleman's club, smelled of his expensive cigars.

Richard was a tall, slim man, who had been in the Guards before qualifying as a barrister. His dark grey suit had come from a Savile Row tailors; not for him the pinstripe trousers and black jacket. His shirt was pale pink with a white detachable collar to allow him to remove it and wear the winged collar and tabs of courtroom dress. He was perched on the corner of his desk, next to the chair in which Eleanor was sitting.

'Ah, Cassie, I was just saying to Eleanor here, do we have enough work for another woman, or should we put the two to one side? What do you think?' He waved his glasses around, as he spoke, then took the handkerchief from the top pocket of his suit, and rubbed them gently.

Eleanor had taken the jacket of her black suit off and put it over the arm of her chair. There was always tension between her and Richard; a stiffness in their relationship that was unexplained. Cassie noticed Eleanor's hands smooth her skirt as if she wanted to brush something unpleasant away.

Cassie was too aware that being offered a tenancy was the last, but most important, hurdle an aspiring barrister faced. She had been instrumental in setting up this committee to inject some objectivity into the process, and Richard's comments revealed how hard it was to change the entrenched behaviour. Sexist attitudes were still prevalent; it was always somebody else who was prejudiced, solicitors didn't want to instruct a woman, male offenders didn't want a woman representing them. No one wanted to say they still preferred the bar to be predominantly a male preserve. She hadn't been in practice long before she had discovered how much work was sent to her male colleagues on the basis of their ability to play cricket rather than their skills in court, and how many female solicitors seemed to prefer men who flirted with them.

Tenancy interviews were often repetitive; the applicant was given a set of papers and asked to prepare a plea in mitigation, or an appeal against sentence. It gave the committee the opportunity to assess the candidates' advocacy skills. Then they would be asked a few questions; somebody always asked why the applicant had chosen to come to the Bar, and invariably they would say something about valuing the independence and how they believed they would be judged on their merit.

No one, not even Cassie, ever disabused them and said that if they aspired to taking silk, becoming Treasury Counsel, or perhaps a Crown Court Judge, they would need to conform to all the unwritten rules to enable them to fit into this institution, like a piece in a jigsaw puzzle.

Even if the format of the interviews was repetitive, the actual meeting could be difficult. Chambers was Richard's fiefdom and he liked to run it his way, including picking tenants. Eleanor always had her own agenda, a favourite pupil, or a member of her own Oxford college, who she thought would be just the right person to be offered a tenancy. Of the other members, only Cassie was totally committed to the objective criteria they were meant to apply to prospective tenants, even Stephen Burnett, her closest friend, could be capricious.

'I think we should consider everyone on their merits,' Cassie replied. This was not the time to argue.

Eleanor shifted in the club chair in front of Richard's desk, one elbow resting on its surface, before saying. 'Jack's not too keen.'

Cassie knew Eleanor meant that their senior clerk would prefer a man; he believed they found it easier to network with instructing solicitors, whether male or female. 'The difficulty for you, is most of our solicitors want to talk about sport and, well, I don't suppose you play football,' Jack had said when she first met him, making it clear he considered her a bit of a liability.

'What's Jack not too keen on?' asked Peter Maynard, as he came into the room. Peter was some years senior to Cassie in Chambers. His cherubic face disguised a sharp mind, but she found him tedious, constantly dropping the names of judges as if they were great friends.

'Apparently, we are letting our clerk decide who is taken on,' Cassie said.

Peter looked at Richard, anxious not to find himself in disagreement with his head of Chambers.

'I've sent Stephen out for a couple of bottles,' Richard said, ignoring him, 'Sit down, sit down,' he waved his arms around the room. Peter sat down in the armchair next to Eleanor, took the application forms out of an envelope and began leafing through them.

'I really haven't had time to read these. Are we going to be long? I've just too much to do,' he said as he glanced at the pages.

'Got something important on, then, Peter?' Eleanor asked. He didn't answer. At that moment Stephen returned carrying a Tesco bag from which he removed two bottles of wine.

'Shall I put these here? We don't want them to get the wrong idea,' Stephen said, as he put the bottles down by the side of Richard's desk.

'They're all here,' he added, nodding in the direction of the waiting room.

Cassie grinned at him. She wanted him to support her, when they came to discussing the applicants. Despite their very different backgrounds they often agreed about the pupils in Chambers and their potential. He and Cassie had been offered tenancies at 3 Burke Court on the same day, their careers were following a similar trajectory. For a while they socialised together, spending evenings in the various pubs and wine bars around Fleet Street and the Temple, until he had become engaged to a very pretty young woman, leaving Cassie to go straight home.

'Let's get started, shall we,' said Richard, 'I suggest we let them do the advocacy test and then we ask them a few questions. Perhaps one each? Is that OK?'

The rest of the Tenancy Committee nodded in agreement.

'Good. Now, Cassie, you've set the advocacy test. What is it?'

'An appeal against sentence in a breach of trust case. Young woman of good character took small amounts of money from the petty cash over about three months. I succeeded in getting a sentence of six months' imprisonment reduced to a probation order.' Cassie handed out copies of the brief she had prepared.

40

'That was a good result,' said Peter Maynard.

'Not really, I was in front of Judge Hamel.'

'Mm, he's such a nice man. Always been a bit of a soft touch,' Peter said, implying he knew the judge.

'Right, who's first?' asked Eleanor.

'I think we'll take Mike Harris, then the other men and finish with the two women,' said Richard, 'Can you call him in, Stephen?'

Mike Harris had been a popular pupil, hardworking and trusted by other members of Chambers, so was the favourite for the tenancy. Cassie liked him, like most of the tenants at 3 Burke Court he had not been privately educated, and he had a robust sense of the ridiculous.

The other male candidates were rather unimpressive. The two females could not have been more different. Cassie was disappointed in the small blonde, but Mitzie Baldwin lived up to the promise of her application. She was a tall, impressive looking black woman, dressed soberly in the compulsory black suit; her voice was melodious and she was a persuasive advocate, she had researched the law and used guideline cases effectively, but when it came to questions, Richard didn't want to ask any and Cassie knew he had already made up his mind.

When they had seen all the applicants, Richard pulled a corkscrew out of the top drawer of his desk and took six glasses from a box he kept in his filing cabinet. Once the wine was poured, he began by saying, 'I really don't think there is much to talk about is there? We'll clearly take young Harris, I thought he was quite impressive.' He beamed around at them.

The rest of the committee murmured their agreement, and began to put their papers away.

41

'Mike Harris is very good, but shouldn't we consider any of the others?' Cassie said, 'We haven't…'

Richard interrupted her, 'I think we ought to take on William Allen as well. His father's a High Court Judge.'

'Is he? Well of course we should give very careful consideration to him then,' Peter said.

'I suppose it might help your application for silk this year, Peter. Always good to have personal recommendations from a senior judge,' Eleanor said as she pushed her glasses up, like an Alice-band, into her red curly hair. Peter scowled at her.

'I just think, we haven't taken on a woman for four years. People might think we are sexist.' Cassie said, trying to keep her voice steady. They had agreed this procedure for selecting tenants after months of arguing, and now the rest of the committee were ready to offer a place to someone who hadn't even applied.

'What about Mitzie Baldwin? She was very good,' Cassie said.

'I don't think she's really one of us, is she?' said Richard.

'It's difficult enough for the clerks to get work for a woman, never mind a coloured woman,' Eleanor added.

'A black woman,' Cassie corrected Eleanor's description and went on, 'The more women, the less prejudice the clerks can show.'

'Why she didn't even go to a half-decent university – where did you go, my dear?' Eleanor asked Cassie.

'Nottingham,' Cassie replied

'—like Nottingham,' Eleanor added.

'I'm for Mike Harris,' said Stephen.

'Yes, I'm sure that's the right choice. And William Allen as well. It'll be good for Chambers.' Richard put his glasses on, rearranged the papers on his desk and smiled round at them.

'I do think we should at least discuss the other candidates. We should consider another woman,' Cassie said, looking round at the rest of the committee. They could be so pompous and arrogant, these males, and that included Eleanor.

''Fraid you're outvoted, old girl,' said Peter.

'Is that decided then?' Richard said, then before anybody could comment further, 'I hear you've had a bit of a disagreement with Marcus Pike, Cassie.'

Eleanor chortled, 'He was telling everyone in the Old Bailey Mess you'd had a real go at him, told him he was doing the prosecution's job for them.'

'Not advisable, disagreeing with your leader. Not if you want to get on,' added Peter.

That was as much as Cassie could take, she walked out of the room slamming the door behind her with the glass of wine still in her hand. She felt like throwing it against the wall of the waiting room, but instead downed the contents in one, before putting the glass down on the stairs.

Chapter 7

On Alex's desk was a small sheaf of papers, held down by a glass paperweight which had an imprint of a dog's pawmark, her family's last pet. She had arrived early for her afternoon shift, hoping she would be able to work uninterrupted preparing the statements the Crown Prosecution Service were asking for in a serious street robbery. On top of the documents was a sheet of lined paper on which a spidery hand had written, 'Can you call, Mr Collins, Cotburn Square,' and underneath was a telephone number, and what she assumed was the time of the call, 12.30pm. Just under an hour ago.

She tapped her fingers on the desk as she weighed up her options: ignore the call and carry on with the work on the court papers, or put them to one side and contact Mr Collins. Tracey at the CPS would be easier to deal with than an irate Mr Collins. She reached for the telephone and dialled the number on the sheet of paper.

'DC Seymour here,' she said, when the call was answered by a male saying hello.

'I've been waiting for you to call. There's been another intruder in the garden. We took up your suggestion of putting a camera on one of the trees, and we've got a recording of a man crossing the lawn. I'm sure it's the same one I bumped into before. Well, I think it's the same one. Shall I drop it off at the police station or will you come to collect it?'

Alex hesitated; Mr Collins continued.

'It might be better if you came here and saw where we positioned the camera. You'd get a better idea of what we've filmed.'

'OK. I'll be with you in ten minutes or so.'

She walked quickly from the police station. There was no point in taking a car, finding a parking space might take ages. The gate to the garden was open when she arrived and there was no sign of Mr Collins. She strode through the arch of yew and followed the path across the lawn in the direction of the garden shed. As she approached Mr Collins's head popped round the door.

'There you are. I thought you were never going to arrive. Come in, we've got the playing device in here,' he said.

She followed him into the shed, where, amongst the piles of empty flower pots and a selection of hand tools, she saw the screen of a small CCTV, showing the route she had just taken.

'We've put the camera in the lime tree, pointing towards the path you've just come along. I check it every day and this morning I found this.' He pushed the play button and the view changed to pictures of the garden in the dark. The figure of a tall man came across the lawn and then vanished, as the camera had moved from left to right.

'Look at the time on the recording. It shows 23:05. Yes?' said Mr Collins.

Alex nodded agreement.

Collins pushed the fast forward button and then stopped it. The recording began to play again, but the time was now 23.26. Another forty seconds passed before a shape rose up from the bottom of the screen. When Alex could see the figure's head and torso, the man turned his face first to one side and then to the other, before walking away from the camera and disappearing through the arch in the yew hedge.

'He must have been sat on the bench below the tree,' Collins said.

'Twenty minutes is a long time,' said Alex.

'Perhaps he was waiting for someone.'

'Maybe. You've not found any more drugs in the garden have you?'

'No, I went to look under the shed immediately and I checked the compost heap as well. Nothing. Of course,' he paused, 'we haven't searched the whole garden, yet. Should we do that?'

'No, I don't think that's necessary. May I take the DVD? I'd like the drugs squad officers to have a look at it.'

Fifteen minutes later she went to see Mel Haskins in the drug squad office. He was sat at his computer terminal, with a pile of documents from which he was transferring information.

Alex put the disc on his desk and said, 'Have a look at this and see what you think. You need to get to about eleven pm, a little after.'

Mel put the DVD in his computer and opened the file, then fast forwarded it to just before 23:00 hours.

'Where is it?'

'Cotburn Square Garden. Taken last night, by the vigilantes of the Garden Committee.'

The computer screen showed an area of lawn, which without lighting was a pale grey. The path made a broad white strip across the grass, and the yew hedge was a black barrier.

Alex began to explain about the gate to the gardens being behind the hedge, and as she did so the male figure appeared and walked towards the camera.

The screen on Mel's computer was larger than the one in the potting shed, and gave a better picture of the man's face. Mel and Alex bend forward to peer at it.

46

'Has he got a beard, or something?' Alex said.

'Not sure. Could be. I don't recognise him at all. I could show it to the lads and see if any of them have seen him before.' He clicked on the pause sign, and looked at the face, but the shadows created by the tree made it difficult to distinguish any of the features.

'The guy vanishes and nothing happens for about twenty minutes, and then he comes up into view as if he's been sitting under the tree. There's a bench there.'

'Seems a long time to be sitting in a dark garden; can't be just admiring the plants.'

'Collins suggested he was waiting for someone. I wondered if it was a meet, and the other party didn't turn up.'

'Could be anything. Let's look at the other part.'

Mel moved the recording forward again and when the figure began to rise onto the screen, he moved his mouse along the tool bar and the sequence played in slow-motion. When the man's profile appeared he paused the picture and examined it carefully.

'I'm not sure about a beard, but there is a shadow or something on his left cheek. Did Collins say he thought it was the same man?'

'Yes, he did.'

The recording continued to play and the figure vanished through the gap in the hedge.

'You've been in the garden. That arch, how high is it?'

'I'm five ten and I would say it's only about eight or nine inches above my head.'

'This guy only just gets through without ducking. I'd say he's over six foot. So, similar description to the man who was there in June. I'll make a note to link the two sightings. Leave the disc with me and I'll try the

47

lads who saw him then and see what they think. And it might be worth contacting Collins in a day or so and see if this fellow has been back or anyone else has trespassed there.'

'I won't need to. Mr Collins will be on to me straight away if he spots anything else.'

Chapter 8

The next evening, when Cassie returned to Chambers, Jack, the senior clerk, told her the trial date for the case of Barker had been moved and it would start the following Monday.

'Does that cause me any problems?' she asked.

'Not at the moment, Colin in the List Office thinks it's going to plead, anyway.'

'I wouldn't bet on it.'

'Right, I'll try to make sure nothing else is listed for you next week; is a week enough?'

'I should think so, it might overrun by a day or so, and I'm sure Mr Pike will want to leave as soon as he's made his speech.'

Jack smiled, 'His clerk will want him too. Right I'll keep you free until Wednesday the following week. Just hope some really good fraud case doesn't come up for you.'

'Not very likely is it?'

Dangling the carrot of a better case was Jack's way of trying to persuade her she should give Barker the same advice as Marcus. Jack wasn't to be trusted; the more solicitous he seemed, the more cautious she became. He began to talk about a firm of solicitors which had a reputation for representing clients charged with fraud, but her attention was distracted by an empty wineglass on his desk. It was the one she had put down on the staircase as she had stormed out of Richard Jago's room at the end of the Tenancy Committee meeting. There were the traces of her pink lipstick on the rim and at the bottom of the bowl was stained red with the dregs of wine. He must have noticed her eyes focusing on it, and he picked it up and put it down again.

Clearly Jack had been told about the committee meeting; but she didn't know who had told him about the discussion or how much they had revealed. She didn't want to tell him anything he didn't already know, but she didn't want him to think she was hiding something.

'I wanted to know what you thought of the candidates for the tenancy.'

'Mike Harris was the obvious choice.'

'I'd heard you were rather upset about the decision.' He stretched his hand out towards the glass.

'Of course not. I like Mike Harris and he's very good. I was surprised when he left, but we weren't looking for a new tenant then.'

'Did you think any of the others might have been any good?'

'I would have liked us to give more consideration to the two women. Shouldn't we look at someone who isn't a white Anglo-Saxon male?'

'You're not one.'

'Obviously, but it's ten years since I was taken on and apart from Ayesha...'

'There you are, another female and a Mancunian to boot.'

'Very funny. It's about four years since she came here. We've given tenancies to six men since then. It's time for another woman.'

'There were two on the short list. I assume they weren't as good as Harris.'

Cassie wasn't going to tell him there had been no discussion at all about any of the candidates other than Mike Harris, or that Richard was determined to offer a

50

place to some judge's son. Her reticence was unnecessary.

'I hear Judge Allen's son has just finished pupillage at Stone Court. He might make a good tenant. Useful connections, you might say,' Jack said. Cassie was aware of him watching her to gauge her reaction.

'I don't know him, and he hasn't applied to come here. We've made a decision.'

'There's room for another couple or so, we've a lot of work at the bottom and we're turning it away. I don't like doing that.'

'No, you don't,' said Cassie as she walked towards the door.

On her way home she called Ben to tell him about the Barker case being relisted.

'Does that mean you will be working all weekend? You haven't forgotten we're having dinner with Philip have you?'

'No, it's not a problem. I'm being led, so someone else has to do most of the work. I'll need to read through the papers again, but it's somebody else's show, not mine. I'll try and get most of the work done tonight. I've just got a plea at Southwark tomorrow so I'll be home early and can finish it off then.'

'I should be finished about six, so I'll be with you by seven.'

She said that would be fine, she was sure she could complete the work before Ben arrived.

She worked on the brief most of Thursday evening, leaving the papers spread out over her desk, so that she could begin again where she had left off, when she got back from court.

She was back in her flat in time to prepare herself a plate of pasta with a sauce made of leeks, pancetta and

51

crème fraiche. She took a bottle of Argentinian Malbec out of her wine rack, but put it back. Drinking at lunchtime wasn't on when she needed to work.

Once she had finished eating she returned to the Barker brief. The copy of the Evening Standard was tucked between the files; she pulled it out and began to read the article about the murder of Shelley Paulson. She turned the paper over and looked at the report of a football match on the back page. The game was between Chelsea and Everton, and the photograph was of one of the Chelsea players; she didn't take any notice of the name.

She put the paper down and returned to reading. She had completed the statements of the witnesses who would be called at the trial and turned her attention to the rest of the documents, the unused material which the Crown would not use. She winced as she reread the report of the fingerprint expert, Dr Pretty, and skipped through the statements taken from Shelley Paulson's friends and clients. Then she started on the transcripts of the recordings made by the undercover police officer, Rose Cummings, and flicked through them until she came to the section where Lenny said he'd been to a football match with a friend he called Hinds. The words 'Chelsea' and 'Everton' seemed to leap out of the page. She slowed down and read the passage again. The game he had gone to, he told Rose, was at Stamford Bridge and the home team had played Everton. Cassie fumbled through the papers for the copy of the Standard, turned again to the back page and checked the date of the newspaper. It was 19th September and the game had been the night before, the same day as the murder. Cassie pushed her hair back, she must make sure she had read the dates correctly.

She traced the details of the match with her finger, first in the newspaper, confirming the date and the time of the game, and then in the transcript. She went back to the newspaper, to check again and to ensure it had been played at Stamford Bridge, the Chelsea ground; it had, and it followed that if Lenny had gone there that night he was not in Holland Walk and he was not the murderer.

The case against Barker had seemed unanswerable and she had been sure he would be convicted. Now there was everything to fight for; her client had an alibi and what's more a witness who could say where he was on the night of the murder. Innocent until proved guilty. She knew she shouldn't have assumed Lenny was guilty; she wasn't the judge or the jury, and sometimes the evidence could change.

For a few moments she sat at her desk, then she picked up a yellow highlighter and marked the passage in the transcript and the date of the football game in the newspaper. The next step was to ring Tim Durrant, tell him the news and he could then contact this man 'Hinds' and get a statement from him. As soon as he answered she said, 'We have an alibi.'

'What do you mean?' he asked.

She explained about the reference to the game in the transcripts and the report of the same game in the Evening Standard. 'So he was at Stamford Bridge, not in Holland Park,' she said.

'Calm down. It's not what he said in interview. Why didn't he remember when he was shown the newspaper? Anyway we'd need to find the witness and how are we going to do that in two days? Particularly now our boy is in Brixton.'

'What?' she yelled, 'What's happened?'

'He broke his curfew on Tuesday evening.'

'Can't we go and see him?'

'It's too late to make an appointment for tomorrow, the office is closed and the weekends are impossible, they're always fully booked.' Tim paused, and then said, 'I'll see if I can speak to him on the telephone.'

'Ring me as soon as you've spoken to him. Have you got my mobile number?'

'Yes. But I don't know what we can do even if he says he was at the match now.'

'Look, just ring me if he says he was. We need to get hold of Hinds. Lenny should know where he lives.'

'I wouldn't bet on it,' Tim replied. 'I think you should ring Marcus and tell him. See what he wants to do,' he added before ringing off.

She tried to contact Marcus at his chambers, but was told that he had already left for the weekend. She tried his mobile number but either the phone was switched off or there was no reception, so she sent a text asking him to contact her. She slumped forwards, put her elbows on her desk and held her head in her hands, trying to work out what to do next. Who was Hinds? Where was he? Could he be found in time? The questions went round and round and she couldn't see any answers, any way to solve the problem of the missing alibi.

Chapter 9

Cassie usually looked forward to Friday nights, but the discovery of a possible alibi witness, a witness whose whereabouts were unknown, had made her anxious. She didn't have a clue where to begin looking for him, even if the name Hinds was his real name, after all what kind of name was that?

She had anticipated spending an uninterrupted weekend with Ben, with nothing to do on the Barker case, she should have been able to put any thoughts of work from her mind, but the discovery of an alibi for her client had unsettled her and left her worrying about how they might find the missing witness.

As soon as Ben arrived, she slipped an arm under his and began to tell him about Hinds. She was pleased to see him, she needed his objectivity; her own judgement, usually so good, had abandoned her with the sudden shift in the weight of evidence.

'Hey, have you forgotten we are going to Philip's for dinner tonight?' Ben said, before pulling her to him and kissing her.

'I knew we were going somewhere but with all this going on, contacting Tim and trying to get hold of Marcus, it had completely slipped my mind. I want to tell Marcus about this alibi and ask what he wants to do, but he's away for the weekend. How can he with this trial about to start?'

'Murders are two a penny for him, aren't they? Isn't that why Tim chose him for this case?'

'Yes, but...I'm going to try again.' She was too anxious; there was very little anyone could do, but she wanted to feel something was happening and, if she was honest, impress Marcus Pike with her abilities.

While she waited for the phone to be answered, Ben picked up the DVD she had left on the coffee table.

'What's this?' he asked.

No one answered the phone and, after closing the connection, she said, 'It's the recording made of the identification parade. Do you want to see it?'

'Sure. How long is it? '

'About twenty minutes. Is that OK?'

'Sure. It won't take that long to get to Philip's. Anyway he was still in his office when I left.'

He placed the DVD into Cassie's computer and started to play it. She came and stood next to him.

The first pictures were of the long dimly-lit viewing gallery and then a view of the parade room, where a crowd of fifteen or so young men milled around under bright fluorescent lighting. They were all in their early twenties, dressed in jeans and a variety of shirts and sweaters. The soundtrack picked up snippets of their conversation and their nervous laughter. Someone said, 'What happens if one of us gets identified?'

No one replied.

A few moments later, a uniformed police officer in shirtsleeves came into view, followed by Tim Durrant.

'That's Tim,' Cassie said to Ben.

'Now lads,' said the police officer, 'Can you just stand in a line please. We won't be long now.'

Tim began to walk along the row of men, stopping in front of each one.

'They need eight, and Tim is trying to get lads who are similar to Barker in height, and eliminate those who are too obviously different,' Cassie said.

'Trying to confuse the witness,' Ben said.

'That's one way of looking at it. You could say trying to make sure he really does remember what the killer looked like.'

The screen went back to the empty viewing gallery, but Cassie and Ben could hear the voice of the officer say, 'You lot can go now. The rest of you, can you stay lined up.'

The camera returned to the parade room where eight young men stood behind a row of numbers. Lenny Barker was led in by a man in plain clothes. Somebody had supplied him with a pair of jeans and a sweatshirt. His face was tense and his left cheek twitched. Tim went over to him and whispered something to him.

'Take up any position you like,' said the officer.

Lenny looked at Tim, who pointed to a position two in from the left; in front of him was the number 3.

Now the screen switched to the viewing gallery again and a different uniformed officer holding a clipboard came into view, and with him was another man in a dark raincoat.

'I want you to walk slowly along the gallery and look carefully at all the men and if you recognise the man you saw in Holland Walk, please tell me the number. Do remember the man might not be there.'

'That's the eyewitness, James Compton,' Cassie said.

Compton walked slowly along the gallery. He stopped for a few moments and looked at the man stood at number 6, and then turned towards number 5, as if he was comparing them. They were the two tallest men in the line-up. Then he moved on to the other end of the gallery, before swivelling round and making his way back towards the officer. He stopped and looked

57

down at Barker and then asked the officer if the men could turn to their right. The request was relayed to the police inspector in the parade room and he asked them to do so. Some went left and had to be asked to turn the other way. By the time they were all standing with their left cheeks towards Compton he had moved on and was looking down at number 5 again. He lifted his head and began to shake it as he quickened his pace towards the door.

The policeman asked him again if he could identify the man he had seen in Holland Walk, but Compton just continued to shake his head and walked out of view of the camera. As the officer turned to leave and was blocking any view of the witness, the words, 'I think it's number three' could be heard clearly.

'Would that persuade you he was sure Barker was the right man?'

'I'd want to know why he hesitated, but if he had a good explanation, I think I could accept it. He was looking at your man when he asked if they could all turn. Something about Barker made him want a view of his profile,' Ben said.

Cassie wasn't too disappointed by Ben's reaction; she had thought the same before the evidence of the alibi had emerged. There was nothing further she could do now except wait for Tim to find out from Lenny where Hinds lives. For now there was the dinner party at Philip Stanmore's, a fellow lecturer of Ben's.

Cassie and Ben were the last to arrive. As Philip helped her out of her coat, she noticed two people standing looking out of a large window, towards the Thames and the lights of a building on the other side of the river. She couldn't see their faces, apart from a blurred reflection in the glass. From the way they were

58

leaning, she assumed they were a couple. They were both tall and slim, the man had a mop of dark hair, the woman's was blonde and shoulder length. They were talking in hushed tones but she could hear the man say, 'That's the former Billingsgate Fish Market.'

Sitting on a low leather sofa was a woman of about her own age, wearing a white dress with an asymmetrical hem. Her make-up was pale and contrasted sharply with the large round black rimmed spectacles on her nose. She had a wine glass in her hand, the remains of some red wine staining the base.

Philip got them two glasses and poured them each a glass of wine before saying, 'Alex, Aubrey, another drink?'

The two turned towards Cassie and Ben. The man came towards them and said, 'I'm Aubrey.'

'What about you, Tamsin?' said Phillip.

'Yes. Desperate. Had a bloody awful day.' She held out the glass and watched whilst Philip refilled it. 'Thank God it's Friday.'

Cassie felt the short stab of jealousy as she saw Ben smile and say, 'Then you must be Alex?' The woman, who had been stood by the window, was dressed in a pair of black trousers and a dark grey silk blouse, whose buttons were open so that the curve of her breast was just visible. Cassie's clothes, a simple navy dress and low heels, were rather dowdy by comparison, but she reassured herself, it wasn't important.

After he had poured wine into Tamsin's glass Philip left them, to finish making their meal, declining Cassie's offer of help saying, 'No way, Ben says you're an ace cook and I wouldn't dare let you see the state of my kitchen.'

She walked over to the window and looked out at the lights reflected in the dark swirling mirror of the river. She was distracted by the Barker case, planning new tactics for the trial in her mind, and only heard snippets of conversation.

'Cassie lives near there, Chepstow Road,' Ben said to Alex. Then Tamsin's voice, 'Oh Aubrey, don't be such a bore.'

From her handbag she took her mobile phone and checked to see if she had missed a call from Tim whilst they were on the underground, but there was nothing. She turned the sound off, but left the phone on vibrating mode, and slipped it back into her bag.

'I do think we ought to have a rule, no mobile phones on Friday nights. Don't you think?' said Tamsin.

Tamsin must have seen her take her mobile out. For a moment she felt embarrassed, but then Alex said, 'Not everybody works fixed hours.'

Over the meal they talked of the difficulties of getting around London; how much they disliked traveling by tube, but how indispensable it was; the price of property in different areas of the city. Apart from Cassie and Ben, the others had met on a skiing holiday, and there was talk of the thrills and spills of racing down snow-covered mountain slopes.

After they had finished eating, Tamsin began to tease Philip about his cooking skills, asking him if he had bought the dishes at Borough Market. He insisted he had prepared the meal himself.

'I heard Philip say you are a good cook, are you a chef then?' Aubrey said.

Cassie laughed, 'No, I'm at the Bar.'

'Really,' said Tamsin, 'That must be interesting.'

'I enjoy it.'

'What sort of work do you do?' said Alex.

'Mainly defending in the Criminal Courts.'

'How can you defend someone you know is guilty?' said Aubrey.

Cassie looked at Ben and grinned at him; he hadn't believed her when she told him how often she was asked that question.

'It's not my job to decide if he's guilty or innocent. That's for the jury. Anyway it depends what you mean by know. If a defendant says he committed the offence, I can't represent him unless he pleads guilty.'

'But you must have an idea?' Aubrey said.

'I might be wrong. The case I'm doing now, I thought the guy was guilty. He'd been identified by an eyewitness, but then some extra evidence was disclosed by the police, rather late in the day, and now I think he may be innocent.'

Cassie looked round the table and noticed Alex was observing her closely.

'I think we've met before,' Alex said.

'Really? I can't think where.'

Philip intervened, 'Alex is in the police force.'

'Perhaps in court somewhere?' Cassie said.

'I assume so.' There was a pause before she continued, 'I think it was at Snaresbrook; you were defending in one of those drug trials from the investigation around Kings Cross Station.'

'Yes, I did a couple of those cases.'

'I hadn't been involved in the observations, but they were short of an officer to handle the exhibits. Most of the defendants pleaded guilty, but there was one where the handover of drugs in exchange for cash had not been caught on camera. There was a large traffic sign obscuring the scene, but two women officers gave evidence they had seen the transaction.'

'That was Sara Leighton's case.'

'I was very impressed by your cross-examination. You made those witnesses look totally unreliable. I was glad it wasn't me.'

Cassie grinned, 'Their shadows on the video gave them away. They couldn't have been in a position to see the drugs handed over.'

'Tell us about the other case. What's the guy charged with?' said Tamsin.

'Murder. A young woman was killed in Holland Walk last September,' Cassie replied.

'How awful. But why do you think he's innocent?' Aubrey said.

'That's the Paulson case isn't it?' said Alex. She didn't want Cassie to reveal anything about the case that might cause any difficulties for either of them later.

'Yes. It is,' Cassie said.

'Poor girl,' Tamsin said.

'There's always a victim,' Alex murmured.

'Victims. Any crime is like a stone dropping into a pool,' Cassie said.

Tamsin took out a packet of cigarettes.

'I'd rather you didn't smoke,' Alex said.

Tamsin put the packet back, and said she'd go outside, but Philip said she could go into the bedroom, where there was a small balcony.

When she had left Alex said to Cassie, 'I gave up two months ago, but get desperate as soon as I smell someone else's, particularly after dinner.'

As she spoke the two of them moved from the table to the sofa. Cassie was about to say she hadn't smoked since she was at university, when she felt her handbag, which was on the seat next to her, tremble, and realised it was her mobile phone vibrating. She pulled it out and looked at the screen. She didn't recognise the number, but pushed the answer key, hoping it was Tim's home telephone.

'Cassie, it's Tim.' said the voice on the other end, 'I've managed to speak to Lenny, after a lot of trouble with prison officers.'

Cassie interrupted him, 'And?'

'He says he did go to the match with this friend, Hinds. They walked home after the game. If he's telling the truth, he couldn't have been in Holland Walk when Shelley Paulson was murdered. The bad news is he doesn't know Hinds's real name, or where he lives.'

'What!' Cassie walked into the centre of the room, oblivious of the conversations going on around her. 'No. How are we going to find him?' she squealed.

There was a sudden silence, and she looked round as Tim said, 'Lenny did say that he thought Hinds worked on the Portobello Market. At least that's where they would meet up.'

Cassie lowered her voice and said, 'Did he say anything else? Give a description?'

'He's mixed race.'

'What ethnic groups?'

'I assume White Afro-Caribbean, if he lived in North Kensington. About six foot. Possibly plays football for a local side. That's as much as I could get from him on the phone.'

'Not very good, is it? And by the way, I can't get hold of Marcus.'

'There's not much we can do at the moment. If I think of anything I'll give you a ring. OK.'

She walked back to the sofa and slipped the phone into her handbag.

'Anything wrong?' Alex asked.

'That was the defendant's solicitor. We've a witness missing and the trial starts on Monday.'

Chapter 10

Over breakfast Ben asked Cassie whether there was anything she particularly wanted to do.

'It's a nice day. We could go down to the river for a walk or to Kew or...' he trailed off as Cassie was turning a spoon over and over in her hands.

'What did you say?' she asked, realising he had been talking to her.

'I asked you what you wanted to do.'

'Find this Hinds,' she replied.

'How can you do that? You don't know if it's his real name, no address, nothing.'

'I know. Barker's mother lives quite close. I think I might go and see her.'

'Isn't that for Tim to do? I thought barristers were meant to keep themselves detached from witnesses?'

'I know, normally I wouldn't get involved. Not the done thing. My colleagues would disapprove but we need something by Monday; some details, the guy's real name, an address, something to identify him, if we want to get an adjournment, and Tim lives somewhere out in Kent.'

Cassie began looking through the case papers again.

'What are you doing?'

'Looking for the full address.'

She pulled out a file and opened it, 'It'll be on his custody record.' She thumbed through the pages, then stopped and read out 'Twenty-six Lancaster Close.' She looked at the exasperated expression on his face, 'Ben, I have to do something.'

'OK. Do you want me to come with you?'

'I'm not sure. No. Yes. At least walk up there with me.'

Once they got to the low-rise concrete blocks of the Lancaster Estate, they had some difficulty locating the exact address. Eventually, they were stood on a narrow walkway in front of a door marked twenty-six; the green paint was peeling away, but the glass panel sparkled. Cassie pushed the doorbell. After a few minutes, it was opened by a thin-faced woman wearing a track suit. She had no make-up on, and her hair looked as if she had not brushed it yet. It was difficult to estimate her age, but she looked a little young to be Lenny's mother.

'Mrs Barker?' Cassie asked.

'Yes,' Mrs Barker replied, worry lines appeared on her forehead, as she inspected Cassie, 'You're not the police are you? Social worker?'

Cassie was taken aback by the question, 'Mrs Barker. I'm Miss Hardman, Cassie Hardman. Lenny's barrister.'

'You're too well dressed for round here. Thought you were the police again.'

'Am I?' Cassie smiled, her dark brown eyes warm and reassuring.

Mrs Barker beckoned her in, 'Come in, come in' and shouted back into the flat, 'Jane. It's Lenny's lawyer.'

Cassie turned towards Ben, but he had moved away down the walkway. 'I won't be long,' she mouthed at him.

Once through the door, Cassie followed Mrs Barker along a lino-covered corridor, past a battered bicycle and into a sitting room, where Lenny's elder sister was sitting on a worn sofa. There were magazines on the floor, a full laundry basket on a chair, and in front of the television where a quiz programme was in full swing was an ironing board, with a pair of blue denim jeans draped on it. Cassie could smell freshly washed garments and the hot iron.

On the mantelpiece, above an electric fire, a photograph of a young boy wearing a bright red sweater leant against the wall. The face was chubbier and the hair much curlier, but it was recognisable as Lenny.

Mrs Barker saw Cassie looking at it and said, 'He was five when that was taken. First year at school. He was such a good boy, despite me and his Dad separating. Lenny went to see him regular, until he remarried and went to Australia. At first there was talk of Lenny going out there, but then the letters tailed off, and now it's just a Christmas card. Lenny's never grumbled or complained about it, but then he never says much.'

She unplugged the iron and pushed the board to one side. 'Never had the police at my door before this either. Not like some round here.'

When her mother paused, Jane said, 'It was awful, really awful. They had him stood naked while they searched everywhere. They'd forgotten to bring one of those white overall things.'

'Sit down, will you. Sorry we're a bit of a mess. I was just doing some ironing,' Mrs Barker said. 'Do sit down. Can I get you a cup of tea?' she added.

'Thanks, but I'm OK. Could I see Lenny's room?' It had suddenly occurred to her that she might get some insight into her taciturn client.

'No problem,' Mrs Barker said and she led the way along the corridor to a bedroom at the back of the flat.

The room was tidy, too tidy, Cassie thought, no clothes on the floor or empty cups by the bed. The walls were painted blue over a striped paper, the curtains were blue but the duvet cover was pink with a Barbie Doll pattern. There was a flat screen TV on a low table, and besides it a pile of magazines. Cassie picked up the couple on the top, one was a copy of Match and the other Muscle and Body.

'The police looked through the ones he had, trying to see if he had any of those pornographic ones. I told them if he'd brought any of those here he'd have been out on his ear.'

Behind the TV the wallpaper had been pulled away, leaving strips hanging. 'The police did that,' Mrs Barker said, 'And that,' pointing to a similar area by the bed. 'At least they didn't damage the TV. He'd have gone mad about that; bought it out of his wages so he could watch the football when he wanted.'

'Mad about it?' Cassie said.

'Upset, I mean, upset. The bedcover is an old one of Jane's; the police took his, for the scientists, they said.'

When they had all returned to the living room, Cassie said, 'I've come because we need to find a friend of Lenny's who might help his case. Lenny calls him Hinds, but doesn't know his real name or where he lives.'

'Hinds. I don't know anyone called Hinds. Do you Jane?' She shook her head. 'I'm not sure,' Jane replied. 'There's that football team Lenny played with. Might be one of them.'

'Yes, it might be,' Cassie said, echoing the words. 'Do you know which football team it was?'

Cassie was beginning to wish she hadn't come, there was a tension between the two women and Jane

68

appeared wary of her. Were they hiding something, or did they genuinely not know who she was talking about. Underneath the friendly exterior she detected distrust.

There was silence while Mrs Barker and Jane looked at each other, and then at Cassie before Mrs Barker replied, 'No. Might have been something to do with the sports centre.'

'Which sports centre? The one under the Westway or the one just along the road here?'

Mrs Barker shrugged her shoulders and frowned at her daughter.

'Don't look at me. I don't know,' Jane said.

Cassie tried to hide the irritation she was feeling, 'Mrs Barker, it's really important to try and find this man. It will help Lenny's case. Just try and think where he played football.' Cassie was silent for a moment, casting around for a way of prompting their memories. 'Did he have any football kit?'

'Only his boots. If he was playing he took his boots,' Mrs Barker said.

Jane chipped in 'I'm not sure if it was a real team or he just got together with a few mates, and they kicked a football about.'

'Have you any idea where they played?'

'No,' Jane replied.

'Or who with?'

'No,' they both said.

They seemed to know so little about Lenny's friends, what he did or where he went. Was he very secretive and if so why? Did he have something to hide or was he just trying to avoid being pestered? Perhaps he was supressing his sexuality, or was there something else, some other behaviour he wished to

69

conceal? Cassie could see no point in continuing to ask them about his friends, not here, not now. 'Look if you think of anything, or can find out about this man, please ring Mr Durrant straight away.'

Cassie left the flat and returned to the street, where she found Ben leaning against the wall.

'They're useless. They have no idea who Hinds is. They don't know if Lenny played football with some team or just with friends. His mother thinks it was something to do with a sports club, but doesn't know which one,' Cassie told him. 'I don't know what to do now.'

'What about trying the sports centre? It's just round the corner isn't it?'

'Mm. Yes, I used to swim there,' she said as she led him back along the walkway.

They could see the entrance to the sports hall as soon as they turned the next corner. In front of them at the ticket booth was a group of young Afro-Caribbean boys and a pretty golden-skinned girl. They were laughing and shouting, and two of them were pretending to throw punches. The attendant in the glass fronted ticket booth, a middle aged Asian man, shook his head at them. 'Kids, I suppose they'll grow up,' he said and then, 'What can I do for you?'

'I'm trying to find out if a young man called Lenny Barker played football here.'

'I don't know the name. What'd you want him for? You're not the police are you?'

Cassie looked at Ben and then back at the man, 'No. We're not police. I'm a lawyer. I'm representing Lenny Barker. He's charged with a serious offence and I think someone he played football with may be able to assist us.'

'Well, I don't know.' He spoke slowly, giving himself time to think, 'It's confidential information you want.' There was a pause. 'That's if he played here,' he added.

Cassie was tapping her foot gently on the floor, as she searched in her pocket for the business cards she had put there. 'It's very urgent.' She was irritated by the petty officialdom, but smiled to reassure him, and handed him one of the cards. Eventually he got down from his chair and went towards a door in the right hand wall.

'I'll get Bob Maddox, he's the football coach,' he said as he left the ticket booth. 'Wait there.'

A queue formed while they waited but the attendant soon returned followed by a tall athletic black man in a navy track suit. 'Miss Hardman?' he said looking at Cassie.

'Yes.'

'Come through.' He held open a gate for her, and she walked into the hallway, followed by Ben. Mr Maddox escorted them into a small office, the walls covered in cork boards with team fixtures and tables pinned to them. He invited them to sit down on the plastic chairs in front of a desk and closed the lid of his laptop computer.

Once seated Cassie introduced Ben and then explained that they were trying to find out if Lenny Barker played football with one of the centre's teams.

'You're his lawyer, I understand?' Bob asked, turning her card over in his hands.

'Yes,' she replied.

'And Ben?'

'A friend of mine.'

Bob Maddox continued looking at the card, paused and looked at Ben and then Cassie.

'He's been charged with murder, I hear. Is that right?'

'Yes,' said Cassie. 'Did he play football here?'

'If he did?'

'I think he may have been at a football match on the night of the murder, with another member of the team.'

'Do you know his name?'

'The name I have is Hinds. I don't know if that's a surname or a nickname.'

'OK. I think I can help but I don't think it's going to get you very far. Lenny did play here. So did Hinds. It's a nickname, but don't ask me how he got it.' He got up and went to a filing cabinet, and rifled through the files in the bottom drawer before pulling one out and opening it. 'His real name was Edwin Walker. I don't have an address for him, only a mobile number.'

'Can you let me have it?' Cassie moved forward to the edge of her seat, her eyes fixed on Bob Maddox.

He was clearly reluctant. 'Look, I've gone as far as I dare. I don't really know who you are, and I can't hand out someone's personal details just like that.'

Cassie leant back, pursed her lips and opened her mouth to speak, when Ben said, 'Why don't you ring the number, Mr Maddox, and see if he'll talk to us?' Cassie shot him a glance of approval, impressed by his quick thinking, but disappointed she hadn't thought of it first.

Bob Maddox picked up his phone, looked at the file he was holding, and dialled a number. They could hear the ringing tone, followed by a voice telling them the number was no longer in service.

'Thank you,' said Cassie, trying not to look disappointed, 'Can you tell me anything else about Hinds which might help us find him?'

'Not really. He played with us for a season about a year ago, possibly two. I heard he'd been sent to prison for something. It couldn't have been for long because I saw him on the market a couple of months later.'

'What about his age? Do you have a date of birth?'

'I would say he was about twenty-three or so. I don't appear to have a date of birth for him but he must have been over eighteen when he started playing with us. I'm sorry I can't help you.'

Cassie got up and thanked him, apologised for taking up his time, and asked him to ring the number on her business card if he thought of anything that might help. He had placed the card on his desk, but he picked it up again and nodded at her. She got up and left the office. Ben echoed her thanks, then followed her out and into the street

'At least you have his real name. Edwin. Bit posh. No wonder he preferred a nickname, even if it is a bit strange,' he laughed.

'It's not a laughing matter,' Cassie said as she strode off in the direction of Portobello Road leaving him behind.

'Don't be silly, Cassie. What are you doing now?' Ben said, following her.

She stopped at the traffic lights on Ladbroke Road, turned to Ben. 'I don't know what to do. I suppose it's best to wait until Monday and get the police to trace him. If he's been convicted, they should have an address for him. Let's go home.'

73

Chapter 11

Cassie arrived at the Old Bailey as the clock on the church tower of St Martin-within-Ludgate struck nine. She was loaded down with the bags containing her robes, the criminal barrister's bible, Archbold, and the four files of the Barker brief. There was a long queue leading from the entrance to the courts, along the street and past the steps to the now permanently-closed doors of the Edwardian building, where the famous number one court was situated. Lawyers, witnesses and jurors were all waiting to get through the security procedures beyond the revolving doors. The queue moved slowly, too slowly for her, impatient as she was to get into the building and start the final preparations for the trial.

Once she was through the scanning machines, she walked past the glass pen, where defence witnesses and prisoners' families were held, and down three steps to the lift lobby. As she waited for a lift to the fifth floor, David Jennings, the junior barrister for the prosecution, rolled down the steps towards her. They had co-defended in a trial at the Old Bailey some years before and were good friends. It had been a prank; a drunken escapade by a group of young men, who had driven a road roller a few yards along the highway. Their opponent, a very serious young woman, seemed to think it was a state trial.

'Well, I suppose it did take place outside the Tower of London,' David had said. Cassie had burst into laughter, but prosecuting counsel didn't seem to get the joke. However, today he was the opposition, so she was a little more distant than she would have been if they had simply met up at court.

'I hear you've come up with an alibi,' he said.

'News travels fast. We wouldn't have known about it if the police hadn't set him up with the WPC.'

'I guess we'll have to try and defend their actions,' he replied. He didn't sound particularly pleased by the prospect.

Once upstairs in the female robing room, Cassie pushed aside a pile of papers to make room for her bags. She put her robes on, checked the tabs were straight in the full length mirror. Under the harsh lights, turned on because the bomb-proof net curtains made it dark, she peered at her reflection, wished she was taller and more imposing, and then dismissed the thought. She put her wig on top of her files and tucked them all under her arm and left the room.

She had just started to climb the stairs to the Bar Mess, when she heard her name called on the tannoy summoning her back to the front door. She had no idea why she was wanted, but she turned back to the lobby and trotted down the four flights of stairs to the ground floor. Tim Durrant had arrived with Lenny's mother, who was dressed in a grey suit, her hair combed and her face made up, so that Cassie failed to recognise her at first. Jane hadn't paid so much attention to her appearance. She was casually dressed, wearing a pair of faded jeans with a dark blue parka. When Mrs Barker saw Cassie her eyes lit up, and she jumped up from the bench on which she was sitting.

'Miss Hardman.' The words shot out of Mrs Barker's mouth, 'Miss Hardman. I've been making some enquiries about the football.'

'Yes?' replied Cassie.

'The team was Westbourne Wonders. They played for the Sports Club next door to us. I found a card.

75

Look,' and she held out a battered white card with a list of fixtures on it. Cassie took it from her. Against each fixture the results had been written in a blue biro. The last game marked had been played on the 28th October, just before Lenny had been arrested. Cassie looked at the dates of the previous games and noticed one on the 23rd September, five days after the murder, and was struck again by how Lenny's behaviour, going to work, playing football, appeared to have been unaffected by the murder of Shelley Paulson. Could he have behaved so normally if he had killed her?

'I asked around the estate if any other kids played for the same team. There's a couple who do, and they say this guy Hinds played with them until about a year ago. Then he left but they think the family has moved to Willesden,' she paused 'Or was it Wembley? Anyway I thought the council might have an address for them for forwarding stuff.' She looked at Cassie, her eyes pleading for approval.

Cassie hesitated before saying, 'I think his name was Edwin Walker. Does that ring any bells with you?'

'No, it doesn't,' she shook her head. Cassie smiled at her but said nothing. There was nothing to say.

Mrs Barker turned away from Cassie and, after a moment's hesitation, asked Tim if she would be able to watch the trial. He walked with her to the exit door, and directed her out of the building to a side passage where a queue had formed at the entrance to the public gallery. 'We'd better go and see him,' Tim said when he returned, and together they went down the small flight of stairs that led to the basement and the entrance to the cell area. The custody area was a parallel world, a maze of harshly lit corridors, where keys jangled,

76

boots thumped, and the stale air smelt of urine, overcooked cabbage and fear.

The interview room was the size of a hermit's cell, painted in institutional cream and decorated with mundane graffiti. Cassie put her papers down on the battered table, pushed the seats back against the wall and eased herself into the space. Tim remained standing at the door to catch Lenny when he was brought from his cell.

They didn't have to wait long before he came along the corridor. Tim ushered him into the room and told him to sit down on the chair furthest from the door. Cassie was aware of the risk a defendant might pose if he didn't like the advice he was being given. At least if she was closer to the door than Lenny and he threatened her she could escape easily. She didn't think Lenny would assault her, but the habit was totally automatic, and she assumed it was for Tim as well.

Lenny pushed his hands through his hair and pulled at the collar of his white shirt.

'Do I look OK? My mum wanted me to wear a tie but I wasn't sure.'

'You're fine. You're better off being comfortable. We don't want you pulling at your collar or wriggling too much, the jury may see it as a sign of guilt,' Cassie replied. She went on to explain how they had found out about the football match. Lenny's fingers played on the table and he chewed on his lower lip. 'Don't worry about it now,' said Cassie, 'Can you help us any more with Hinds? I've spoken to Mr Maddox at the sports centre, and he told us he was called Edwin Walker. Your mum thinks he's moved from the Lancaster Estate to Willesden. Do you have any idea where he lives?'

'No. I don't.' Creases appeared across Lenny Barker's forehead. 'He used to just turn up on the market. Sometimes he worked for one of the stall holders up by the flyover, you know. Helping to move boxes of fruit and veg. Other times he just hung around. We'd go and have a drink together, like, talk about football. We both support Chelsea.'

The door opened and Marcus Pike erupted into the room, filling the remaining space. Cassie sat back and let Marcus take over the conference.

'I assume Miss Hardman has told you that you appear to have an alibi, if what you told this policewoman was true and you weren't just boasting,' Marcus began. It wasn't a question and he didn't wait for a reply. 'Two things. First, why did you not say you'd been at the football to the police?' Marcus held his hand up to stop Lenny replying, 'And second, what do you know about this man Hinds that may help us find him?'

'I've been thinking about it, like, since Mr Durrant called. We played football and, well, the market, you know. It was all casual.'

'Did he have a girlfriend or anyone who might know where he is?' Marcus asked.

'Not anyone I know,' Lenny replied, 'We didn't go around together or anything. Just the football.' He paused before adding, 'And he hasn't played for some time, you know, not since he was locked up.'

'Let's hope the police can trace him. Now, why didn't you tell them you'd been with him to the match?'

Lenny looked first at Tim, then Cassie before answering Marcus. The twitch in his left cheek returned. 'The date, you know; it didn't mean anything.

I'd been in the park round then. They said there were cameras. I thought they might have photos. I don't know really. Then that guy identified me. You know, it seemed silly saying I couldn't remember.' He tailed off.

He sounded unconvincing; of course defendants, even well-educated ones, found being arrested and held in custody so intimidating that they frequently made mistakes during police interviews, but, still, his explanation didn't sound credible. Marcus went on to explain that they would be applying for an adjournment in order to try and find Hinds. 'But,' he warned Lenny, 'If we get it you'll have to stay in prison for the time being.'

Lenny's face sagged, his shoulders drooped and he leant back on his chair.

'It's for the best. If we find Hinds, I don't want any suggestion that you have tried to concoct an alibi with him. Do you understand?' Marcus said.

Lenny nodded and sighed. 'I want to go home.' Cassie leant over and patted his arm.

'Let's take one step at a time,' she said, although unless Hinds could be found, there was a real risk he would be spending a long time in prison. The police investigation had stopped, the prosecution believed Lenny was the killer, and there was enough evidence for a jury to convict him.

Chapter 12

Court number 12 was in the new part of the Old Bailey and lacked the character of the older courts. The room was panelled like the inside of a ski chalet, lit by banks of fluorescent lights in the ceiling, which flickered subliminally. The only decoration was a large, Disneyesque version of the Royal Standard with its motto 'Honi Soit qui Mal y Pense' in a girdle around it, on the wall behind the elevated judge's bench.

Cassie was the first to arrive, and she walked along the back of the court past the dock and put her papers down on the second row of workbenches, close to the jury box where, by convention, defence lawyers always sit. Marcus Pike would take the place in front of her and Tim behind. Seconds later Howard Alsopp arrived followed by David Jennings, who was struggling with both his and Howard's files. A police officer came in and spoke to them, but she was too far away to hear what he said. Howard opened his lectern and placed it on the bench, then he and David continued to sort their papers.

Cassie looked up at the public gallery above the witness box, and saw Mrs Barker and Jane had found seats on the front row; she put a hand up to acknowledge them, and Jane waved back. Then Marcus arrived, rushing across the front of the court saying, 'I'm not late, am I?' as if he was a guest at some Mad Hatter's tea party, before sitting down.

While they waited for the judge to come into court, Cassie arranged her papers, checked that her files, which she had placed upright in front of her, were in the right order, put a new notebook on the bench, and positioned a fountain pen, two ball point pens and two pencils to the right of the notebook, and three different coloured highlighters to the left. She rearranged them from time to time, moving the pencils from left to right and then back again, as they waited. The beginning of a trial was stressful, the uncertainty about the witnesses, the unknown nature of the jury; and the unpredictability of prosecuting counsel, who would probably create lies out of misunderstandings, facts out of opinions.

When the judges' door opened, instead of the judge coming in, the court clerk, a slim, young woman wearing dark clothes under a lawyer's gown, her light brown hair pulled back from her face, told them the judge would like to see counsel in his room. She held the door open and the four barristers filed out into the judges' corridor. These corridors were hushed, the carpets thick to absorb the sound, like those in an expensive hotel, and so different from the clatter of the cells.

They followed the clerk to His Honour Judge Stewart Crabtree's chambers a little way along. 'Counsel in the case of Barker to see you, my Lord,' said the clerk as she ushered them into the room.

Judge Crabtree was a handsome man, square faced, lightly tanned with wavy, dark blond hair. Cassie had never seen him without his wig before and he looked much younger than his fifty-three years. Hung on the walls, as well as the usual photographs of him in robes at judicial functions, was one of him stood by what looked like the Round Pond in Kensington Gardens. He was dressed in beige slacks and a white open necked shirt, the sleeves rolled up, his right arm

81

stretching out to hold the top of the mast of a model yacht. He looked almost human.

'I've asked you to come and see me because I've heard that the police have been playing silly buggers again.' He paused and looked at Cassie, 'Sorry for the language.'

Then he turned his attention to Howard Alsopp, 'Is that right?'

Howard pursed his lips before replying 'I'm afraid it is. They got worried about the evidence, something said by the CPS, and decided to try and get either some confession out of him, or information they could work on. It seems to have back fired.'

'What do you mean by that?' the judge asked.

'During the course of the conversations with the undercover policewoman, the defendant told her he had gone to a football match at Stamford Bridge,' he paused, 'and investigation has revealed it was the same night as the murder.'

'Police investigation?'

Marcus chipped in, 'No, My Lord, my junior made enquires about the date of the game.'

'You've not served an alibi notice?' he said turning his attention to the defence. Cassie groaned inwardly, it was typical of a judge to find fault with the defence, rather than keep his mind on the prosecution's misdemeanours.

'No, we were only served the bundle relating to this part of the investigation on Thursday of last week,' Marcus said, leaning forward towards Judge Crabtree. 'We are in some difficulty because Barker did not go alone to the game, and we will be applying for an adjournment to try and find the witness.'

'What do you say to that, Howard?'

'We don't accept the alibi. We realise the conversation was spontaneous; we cannot say he has made it up, but we do think he is mistaken. Also he only knows the man he went with by a nickname. We think it will be difficult if...'

Cassie had anticipated the prosecution would say there was no means of finding Hinds without his real name and, if possible, his date of birth. The Criminal Records, Electoral Roles, Social Security files would all be in his proper name and knowing his age would narrow the possible number of men who could be their witness. If the prospect of finding him was remote, the judge was very unlikely to grant an adjournment, and the trial would go on with only Lenny saying he was at the football match. She interrupted 'We do know his name and an approximate age.'

Howard went on, 'Even if we have the name and date of birth, it may be difficult to trace him, if not impossible, and we have a witness problem too.'

'What's that?' the judge asked.

'The eyewitness, Mr Compton, is due to return to the United States at the end of the week. He normally resides there.'

Judge Crabtree picked up a pencil and drummed it on the desk, looked up at the ceiling and then said, 'Right. I think the best course of action is for the defence to give all the information they have about this alibi witness to the prosecution, the police should, no I direct that the police will, assist in trying to locate him. We'll swear in a jury, send them away until tomorrow, then begin the trial so that your eyewitness will be able to return to the States.'

Cassie suppressed her disappointment, the decision was unfair, but not surprising as the most important

83

witness lived so far away. Judge Crabtree was relying on the police finding Hinds before the trial was over; there was no certainty his confidence was well placed.

Once back in court and in their places they waited for the knock on the door informing them that the judge was about to enter. A male court official held the door open as the judge swept onto the bench, took his seat in front of the royal crest, opened the red ledger in front of him, and then asked for the jury panel to be brought in.

Marcus leant back and asked Cassie to speak to Lenny Barker, who was now in the dock behind them, segregated from his solicitor and barrister, as if his point of view was unimportant. She would have preferred to have Lenny sitting next to her or at least on the seat behind, although he couldn't keep tugging at her gown, disturbing her concentration while he was at the back of the court.

The panel, consisting of sixteen men and women, stood under the public gallery as the court clerk opened a wooden box on the bench in front of her and took out a number of white cards. She told the members of the jury panel that if their name was called they were to walk across the court and take a seat in the jury box, beginning in the front row. Cassie scanned them, trying to make an assessment of their prejudices, from their age and appearance; it was the only information available.

One by one twelve names were read out, and an assortment of men and women took their places. One by one they took the oath, most reading the words from the card they had been given; some stumbled and were sworn in by repeating the phrases, as the jury bailiff read them out. Unless Lenny said he recognised any of them, the defence could not challenge them, nor did Cassie anticipate the prosecution would have any reason to object.

She made a note of their names as they were called, she had an indefinable blueprint in her mind; the older they were the more likely to convict, women tended to acquit, regimental ties were bad news, so were women in smart suits and thirty something men trying to dress down but whose expensive jeans and smart polo shirts gave them away. Newspapers were another clue, readers of the Daily Telegraph and the tabloids were thought to be prosecution-minded, only the Guardian indicated a more open approach. Cassie thought it was a myth, but she still tried to identify the newspapers prospective jurors were carrying.

Once they were seated the jury began to look around them, at the judge, the defendant in the dock and counsel. Two of the younger women looked directly at Cassie. She liked the look of them; they were a similar age to herself, and casually dressed. She smiled at them, trying to engage with them, because at the end of the trial they would have to look them and the rest of the jury in the face, tell them the defence version of events and persuade them it might be true. She wrote 'friendly' by the names of the two women, Anna Fry and Amanda Conrad.

When they were all sworn, the clerk told them that Barker had been charged with the murder of Shelley Paulson on 18th September last and they were to say, having heard the evidence, whether he was guilty or not.

'Now you've just sat down, I am going to ask you to go away until tomorrow morning so that some further enquires can be made. If you go now with the jury bailiff, she will tell you what to do tomorrow, you can then go home. In the meantime I must ask you not to talk about the case you are about to try. I should also warn you not to do any research on your computers; you try the case on the evidence given in this courtroom, not on the internet. It isn't fair on the defendant if you come to a decision on the basis of something of which he is unaware, and of which he has no way of rebutting. I know you've heard nothing about it yet, but it's better to begin as you mean to go on, and not discuss the case at all. Thank you.'

And with those words His Honour Judge Crabtree rushed out of the room.

Marcus turned to Cassie. 'Gone to sail his model boats somewhere, I guess. We must go and see our hero again.'

Back down in the cells, Marcus explained what had happened. And asked Lenny to give an account of the night he went to Stamford Bridge. He told them he had met Hinds as he was leaving the sports centre. He wasn't sure of the day. It might have been Thursday or Friday. He hadn't seen him for some time and Hinds asked about the team they had both played for, Westbourne Wonders, and then they had talked about the Chelsea team. Hinds had asked him if he wanted to go to the game against Everton the following Tuesday.

'He told me he might be able to get some tickets. Wicked, I thought. Particularly free tickets.' Tuesday evening he had met Hinds outside the pub, Portobello Gold, and they had gone to catch the bus to Fulham Broadway. The game started a bit late, and then there was injury time, so they left the ground at about nine thirty, quarter to ten and walked up Warwick Road to

Shepherds Bush, where Hinds left him. From there he continued on to Ladbroke Grove, and then to the Lancaster Estate, getting home about ten thirty.

Marcus asked him if he was sure of the time.

'No,' replied Lenny, shaking his head.

Tim chipped in 'Shelley was killed at about nine minutes past ten. At least that's the time of the 999 call. If the match started at seven thirty, the earliest it would have finished would be nine twenty, and it normally takes at least ten to fifteen minutes to get out of the ground.'

'Not a great football fan myself but I can see it takes time to get away. What about you, Cassie, been to any football matches recently?'

Cassie laughed 'Actually, yes. My boyfriend's a Liverpool fan and we went to watch them at Arsenal.'

'Do you have an Oyster Card, Lenny?' Marcus asked.

'Yes. The police took it.'

'We'll have to ask them to find the record of the journeys you made. Miss Hardman, can you ask David Jennings to do that, they'll be quicker.' Cassie nodded, vexed with herself for not thinking about it.'

'What do you think of the jury?' Marcus said looking first at Cassie and then Tim.

'Looks OK,' said Tim.

'I think so. Seven women, most of them under forty. Didn't spot any Telegraph readers. Let's hope they go to football matches.' Marcus paused and then added 'Of course with that number of women it's good to have one on the team. Shows you don't hate women.' With that comment, he left the room, leaving Cassie angered by his remarks, but not wanting to reveal her feelings. Nor did she want Lenny to know how pessimistic she was about the police finding his friend before the trial was over.

Chapter 13

'We've got two jobs to do this morning,' said Chris Dundy to Alex. 'One, we've to check out this guy, Edward Walker, lives at flat three, forty-eight Cambridge Gardens. Then there's these robberies. Sarge'll be furious if we don't make some headway today. We've got this witness to get a statement from. She's a bit of an old battleaxe apparently, bit upper crust like you. Sarge thought you'd be the best at getting a decent statement from her.'

'Which first?' Alex asked.

'Cambridge Gardens, I think. Walker may be a witness in a murder trial. You know, the hooker from Cotburn Square, who was killed last September. Some guy is standing trial and has put forward an alibi, at the last minute, says he was at Stamford Bridge for the Everton game.'

'Walker is the alibi witness?'

'I think so.'

'That's a coincidence.'

'What, putting up an alibi at the last minute? I call that convenient.'

'No. I met the defendant's brief on Friday, at a dinner party,' she said.

'Hobnobbing with your posh friends then.'

'No more up-market than yours. She's convinced he's innocent. Said something about some evidence being served late.'

'Blame us again. I suppose he'd just forgotten he'd been at Stamford Bridge on the night of the murder. Come on, that's unbelievable.'

Alex wasn't really listening to him.

'She was stabbed wasn't she and, well, do they have the murder weapon? A couple of weeks ago, I went to Cotburn Square to retrieve a knife they'd found in a compost heap. The gardener thought it had been there for some time. Hidden,' she said.

'Don't know. Come on let's get on.'

Forty-eight Cambridge Gardens was a Victorian house divided into six flats. Number three was on the second floor. Although they rang the bell several times, there was no reply. Just as they turned to leave, a window on the ground floor creaked open and a young woman wearing a worn dressing gown and a wet towel wrapped round her head leant out.

'You're making a lot of noise, waking people up. What you doing here?' she said.

'Sorry, love. We're looking for Mr Walker, Edward Walker. He's not in trouble or anything,' Alex added quickly, seeing the suspicious look on the woman's face.

'Ed. I've not seen him for a couple of days.'

'D'you know where he works?' Chris said.

'Naw. Sorry.' The window was slammed shut and the curtains briskly pulled across.

'Friendly,' said Chris, as he pulled his radio out and informed control at the station the potential witness was not at home.

'Now for Mrs Bampton.'

The house on Aubrey Walk was tall and narrow, the front door painted black with a lion's head door knocker. Chris banged the head energetically. A slim woman in her fifties dressed in a pair of well-cut jeans answered the door.

'Mrs Bampton?' Chris enquired as he produced his warrant card and stepped forward, his foot in the door to prevent it being closed. The woman nodded and looked at the card he was holding. 'I'm Detective Constable Dundy and this is Detective Constable Alexis Seymour. Can we come in please?'

Mrs Bampton moved back and held the door open wider, 'Is it really necessary? If it's about that robbery on Holland Walk, I told the officer all I knew about it at the time.'

'We need to take a statement from you, fill in the details. I'm sure you understand.' Alex replied keeping her voice as neutral as possible. She glanced round trying to get some impression of the woman they had come to interview. Like many houses in this part of London, this one had been purchased for its smart address rather than the space it provided. Alex guessed there was one room on each floor, so she wasn't surprised when Mrs Bampton led the way up the stairs to a sitting room.

She directed them to a couple of armchairs and sat down herself facing them. 'I'm busy, but I'll try to help. What do you want to know?'

There was an almost full glass of white wine on the coffee table and a glossy magazine next to it. Mrs Bampton wasn't that busy. Alex turned on her professional smile and asked her to start from the beginning; what was the first thing she had noticed?

'I was sitting where you are now, when I heard someone say something like, "I haven't got any." Then someone else began to shout, but I couldn't hear what they were saying. So I got up and walked to the window.' Mrs Bampton demonstrated her actions; Alex followed. 'As you can see, there is a good view of

Holland Walk from here.' Alex looked down into a small paved area, surrounded by a dark brick wall about seven foot high, in which there was a white gate and over the wall there was a view of the path, as it climbed steeply southward.

'I saw this girl holding on to her handbag and a man pulling at it, trying to take it from her. After a short while, probably seconds, she let go and the man turned and ran down the Walk towards me. I immediately dialled 999. The girl was in the Walk, screaming and crying, when two uniformed officers arrived. I went out of that gate at the back of the house and gave them my name and address. It's only about six months since that awful murder in Holland Walk. I was frightened, well, that this girl might have been killed.'

Alex asked her to describe the man she saw.

'He was fairly average really. He had close cropped hair, dark, with a tiny ponytail at the back.'

'Height?' Chris queried.

'I'd say about five eleven, six foot, but slim.'

'Colour?' Alex asked.

Chris Dundy's radio crackled into life. 'Excuse me,' he said to Mrs Bampton, and replied to the caller, 'We'll go right back as soon as we've finished here.'

'He was white. When he turned and ran, he had quite a thin nose, dark eyes. He was dressed in a black track suit with pale blue strips down the side.' She stopped suddenly, 'That's all I can remember.'

'Would you be able to pick him out, if we held an identity parade?' Chris asked.

'I think so. I did have a good view of him.'

Chris had been writing down the description Mrs Bampton had given of the incident and asked her to sign it.

Once out of the house, Alex asked Chris if he had a suspect in mind when he had suggested an ID parade. He told her there were one or two who had been doing similar robberies in the area, and who they were considering pulling in.

'You have it down as robbery? Not drug dealing?'

'The victim said the guy was trying to take her handbag; same as Mrs Bampton. It's obvious isn't it?'

'She also said the first words she heard shouted were "I haven't got any." That could be a reference to drugs. And the girl's not going to tell the truth if it was.'

'There are three or four similar cases, all handbag snatches and the descriptions are the same. We'll just have to arrange a parade. We've to go back to Cambridge Gardens, see if this man has turned up.'

This time they were in luck and a large black male answered the door. 'Mr Walker, is it?' Chris said.

The man nodded but said nothing.

'Can we come up?' Chris said.

'I suppose so.'

Once in the flat they remained standing as Chris explained he fitted the description of a person who may be an alibi witness for a Lenny Barker.'

'Who? I don't know anyone of that name. Who says I know him?'

'The information we have is that someone with the same name as you and about your age is a friend of Barker's and went to a football match with him.'

While the two men talked, Alex looked round the flat and saw a blue and white scarf, hung over a chair.

'Support Chelsea, do you?' she asked. The man nodded, suddenly wary.

'Did you go to the game against Everton last September?'

'I might have done.'

'Name Hinds mean anything to you?' Chris asked.

The man relaxed and shook his head. 'No, no, never heard that name before.'

'OK, Mr Walker. We'll leave it there for the moment.'

Once outside, Chris said he didn't think he was the person they wanted.

'No, but he was a bit leery, wasn't he.'

Back at the station, Chris said he would start organising the identification parade and handed her the paper with the contact number for the officer searching for Walker. 'Can you give him a bell and tell him what we found.'

She rang the number and was put through to the police room at the Old Bailey.

'O'Connor,' said the voice that answered.

Alex told him the result of their enquiries, and then asked him if the murder weapon had been recovered. He told her no, and asked her why she wanted to know. She explained about the knife which had been found in Cotburn Square.

'Detective, what did you say your name was, Seymour, was it?' The voice at the other end sounded impatient, 'It can't possibly be relevant. I really don't want to be bothered by silly speculation. Goodbye.' The phone was slammed down.

Alex looked over Chris's shoulder at the file for the robbery, and jotted down the crime number. She attached to the plastic bag containing the knife a request form for a forensic examination that asked the scenes of crime officer to examine it for fingerprints and possible blood stains.

'What're you doing? Chris asked, 'that knife wasn't used in the robbery.

'I know but I'd just like to get it checked out. We found a pizza box containing drugs hidden very close to this knife and I want to know if the same person hid them both.'

'And the blood stains?'

'Well, you never know?' she said and grinned like a satisfied cat.

Chapter 14

As Cassie walked towards Court 12, on the second day of the trial, she heard a voice behind calling her name. She stopped, and a moment later David Jennings was by her side. 'I've just been talking to Sergeant Dean,' he said.

'Have they found Hinds, Walker, whatever his name is?' she said interrupting him.

'No. Not yet. They did a CRB check and it came up with four names. Three are recorded as Edward but they fit the age and description.' Cassie nodded and David went on, 'They've checked out a couple of the addresses but didn't find anyone at home. Officers are visiting the others at the moment. They'll try them all again if they don't get a result.'

'Right. I was hoping we might have got something.' Cassie knew how unlikely it was the police would have found Walker so quickly, but she also knew they could be dilatory when it came to helping the defence. She was determined to keep them on their toes.

'David, I've prepared the alibi notice, I just have to let Marcus see it before I give you a copy. In it I've said Barker caught the bus to Fulham Broadway. I assume you'll check his Oyster Card to see if it was used. I understand the police have it.'

'I'm sure we'll want to look at that. I'll ask Sergeant Dean. Incidentally, he tells me he's a regular at Stamford Bridge and thinks that it takes about twenty minutes to get out of the ground. Rather supports your alibi.'

Cassie nodded. 'There's another thing as well. I know these games are fairly heavily policed. Don't they use CCTV, looking for known trouble makers?'

'I'm not sure how often they do that, but I can ask. If they did at this match, they may still have the DVDs, but it's unlikely.'

'Can you find out for me? It may just be another way of establishing an alibi.'

'Cassie, I'm not happy about sending the police off on a wild goose chase. I'll think about it.'

'I know, but it's worth trying. The police have screwed this inquiry up. If they'd investigated it properly they would have got the DVDs, the least you can do is chase it up now.'

'Cassie, there are limits. I know you think this alibi is genuine and he's innocent, that's tough – but,' David shrugged his shoulders, 'I know it's hard.'

She didn't reply, it was difficult because however much she believed juries reached the right verdicts, she knew there was always the possibility they might find the Crown's case compelling.

Instead she asked him if she could see Shelley Paulson's clothes.

As they waited for the Judge to come into court, a tall slim woman in her late forties came through the door. She was wearing a dark suit, possibly navy, the lack of light under the public gallery made it difficult to see, and carrying a pale pink mac, which she pushed under a chair as she sat down. She was accompanied by a man, whose long dark coat was open revealing a similar sober suit. The woman was, unquestionably, Shelley Paulson's mother – the same high cheekbones, the same bow-shaped lips and the same snub nose –

97

but Cassie wasn't sure who the man was; there had been no mention of Shelley's father in the statements. It had been Mrs Paulson who had identified the body, and now she would listen while the last moments of her daughter's life were scrutinised in minute detail. Cassie refused to think about the horror of the experience Mrs Paulson was about to endure, she could not let her professional judgement be influenced by her compassion, a compassion not yet warped by cynicism.

Cassie turned over the cover of her notebook just as the judges' door opened; she stood, as did the rest of the court, while Judge Crabtree walked onto the bench, nodded towards them and the jury, before sitting down.

'Mr Alsopp, are we ready to proceed?'

'Yes, My Lord.'

The judge indicated the prosecution was to begin their opening speech. Howard Alsopp turned towards the jury. His voice was light for such a big man, a pleasant tenor, and he spoke fluently with a newsreader's classless precision, rarely hesitating to look at his papers. Once the formalities were dispensed with he began to explain what the case was about. Having told the jury the murder had taken place soon after ten o'clock on the night of 18th September last in Holland Walk, he went on, 'The victim was a twenty-eight year old woman who appears to have worked as an escort to overseas business men visiting this country. Make of that what you will. It is not relevant to this case.'

Cassie tapped her pen on her notebook. How typical, the throwaway line that implied he wasn't prejudiced and the jury should not be either. Why didn't he just say that she didn't deserve to be murdered even if she was a prostitute?

'She lived in a top floor flat in Cotburn Square, Notting Hill. We know that on the night of her murder she hailed a taxi in Ladbroke Grove, not far from there, and was driven to Campden Hill Road, where she got out close to the Windsor Castle public house. She paid the driver, who continued on towards Kensington High Street. In his rear view mirror he saw somebody approach her; he thought it was a man. The person put an arm round the woman's shoulders in what appeared to be an affectionate manner. She was next seen by the most important witness in this case, James Compton. He was walking north along Holland Walk.'

Howard Alsopp paused. 'My Lord, I think it may help the jury to have a bundle of photographs at this stage and a map of the area.'

'Any objections, Mr Pike?'

'No, My Lord. Of course they are taken in daylight and it would have been dark. Also these are in winter and in September the trees would still be in leaf.' Cassie nodded, it was important the jury didn't think this was the view the eyewitness had.

David Jennings handed the bundles of photographs and sheets of paper to the usher, who gave them to the jury.

'One between two,' Howard Alsop said, 'Now turn to page two of the bundle.'

Cassie opened her set. The picture showed a view along a broad pedestrian footpath, the width of a country lane. On the left was a wide grass verge, street lamps of nineteenth century design were set at regular intervals, and then iron railings divided the Walk from Holland Park. Large trees, on both sides of the lane, created a tunnel of branches; further north, on the right, a high brick wall protected the gardens of the houses behind.

Howard Alsopp continued, 'Now turn over to page three. As you can see the path is now between the railings on the left and the wall on the right. When Mr Compton reached about the position in this photograph, which, if you look at your map...'

He stopped as the jury unfolded the papers they had been given. Cassie took out her copy from a lever-arch file and opened it, placing the bundle of photographs on top.

He went on, 'This photograph was taken from the entrance to Duchess of Bedford Walk. Mr Compton saw, first, a young woman and then a man, who grabbed her arm. At first he thought they were just a young couple having an argument, then he saw the woman turn towards the man and her hand went up to his face. The man pulled the woman in front of him, and the next thing Mr Compton saw was the woman slipping to the ground. At that point Mr Compton shouted, and ran forward; the man looked up towards him, then ran back along the lane and vanished, probably under a bridge between parts of Holland Park School.'

Cassie knew the reference to the school was deliberate, drawing attention to something the prosecution would play on: Lenny's knowledge of the area as a former pupil.

'Mr Compton was about to give chase, but realised that the young woman, who we now know was Shelley Paulson, was seriously injured, and instead he used his mobile phone to dial 999. That call was timed at nine minutes past ten. It may be that the time of that call will become important in the case, as it fixes within a few seconds the moment that Shelley was murdered. Both police and ambulance arrived quickly at the scene, but too late to save her life. Now if you could just turn to page nine of the photographs.'

Marcus turned to Cassie, 'The happy snaps.' Cassie grimaced at the remark; she didn't like that way of referring to the autopsy photographs even though comparing them to holiday pictures made them less disturbing. There was no need for the prosecution to show the photographs of the dead woman, but Howard Alsopp wasn't going to miss the opportunity to excite the sympathies of the jury.

Howard apologised to the jury for showing them the pictures. Cassie turned the pages of the bundle to a picture of the naked body of a young woman. She looked over to her left, where Mrs Paulson was sat, immobile, at the side of the courtroom where the jury could see her; the resemblance between mother and daughter was striking. The man was no longer there, and fleetingly Cassie wondered again who he was, before she turned to look at the jury and saw Amanda Conrad watching the living woman rather than looking at the photographs of the corpse.

'Shelley Paulson was killed as a result of a single blow with a knife to the right hand side of her body, which pierced the ribcage, and entered the heart. The pathologist will tell you that death was virtually instantaneous. There were bruises on her right wrist but no other injuries. The bruises we say were made by this defendant as he struggled with Miss Paulson, and it was he who used his knife to strike the fatal blow.' Howard gestured with his left hand towards the dock. Cassie saw all the jurors look at Lenny. She turned herself to have the same image they would have. He was looking down, and didn't seem to be aware of the attention he was receiving. Would he look as young and vulnerable to the jury as he did to her? She looked at the two young women, the 'two As', as she had named them, but could not see in their faces any reaction to her client.

Howard paused as the jury turned their attention back to the bundle of photographs. Some of them looked at each picture for a few moments, others for hardly a second before passing on to the next page. He continued, 'Forensic examination of Miss Paulson's clothing revealed fibres that matched a sweatshirt taken from Barker's address. In fairness, I should add that the sweatshirt is of a common make and thousands of them have been manufactured and sold, but it is another piece of evidence that points to Barker being the killer.'

Howard had made the evidence of matching fibres sound much more significant than it really was, particularly as there was no blood staining on the sweatshirt. Up until now, Howard had been fair, but not now, not with those phrases.

'At first police investigations, although thorough...'

Tim whispered, 'Cassie. That'll help his image with the police. Sergeant Dean has just come in.' Cassie looked over towards the chairs under the public gallery and saw a clean-shaven, rather attractive man standing by the end of counsels' row and beckoning to David Jennings, who got up and the two of them left the room.

By the time Cassie began to listen again to Howard Alsopp, he was describing the arrest and interviews of Lenny Barker. As he began his closing remarks, David

102

Jennings appeared at the door of the courtroom and beckoned to Cassie to come out of the room. Outside Number 12 court, in a waiting area, the width of a two lane road, which ran the length of the building and overlooked the street, from which the Central Criminal Court got its name, she saw a dark haired man sitting with his back to her, reading a copy of The Financial Times, whom she assumed was the eyewitness James Compton. David Jennings was stood a little way down the hall with the officer and she went towards them.

'This is Sergeant Dean. I've asked him to keep me informed of any developments.' Then addressing the officer, 'Miss Hardman is representing Barker. Can you tell her where you are with trying to find Walker?'

'We've identified four men who might be your witness. We have them all as Edward Walker not Edwin, but that's probably a transcription error. Can your client help us with any more information?'

'I don't think so, we've asked him about Walker several times, but he can't add anything. He didn't even know the man's real name. His mother thought he'd moved to Willesden or Wembley, but she wasn't sure of that.'

'We'll continue our enquiries but...' A crooked smile played on his face, as if to warn her he was not optimistic about finding Walker.

Cassie looked up at him and thought for a moment, 'Do you have the mugshots of the men? We can get Barker to look at them and see if he can identify his friend.'

'I can get those. The Oyster Card, we're checking that out, and as soon as we have the result I'll let Mr Jennings know.'

'Thanks. What about DVDs at the football match? Can you check if any were taken and if they still exist?'

Colin Dean rolled his eyes upwards before looking at David Jennings.

'She's entitled to ask, and I think we should at least make some enquiries. Wasn't a special team set up to try and counter football hooliganism?'

Dean agreed there was, and he thought the match between Chelsea and Everton was probably targeted. He would try to find out if the DVDs still existed, although he thought it unlikely unless there had been any trouble that night.

He walked towards the lift and the two barristers returned to the courtroom, just as Marcus Pike said that he wished to raise a matter of law. Judge Crabtree turned to the jury and apologised to them. He said he hoped it would not be long, but perhaps they could use the time by electing a foreman. As they left the jury box, Cassie noticed a young man pick up his set of photographs and take them with him. Would he be elected the foreman? She liked the way he was dressed casually but neatly in jeans and a pale grey sweater. He reminded her of Ben and that made her think he would approach the evidence like a scientist, carefully and objectively.

Once the door had closed behind them, Judge Crabtree said, 'Mr Pike, I assume the argument is about the admissibility of the identification parade evidence.'

'Yes, we are asking Your Lordship to rule it inadmissible; that the prejudicial effect of the evidence outweighs its probative value.'

Cassie listened with care to Marcus using lawyer's shorthand, words Lenny would not really understand. She turned to look at him; he was gazing at the public gallery, not listening to what was being said. They had explained to him they would try and persuade the judge that the evidence identifying him as the killer was problematic and the judge would have to warn the jury, when he came to sum up, that they should not take it into account, but she thought Lenny didn't really understand.

Marcus outlined their argument to Judge Crabtree, saying the eyewitness's view was very limited, in poor light and for a few seconds only.

'A mere glance,' he said.

These last three words were taken from an important judgement in the Court of Appeal, every lawyer knew them, and by using them Marcus was trying to persuade the judge that the facts of this case were similar.

'What do you say about the admission by Barker that he was in Holland Walk on the night of the murder? Does that not support the identification?' the judge asked.

Cassie's face was impassive, that was part of the job, not revealing your feelings. She felt she wasn't always very good at disguising her emotions, but she reassured herself that at least she was still capable of them, unlike some of her fellow lawyers who were so clever at concealing any sensitivity that they ceased to have any feelings at all. Neither she nor Marcus expected him to rule in their favour, but they had to make the submission to keep open their options, if Lenny was convicted.

Marcus persisted, 'We hesitate to criticise the police, but we would also ask Your Lordship to consider the circumstances in which the alibi came to light and the lack of a proper and timely investigation of that alibi.'

'Mr Alsopp, what do you say?'

'That it's a matter for the jury, properly directed as we know they will be,' Howard began.

Cassie turned to Tim, and whispered 'Flattery wins every time.'

'The jury will have the opportunity to assess the witness and his explanation as to why he was reluctant to select the defendant at the parade.' Howard went on, 'Furthermore, we say that the defendant's admission supports the identification.'

'Mr Alsopp, I am concerned about the parade and the inadequate nature of the identification made by your witness. There is the alibi as well.'

Cassie stopped making notes. Was the judge going to rule in their favour?

Judge Crabtree asked Marcus if he had anything further to say. Marcus declined. Cassie nodded her head; they didn't want the judge to think their arguments were weak.

'No, Mr Pike,' the judge began, 'You may well have a good argument for the jury but I think the evidence is admissible. Can we have the jury, please?'

While they waited for the jury to be brought to the courtroom, Cassie and David located the brown exhibit bag which contained Shelley Paulson's clothes, each item contained within a smaller plastic bag. Cassie noticed a small package containing the silver bracelet, the bracelet that had been examined by the fingerprint expert, but David pushed it to one side before taking out the packets of clothing; the blood-stained T-shirt, a pair of denim jeans with similar marks down the right leg, a bra which was as badly stained as the T-shirt, a cardigan as colourful as Joseph's coat but remarkably untouched by blood, and then a pair of small white pants with dark lines of blood running through the lacy fabric. Finally he drew out a pair of red high heeled shoes. Cassie looked round to see if Mrs Paulson was watching, fortunately she was talking to Sergeant Dean, whose body shielded the bloody clothing.

The shoes were wrapped loosely in a clear bag, making it difficult to see them properly, but after wriggling them around, the heel of the left shoe was visible. 'About four inches?' David said. Cassie nodded her agreement, her assumption about them was right. It was an important fact that they would place before the jury as they tried to undermine the identification of Lenny Barker as the murderer.

Chapter 15

Chris Dundy picked up the papers from his desk and swore.

'What do they want, blood? There just aren't enough hours in the day. We can't do everything.'

'What is it?' Alex asked.

He thrust a piece of paper at her, 'We've got to try and find this bloody witness for the defence, again. Why can't they do it for themselves? Get some private investigator to find the guy.'

'There's no time, the trial has started,' said Alex.

'Of course, you know all about it. You're friends with the defence barrister.'

Alex didn't bother with replying.

The instructions were to visit two addresses, one in Willesden and one in Devonport Road, Shepherds Bush. They were to speak to the inhabitants at each address to ascertain if Edward or Edwin Walker also known as Hinds, lived there, had lived there or visited there.

'We've no time to be chasing all over London. We've got seven street robberies to investigate. ID parades to set up.' He threw his hands up.

'Look, let's try these two addresses, and then get back to the robberies. It's only eight, we'll be back by nine thirty, plenty of time,' Alex said.

Chris continued to grumble as Alex drove the police car through heavy traffic round Shepherds Bush Green and along the Goldhawk Road, past the entrance to the market, which was only just beginning to stir, until they reached Devonport Road. The traffic coming into town was almost stationary as Alex indicated to turn right. None of the vehicles gave way to let them cross the east-bound lane.

'We shouldn't have taken an unmarked car. They'd let us through if we had a blue light,' Chris said.

Alex didn't reply but concentrated on edging the car forward, until a lorry stopped and the driver indicated they could cross his lane.

There were cars parked on both sides of the street, and as Alex looked for somewhere to park, Chris tried to find the right house.

'That's it, number twenty-eight,' he said.

'There's nowhere to park.'

'I think the Merc is just leaving,' Chris said.

Alex slowed their vehicle to a stop, and waited until the Mercedes pulled out of the space, and she was able to reverse neatly into it.

The houses in the street were three storey, built of blackened brick with white coping around the doors and windows. Number twenty-eight was no different. On the front door, prominently displayed at eye-level, there was a burnished brass door-knocker in the shape of a female hand, and on a pillar to the left hand side, three door bells.

'Do we know which one?' Chris asked.

'No.'

'Let's start at the bottom. Not so far to climb.'

There was no reply from the lowest of the three bells. He pressed the button marked '2' and this time a male voice asked who was there. Chris nodded at Alex to answer.

'It's the police. Can you let us in? We're trying to find a man called Walker.'

They heard the hiss of the lock releasing and pushed open the door. The hallway was dark, even on a bright morning. A child's pushchair was propped against the wall and beyond that the stairs. A male figure appeared on the landing above their heads.

'What do you want?' the man said.

'We're looking for an Edward Walker, or it might be Edwin.'

The man came to the head of the stairs and began to descend. He was wearing a towelling dressing gown over a pair of grey trousers. Alex estimated he was in his fifties. Much older than the man they were looking for.

'Do you know who lives in the other flats?' Alex asked.

'I don't know anyone called Walker,' the man replied.

'Can you help us with who lives in the other flats?'

'There's a girl in there. Got a baby' He pointed to the door on the ground floor flat, and waved at the pram. 'I live on the second and the top floor is occupied by two lads.'

'Do you know their names?' Alex said.

'Nah, I don't know them.'

Alex didn't want to waste time with him, he was clearly not the man they were looking for but his reluctance to let them into his own rooms and the refusal to answer her questions directly made her persist.

'What about their correspondence. You must pick it up from time to time?'

'I never bother, I don't get any letters. Nothing.'

'Not even bills. You must pay for gas and electricity.'

He didn't answer.

'What's your name?' Chris asked.

'Why do you want to know?'

'We believe you may be stealing electricity. Where's your meter?' Chris turned to look round for a cupboard which might contain the meters for the house. He saw a white painted box on the wall at the rear of the door and went to open it, but before he could do so, two young men ran down the stairs, past Alex and towards the front door, pushing Chris to the ground as they flung the door open, and made their escape into the street.

Alex followed them, shouting, 'Police – stop.' It had no effect; the two men jumped into a car and sped off in the direction of Uxbridge Road. Another car came up the road behind and prevented her from getting the number of the vehicle.

'Damn, damn,' she said as the vehicle turned left and vanished. Chris came from the house and stood next to her.

'What now?' he said.

'We go back and into the top flat. They must be trying to hide something.' Back inside the house they climbed the two flights of stairs. The door to the flat was ajar, they pushed it open and walked in. The living room was sparsely furnished, a grey sofa, a couple of matching chairs, a coffee table marked with rings from hot cups and a large flat screen television. On the sofa was an orange sleeping bag. They opened the door to the bedroom. Inside they could see an unmade double bed, and, all along one wall, boxes of cigarettes.

'Dodging the tax, do you think?' Alex said, 'It's a job for Customs. I don't think either of them is the man we're looking for. He's mixed race and they were white. Let's go.'

111

Chapter 16

When all the jury was seated Judge Crabtree asked Howard Alsopp to continue, and call the evidence.

David Jennings got to his feet and told the judge that the first witness was the taxi driver, Jason Turner, and the defence had agreed the statement could be read to the jury.

The judge explained to them that, although they would not see the witness, the evidence was just as important as if he had come into court and stood in the witness box. He nodded at David to begin reading.

'On the evening of 15th September I was working, driving my taxi in Ladbroke Grove, when I was hailed by a young woman. She wanted to go to a block of flats on Campden Hill Road near to the Windsor Castle pub. She was an attractive blonde wearing tight fitting blue jeans, a white T-shirt and a multi-coloured cardigan that came down to her thighs. Her shoes were bright red high heels.'

Cassie had asked David to exhibit Shelley Paulson's shoes, during the course of reading the statement. David had refused at first, but relented if she would agree to the rest of the clothes being shown at the same time. The dead woman's jeans, shirt and underclothes were heavily stained with blood, and displaying them would detract from the impact on the jury of the high heeled shoes. Also amongst the items was the silver bracelet, with the coating of grey powder that showed it had been dusted for fingerprints. There was a risk that one or other of the jury would realize the bracelet had been examined and ask questions about any findings. It was a gamble she decided to take.

Each item was in a plastic bag, squashed and almost unidentifiable except for the exhibit label. The bloodstains had turned brown, dirty rather than shocking. Mrs Paulson closed her eyes as her daughter's clothes were held aloft, and then passed along the two rows of jurors. The 'two As' turned the bags over in their hands looking at each item carefully, a look of revulsion on their faces. The young man, whom Cassie had identified as Colin Heap, hardly glanced at the jeans, shirt and cardigan, but tried to hold the shoes by the heels. She leant forward and suggested to Marcus he should ask for that bag to be opened.

There was a delay as plastic gloves were produced by the court usher. Judge Crabtree tapped on the bench as he waited. Howard spoke softly to David, his back to Cassie so that she couldn't hear what was being said. She picked up her pen and then put it down again, there must be no distractions for the jury.

'If the usher could kindly hold them up, that would be sufficient,' Marcus said.

The usher walked slowly in front of the jury box, holding the shoes by the toes in a plastic-gloved hand so that they all could get a good look at them. The shoes were a bright red lizard skin; they appeared saucy and inappropriate in the courtroom. Some of the jurors leant forward and then wrote on their notepads. Even better, Cassie saw Amanda Conrad was using her pencil like an artist, clearly sketching the shoe as well. The jury must not forget those shoes.

David Jennings continued with reading the taxi driver's statement. 'After she had paid me, I drove away in the direction of Kensington High Street. Through my rear view mirror I saw the woman walking slowly across the road; she turned slightly to look behind her, as if someone had called out to her. Somebody, I thought it was a man, came up to her and put an arm round her shoulder. I then turned my attention to the road and by the time I checked my rear view mirror again, they were out of sight.'

David sat down and Howard Alsopp stood up and called for the next witness. James Compton.

The man Cassie had seen in the corridor came into the court and walked the few paces to the witness box without hesitation. He grasped the bible firmly in his right hand and read the oath from the card the usher handed to him, his accent that of someone who had learnt to say trash can rather than rubbish bin.

Cassie observed him carefully. He seemed confident with no trace of the indecision he had displayed at the identification parade. Cross-examination would be difficult; the witness had no reason to lie, all the questions must suggest he was mistaken, and he didn't look like a man who made mistakes, or if he did, would admit to doing so. He had shown himself to be public spirited and the jury might react adversely if the questioning was too robust. Marcus would need to take a careful line between attacking the witness's reliability and allowing him to retain his dignity.

Before that he would be questioned by Howard Alsopp, guided but not led through his account of the events in Holland Walk on the night of the murder, and the subsequent identification of Barker as the killer. Much of the case against their client would depend on how well he gave his evidence.

114

Howard stood up and turned so that he could see the jury while still aware of the witness, and began his examination-in-chief by asking Compton where he had been on the night of 18th September.

'I had gone for a meal with the guys from work and decided to walk home.'

'Did that take you along Holland Walk?'

'Yes, Sir. I live north of the park and it's the obvious route from the High Street.'

'Can you look at the bundle of photographs? Exhibit One, My Lord.'

James Compton picked up the bundle and opened it. His face blanched. He must have opened it at one of the pictures of Shelley Paulson's body.

'No, page one,' Mr Alsopp said, 'Is that the direction you were walking?'

'Yes, I walked north.'

'Any idea of time?'

'There's no dispute, if my learned friend wants to lead,' Marcus said.

'Just after ten pm?' asked Howard.

'Yes, Sir.'

'What was the weather like?'

'It was fine, quite dark. No moonlight that I can remember,' he paused, 'Although there was street lighting.'

'Was there anyone else in the lane?'

'Not at first.'

James Compton went on to give his account of the incident that had resulted in Shelley's death, before he was asked to give a description of the man he had seen.

'He was white, about five foot eleven. His hair was short and I thought he had a beard.'

'Could you see his face?'

'Not at first, but after the girl fell, and I shouted, he looked straight at me, then I had a good view.'

After the initial hesitation, Compton had regained his composure. He was careful with his answers, not exaggerating. The jury would think he was a good witness.

'Can you describe his features?'

The witness glanced towards Lenny Barker in the dock and said, 'Broad forehead, quite a square face and rather red, as if he had been drinking.'

He'd made a mistake, trying to describe the person he saw in the dock. Not only was it different from his statement but it contradicted the previous answer about the lack of light. She looked up at the jury to see if they had noticed the change in his evidence. Most of them were watching James Compton carefully, but one of the 'two As', the one with red hair, had a frown on her face and was looking at the photographs. She looked at her neighbour and pointed to something on the picture.

'You've said he was five foot eleven. Was that shorter or taller than the young woman?'

James Compton hesitated before saying, 'I think he was taller. It's difficult to say.'

Howard Alsopp nodded at that reply. Cassie glanced towards the jury but none of them appeared to respond to the answer Compton had given. The witness's memory was not as good as she had first thought.

'Some weeks later did you attend at Kensington Police Station to try and identify the man you had seen attack the woman in Holland Walk?'

'Yes. I saw...' Before he could go any further, Howard Alsopp put up his hand to stop him and asked,

116

'Now just answer the next question yes or no. Did you see on that parade the man you'd seen in the Walk?'

'Yes.'

'Thank you, Mr Compton. That's all I have to ask you, but you may be asked a few more questions in due course.

'I expect you will be a little while with this witness, Mr Pike?'

Marcus rose to his feet, 'Yes, My Lord.'

'Well in that case we'll adjourn for lunch. Back at five past two, members of the jury. Remember the warning about not talking to anyone else about the case.' He rose and left the bench and the room in what seemed to be three quick strides but must have been more.

After lunch the two of them discussed the various points on which they wished to cross examine the witness. 'Where shall we begin?' Marcus asked, 'With the parade. I think he's quite vulnerable on that.'

Cassie told him she agreed; she had not been qualified very long before she realised the advantage of starting to cross-examine part way through the events a witness was describing. They found it unsettling, as it was a bit like having to fast forward a DVD.

Once the court had reassembled, Marcus Pike stood up slowly, pulled his gown up onto his shoulders, and turned to look at the jury before turning his full attention onto James Compton. Unlike Howard Alsopp, Marcus watched the witness, looking for any sign of weakness; long pauses, shuffling of feet, fingers touching the face and avoiding eye contact. His voice, surprisingly deep for such a small man, had just a hint of a public school accent.

'The identification parade, you were hesitant about picking anyone out weren't you?'

'I'm not sure what you mean. I was quite sure the man I picked was the man in the Walk.' James Compton had not been thrown by Marcus beginning with the parade.

'Were you? You walked along the line-up twice and when you were first asked if you recognised anyone you didn't reply?'

'That's right. I was expecting to see a man with a beard.'

'You were leaving the parade gallery, weren't you? Shaking your head? Indicating that you couldn't make an identification?'

'I was trying to think what the man might look like without a beard.'

'You knew the police were anxious for you to pick somebody out?'

'Yes, they were.'

'Did you believe the man who had murdered this beautiful young woman was in that line-up?'

'Yes, I did, although I...'

Marcus interrupted, 'You wanted to...' but the judge stopped him and asked him to let the witness finish. Cassie listened, and stopped writing, the interruption by the judge gave Compton time to think, to compose an answer. Marcus had been about to ask if the witness wanted to help the police, now he would have to wait and rephrase the question.

'Go on,' Judge Crabtree said to Mr Compton.

'I'm not sure. I was told something about the person not being there but...'

'…you thought the police wouldn't ask you to an identification parade if they had not arrested the man responsible, and you wanted to help them?'

Mr Compton leant against the side of the witness box, moving the bundle of photographs from side to side along the top edge of the wooden stand. Marcus looked at the jury to emphasise the point to them. Cassie looked up at Compton, before turning her attention to the jury, hoping to see some expressions that might indicate their view of the witness. Colin Heap was frowning, but the rest of the jury were watching him intently.

'I knew it was serious. If I thought the man wasn't there I would have said so.'

Howard Alsopp turned to David Jennings, smiled at him, David nodded. It was a good reply and could only restore Compton's credibility as a reliable witness. It was no surprise the prosecuting lawyers were pleased.

Marcus was unperturbed; he hadn't finished with the witness yet.

'Let's go back to the evening of the murder. Can you describe the lighting on Holland Walk?'

'I've said, it's not very well lit and the trees hang over the path,' James Compton snapped back, he was beginning to show signs of irritation. A sign of arrogance perhaps that might make the jury less confident about his evidence.

'Creating shadows where it's almost impossible to see?'

'Yes, that's why I'm not sure where the man went when he ran off. He could have run back along the lane or gone through the path next to the school.'

'When you first saw the young woman, you said the man was behind her. Was he directly behind her?'

'No, not directly behind.' Compton closed his eyes, as if trying to catch the scene in his mind, and then opened them again. 'He was, hm, the woman was in front.'

'So you didn't get a good look at his face?'

'Not then. No.' Compton was back in control of himself, thinking about his answers.

'You've described her hand going up to his face. Can you describe what sort of movement it was?'

James Compton held his hand up to shoulder height, with the fingers extended, and made a clawing motion.

'Like a cat scratching?' asked Marcus.

'Yes, a cat, yes.'

At this stage of the trial, the jury were unaware that the DNA of scrapings from Shelley Paulson's fingernails had not matched her own or, most importantly from Cassie's point of view, Lenny's. Marcus was establishing the evidence which he would use in his final speech.

'Later, you have described him pulling the young woman towards his body, facing towards you?'

'Yes that's right.' He looked down at the photographs and then back at Marcus.

'So no clear view of the man's face then, either?'

'No. I don't think I saw his face clearly until I shouted. Then he looked straight at me. I'll never forget that face, pure evil.'

Cassie smiled and then looked down at her notebook hiding behind the wall of files so the jury could not see her face; she didn't want them to see her reaction to the answer Compton had just given. He had gilded the lily and it could be used to criticise his evidence when Marcus addressed the jury.

Meanwhile Marcus ignored the comment. 'He looked at you and turned to run?'

'Yes, almost immediately, when I shouted he turned.'

'You lost sight of his face again and just had a back view?'

'I'm not sure if I had a back view or a side view. It was all so sudden.'

'The whole incident was very quick wasn't it? Very quick and in very poor light?'

'Yes, it was.'

'Yet, you're very sure you could identify the man six weeks later, and without a beard?'

James Compton didn't answer.

Marcus picked up his witness statement. 'Let's look at what you told the police originally. "The light was very dim and I couldn't tell the colour of his hair even. Nor his clothes." Is that right?'

'Yes. The street lighting made everything look the same colour.'

'There is nothing about the broad forehead or the square face in your statement? Do you want to check?'

'No, Sir, I thought I had told the police officer.'

'He's not written the full description down has he?'

'Clearly he hasn't.'

'Nothing about him having a red face like he'd been drinking? Has the officer omitted that as well?'

'He must have.'

'But you said the light was too dim to see the colour of his hair or clothes? So how could you tell the colour of his face?'

The witness was silent, looking at Marcus like an animal caught in a snare, as indeed he was. Marcus waited, letting the jury absorb the witness's discomfort.

Cassie noticed a middle-aged white male juror shifting uneasily in his seat. It was always a good moment when one got the better of a witness.

'Now, Mr Compton. Do you remember being asked by a police officer at the scene, probably a uniformed officer, to give a description of the man you had seen?'

'Yes. I think so, yes.' He wrinkled his forehead.

'The incident was very fresh in your memory, wasn't it?'

'Yes, sir.'

'I assume you were trying to be as accurate as possible?'

James Compton drew himself up and said 'Of course, I knew it was very important. A young woman was dead. I had seen the man who killed her.' He sounded rather pompous again, too sure of himself; his attitude might alienate the jury.

'Quite, quite. What you told that officer was that the killer was, and I quote, "definitely taller than the woman"?'

'Yes,' he paused 'Yes I did.'

'Thank you, Mr Compton. No further questions, my Lord.'

The 'two As' turned to look at Marcus, and then at Cassie, who looked straight ahead nodding wisely, before taking a mint from the roll she had on the desk in front of her.

'Mr Alsopp. Any re-examination?'

'Just one or two, My Lord. Now Mr Compton, the identification parade. Can you remember what the police said when the parade began?'

'Mr Pike, is there any dispute the Inspector would have said that the man Mr Compton saw in Holland

Walk might not be in the line-up?' the judge interjected.

'Not at all,' replied Marcus.

Howard moved on to his next question, 'Did you make any assumptions about the parade?'

'Do you mean did I think that the man was there? Yes, Sir, I did, but I also knew that I must not pick anyone out if I was not sure.'

'Why, if you were sure, did you hesitate?' Howard stressed the word 'sure'.

'I was trying to remember the man's face and to imagine how he would look without a beard. I was sure it was the same man.'

Cassie watched Howard Alsopp write on his papers, before turning to the jury and then sinking onto his seat, grateful for that last answer.

Chapter 17

Cassie had learnt soon after she qualified that she should not compromise herself for a client. Even if she did not breach the Bar's Code of Conduct, identifying too closely with a client and his case could prejudice her future career. She had heard that somewhere in the bowels of the Ministry of Justice the officials kept files on every barrister containing any details of a lawyer's life they could gather. Any hint of unusual or reckless behaviour was noted and could be used in assessing one's suitability for any appointment. Despite her qualms, Cassie wanted to trace the alibi witness. She persuaded herself, there would be no harm in making a few enquiries on the Portobello Market, and if she got any helpful information, pointing the police or an inquiry agent in the right direction.

Just after six thirty the next morning, Cassie arrived at the junction of Elgin Avenue and Portobello Road. It was not yet light, but the market stalls were illuminated, connected by cables to the bollards on the edge of the pavement. The narrow road was made narrower by white vans parked along one side of the street, their rear doors open to enable a small army of dark coated figures to move cardboard boxes and wooden crates full of vegetables and fruit across the road. Once the boxes were on the barrows, she noted, with some amusement, the stallholders arranging the contents, putting the best looking produce on the pedestrian side of the stall.

Where to begin? Cassie walked slowly along the pavement, between the stalls and the unlit shops, looking at the men and women, wrapped in layers of clothing against the early morning cold. She too had put on an extra sweater under her parka, and wrapped her thickest scarf round her neck. Now she pulled the scarf across her mouth, as she strolled along hoping to see a friendly face, or at least friendly enough for her to approach them and ask questions about Hinds.

When she reached Talbot Road, where the market stalls ended, she turned and walked back, still searching for someone who she hoped might help her. There was a lull in the bustle of people and vehicles as she approached Elgin Crescent again. The vans were beginning to move away leaving the street to early morning office workers. The market traders were opening flasks of coffee and taking sandwiches from their bags, to have breakfast before their first customers arrived. One woman was stood leaning against her stall drinking a cup of coffee, clasping it with her hands. She was wearing striped fingerless gloves tucked into the sleeves of her dark brown jacket, the front of which shone, no doubt, from rubbing fruit, and she had a bright red scarf wrapped round her neck and across her chest. On her head she was wearing a similar coloured knitted hat with a pom-pom that swung as she moved. She caught Cassie looking at her and smiled, 'Can I help you, dearie? Got some nice tomatoes today. Or if you fancy, the leeks are good.' The woman walked to the front of the stall and picked up a solid looking leek and offered it to Cassie, who pulled her scarf away from her mouth.

'I don't want to buy anything at the moment. Thank you.' Cassie hesitated and continued looking at the woman.

'Just looking are you? You'll not find better than here.' The woman took another sip of her coffee, but smiled at Cassie again.

Encouraged by the smile, Cassie said with some hesitation, 'I am looking, but not for vegetables. I'm trying to find someone who works on the market from time to time. Perhaps you can help me?'

The woman put the leek back on the stall and hugged her mug closer, her eyes suddenly wary, 'Why should I? Why are you looking for this man? I assume it's a man?'

'He's known as Hinds. He's about twenty-three or so, quite tall and mixed race. I've been told he used to help out here. Unloading the vans. That kind of thing.' Cassie moved round to the back of the stall as the woman bent to put her coffee cup in a bag under the wheels. 'A friend of his needs his help. Do you know him?'

'I can't say I do,' she said as she straightened up and began to move tomatoes around in a box, taking out some that were damaged and putting them under the barrow. 'You'd do best to ask some of the others. I don't take casual, you never know who they are or what they're after.' She turned her back on Cassie, dismissing her without another word.

Cassie moved away and went back to the pavement. She started to walk back again towards Talbot Road when the woman called after her, 'Try Sammy at stall one four three. He's been here so long, he might know.'

Cassie looked round and said, 'Thanks.'

'He's just by the fish shop,' the woman added.

Cassie thanked her again and strode, purposefully now, along the street. After about twenty yards she was

126

outside the fish shop, its shutters still rolled down, a narrow slit of light at the bottom. On the other side of the pavement was another fruit and vegetable stall, the boxes laid out neatly next to each other on the sloping deck of the barrow. Along the top edge fruit had been arranged in small pyramids which emphasised their roundness. Between the cartons of vegetables were bunches of herbs, rosemary, thyme and bay. Cassie brushed her hand over the rosemary releasing its sweet smell, picked up a bunch, and asked the man behind the stall how much it was. He was big and bulky wearing a dirty green Barbour with a brown corduroy collar. Unlike most of the other traders, he was bareheaded and glove-less, so Cassie could see his fingers were twisted with arthritis. His face was stained by the weather, his grey hair stood out in wings over his ears and there was a roguish twinkle in his eye.

'Twenty-five pence, but for such a lovely lady, take it as a gift.'

Cassie wasn't used to being called lovely and was a bit taken aback. 'Thank you, for the herbs, and the compliment.' She paused and then said, 'Are you Sammy?'

He didn't reply as he replaced the herbs she had dislodged, and she began to think he had not heard her, when he said, 'Why do you want to know?'

Cassie explained that a lady at another stall had told her if she wanted to know anything about the market she should ask Sammy at stall number 143. She pointed up at the number on the upright of the barrow.

'Yeah, I'm Sammy. What it is you want to know?'

Cassie told him she was looking for a man called Hinds and repeated the description she had given earlier.

127

'I don't know anyone of that name who stands the market, and I've been here thirty odd years.'

'I don't think he had a stall himself, he just helped out, unloading the vans, moving boxes.'

Sammy's face was a blank so Cassie decided to try another approach, 'Do you know Mr Boxall; the man who has the hardware shop up the road here?'

'Ay, I know him.'

'What about one of the lads who works for him, Lenny?' She paused, Sammy nodded at her. 'Didn't he help out with the crates?'

'I hear he's in jug. Murdered that girl.'

'Didn't he help with the crates when you needed it?'

Sammy's face softened, 'Sometimes, my hands,' he held them out to show his buckled fingers, 'I need a bit of help, and Lenny, well he was always ready to give me a hand. Never wanted anything either, not like that friend of his.' He stopped, rubbed his nose with one of his deformed fingers, and then went on, 'The half caste kid, is that who you're looking for?'

Cassie nodded, but said nothing.

'I haven't seen him for some time. Not since last year. Heard he'd moved away. Why on earth do you think he can help? He wouldn't help his grandma cross a road unless he was getting something out of it.'

'Lenny says he was with Hinds the night of the murder so I need to find him.'

'Well, I don't know. The lad did help me out occasionally, and a few others but he weren't regular like. Look, give me your number and I'll ask around a bit. If I get anything I'll let you know. Lenny's a good lad and if he didn't do it, well he shouldn't go down for it. No bugger should go down for something they ain't done.' There was a bitter edge to his voice.

Cassie handed him her card, pointing out the mobile number on it. Sammy looked at it and then at her. 'You're Lenny's brief, then? Didn't come like you in my day. I'll ring if I can find out anything.'

She smiled at him, 'You can leave a message. I'll get it.' A small elderly lady pushed in between them, glared at Sammy through her horn-rimmed glasses and asked if they had finished their conversation because she was waiting to be served. 'Never get good service these days. All you people do is stand around and talk.'

'Yes, Mrs. What can I get you? Nice sprouts, a few potatoes, what's it to be?'

Cassie said goodbye to him; he winked at her as she turned away.

Chapter 18

The early morning visit to the Portobello Market had made Cassie short of time to get to the Old Bailey. She just had time to change into the formal black, compulsory in court, before rushing to get the tube to St Paul's.

Once in the building she headed for the fifth floor and the Bar Mess, where she had arranged to meet David Jennings, to discuss the scientific evidence. Both she and Marcus had agreed not to call too much attention to the forensics, such as they were. It was better to lose the information in a number of agreed facts, better to bury the bad news, wasn't that the phrase?

As Cassie walked up the narrow staircase into the large, well lit room she looked round to see if David had arrived. The Bar Mess was busy, there were other barristers in groups at all the rows of tables, eating breakfast or drinking coffee; it was like a school refectory. Amongst them was her roommate Stephen. He beckoned to her and she walked over to him, while she continued to search around the room for David Jennings.

'I'm glad I've seen you. I've heard that Bill Allen is going to another set, and Richard wants to offer the place to one of his friend's sons.'

'And Eleanor, has she a candidate, or Peter?'

'Actually, I think Eleanor does have somebody in mind, but I think it's someone more senior,' he paused and a smile flitted across his face, 'and Peter, well there's that girl who's just finished pupillage with him. She's useless but Peter doesn't half fancy her.'

'You as well, from the way you behaved at the Christmas party,' Cassie said. 'Anyway who told you about this new development?'

'I overheard Jack discussing it with Eleanor,' he took a deep breath, 'That's why I think she has somebody else in mind.'

'And what about judging on merit rather than friendship? Isn't that why we have a committee to make the decision?'

'Yes, of course, but...'

'But what? It's easier if we don't have to go through a tedious selection procedure? Anyway what does Eleanor think about Richard's mate?'

'She's not too pleased about it.'

'And Peter?'

'I don't know. I've not seen him, but he'll be disappointed Allen isn't joining us. He really thought he'd have a High Court Judge backing his application for silk.' Stephen stifled a laugh.

She saw David's head appear as he climbed the staircase from the robing rooms into the Bar Mess and, with some relief, told Stephen she had to go.

When she and David had sat down, she gave him a list of admissions she had prepared. As he studied them, her eyes wandered over the papers he had placed on the table. Amongst them was a thick bundle of photographs, considerably thicker than the one she had been served by the prosecuting solicitors. She had to restrain herself from reaching over and opening the album.

'That seems OK,' Jennings said after he had spent some minutes looking at her list.

David Jennings put the papers to one side and suddenly asked, 'Are you intending to make an application about Rose Cummings?'

'We haven't made up our minds. When are you going to read the alibi notice to the jury?'

'I think Howard wants to get it in as soon as possible. Trying to be fair.'

'Mm.' She wasn't convinced by that argument; what the prosecution wanted was to encourage the jury to think the alibi was a lie.

'Are you going to call your client?'

'I don't know, and I wouldn't tell you if I did.' She was fairly sure Lenny would be giving evidence, but keeping the prosecution guessing was part of the game. 'Any news about Hinds?'

'I've just had a word with Dean. They've eliminated two of the names they had, but the other two are being elusive. After court rose yesterday, as you suggested, I asked them to get the mugshots from criminal records, then you can show them to Barker. If one of them is your witness, they can concentrate on him rather wasting time on the others.'

'Seems a good idea. Let me know when you get them.'

After leaving the Bar Mess, Cassie went straight to the courtroom, where she found Marcus in his seat, reading The Times. He seemed so casual and Cassie wondered if she would ever be as laid back as he was, or appeared to be; was it all an act to disguise the real tensions he felt before his performance in court? She slipped into the row of seats behind him and searched through the files laid out on the bench for her album of photographs. Once she had found them she held them in her hand, and trying to hold the image of the bundle

David Jennings had in her mind, she compared the two. Marcus twisted round in his seat, saw the expression on her face, and asked her if there was something wrong. She told him about the size of the album she had noticed in Jennings's brief.

Marcus grinned at her, 'We'd better ask about that. I don't suppose they reveal anything we don't know, but I do like putting the prosecution on the back foot.'

As they were talking David Jennings came into the courtroom with copies of the admissions he and Cassie had agreed. He handed two of them to Marcus, who began reading the list.

'I've also got these from Dean. They think this one is the right bloke,' he said handing her a set of photographs. 'If you could get your client to confirm that's his mate, the police will circulate it, in the hope somebody might spot him. There are a couple of bail applications in court now, so you'll have time.'

In the cells Marcus and Cassie found Tim trying to explain to Lenny the problems of the identification parade and his interviews with the police. Marcus threw the pictures onto the table and asked Lenny if they were of Hinds. Lenny picked them up, glanced at them, and said, 'Yes, that's him. Have they found him?' Marcus asked him again if the picture was of Hinds. Lenny looked at it a second time and repeated that it was.

Cassie picked up the print, which showed three views of Hinds, full face and his left and right profile. They depicted a young man, unusually for police photographs, smiling at the camera. He was rather handsome, a face the colour of caramel, black hair closely cropped, large dark eyes. Would he make an attractive witness, despite having a criminal record?

'Right, now the police can concentrate on finding him,' Marcus said and then, 'The evidence yesterday could have been worse. Mr Compton was very sure you were the man he saw in Holland Walk, but I think we managed to raise some questions about his reliability.'

Lenny frowned and looked away from Marcus to Cassie, who explained by saying, 'The jury may think that even if he is telling the truth, he's not got it right.' Lenny nodded and sat back in his chair.

Marcus then said, 'I should tell you that I am not confident about securing your acquittal, even with this supposed alibi. If you did kill this girl, there is still time to change your plea. Will you think about it?'

Lenny didn't reply but asked, 'Will they find Hinds?'

Marcus sighed, and then said, 'I don't know. We have to continue on the basis they may not and we have to do without him. We want to try and get before the jury the conversation with that WPC about the football match. That will help.'

Just at that moment, a warder tapped on the glass panel of the door and opened it to tell them they were wanted in court. Cassie knew Compton had been a good witness, but Marcus was being very pessimistic, prompted she thought by his dislike of losing a case. In his eyes, it was better for his client to plead guilty than be convicted after a trial.

'We'll see you up there,' said Tim, as the three of them left the interview room. Cassie picked up the photographs and put them in the pocket of her jacket.

Back upstairs, Howard Alsopp was stood outside the courtroom doors, talking to the usher. He turned towards them and began to walk back along the hall. When he drew level he said, 'They haven't finished; there's another application to go. I'm going back upstairs.'

Marcus turned as well, and followed Howard in the direction of the lifts, leaving Cassie with Tim. They sat down on the seats closest to Court 12, each of them absorbed in their own thoughts. Cassie took the pictures of Hinds out of her pocket and was turning them over in her hands, when she saw Sergeant Dean approaching them. She hurriedly put them back; she didn't want to return them.

He told them he had found two DVDs which had been retained as evidence after the Chelsea–Everton game, and they made arrangements for Tim to take them when they had been brought to court.

As they were talking the jury assembled at one side of the hall; Cassie saw the 'two As' talking, animatedly, to each other and Colin Heap was chatting to an Asian woman dressed in a cobalt blue sari who wasn't responding to his friendly overture. Cassie had not noticed her before and, from what she could observe, she thought the woman might have very fixed ideas about the guilt of someone just because he was standing in the dock.

The jury shuffled into court, where Judge Crabtree was already on the bench. David Jennings was in his usual seat. He had remained after completing the bail application, by tradition, keeping the judge company. Cassie followed the jury, with Marcus and Howard just behind. Once in her seat she checked back in her notes for the woman's name; Deepa Nadswallah.

She then glanced round at Lenny Barker; he was looking up at the public gallery. She followed his gaze and saw his mother and sister, their faces pale with anxiety. When Mrs Barker noticed her, Cassie nodded at her and she responded by smiling warmly. Relatives were so trusting? Judge Crabtree interrupted her thoughts, 'Mr Alsopp, shall we begin?'

'Yes, we have a set of admissions that we propose to read to the jury.' He handed a sheet of paper to the court clerk, who passed it up to the judge, and other copies to the usher for the jury.

David Jennings got to his feet, 'It is agreed by both prosecution and defence that Shelley Paulson was unlawfully killed on eighteenth September last, by a single knife wound which penetrated the heart. The wound was caused by a knife of at least sixteen centimetres in length and four centimetres wide. The murder weapon has not been found. The only other injuries to Miss Paulson were contusions on her lower right arm, that's bruising, members of the jury. Scrapings were taken from under Miss Paulson's fingernails and analysed; the DNA analysis did not match that of Lenny Barker.'

Cassie turned her attention to the jury. She had hoped that the reference to DNA would cause a stir amongst the jury, but although Colin Heap was studying the copy of the admissions he was sharing with one of his neighbours, an overweight woman in her fifties, the others seemed not to notice the piece of evidence that might suggest someone other than Lenny was the killer. Perhaps they should have called the forensic scientist who had done the analysis, but both she and Marcus preferred to rely on using the evidence in their speech to the jury.

136

Heap then looked up as David Jennings confirmed that the clothing taken from the deceased was not damaged other than the cuts needed to remove the clothes from her body at the post-mortem and the one caused by the knife. Her red high heels, he said, were removed by the ambulance men who attended the scene of the murder. Fibres taken from her cardigan matched a sweatshirt taken from Barker's home. Jennings continued reading, telling the jury that despite the extensive search of the scene of the murder and the seizure of all Barker's clothes, that was the only forensic evidence linking him to the murder.

As David Jennings resumed his seat, Marcus got up to inform the judge that there was another matter of law which he wished to raise. Judge Crabtree apologised to the jury, telling them he would send for them as soon as possible. Once the jury had left the courtroom he turned to Marcus and asked him what the point was that he wished to raise.

'My Lord, there are two matters. One we think can be dealt with quickly. The album we have been given contains twenty photographs, and was, no doubt, prepared for the jury, but we believe that there are more photographs and we would like the opportunity of seeing them.'

Judge Crabtree turned towards Howard, who rose to his feet, 'We weren't aware the defence had not been served the full bundle. As usual there is no one from the CPS here, but I will arrange for a copy to be made available over the luncheon adjournment.'

'Quite. I expect nothing less.' Judge Crabtree was clearly irritated. Cassie tried to keep a straight face but couldn't prevent the edges of her mouth turning up a little.

'Now the second matter, Mr Pike.'

'The second matter concerns the alibi. As Your Lordship knows, the defendant did not raise the possibility of an alibi in his interview. It came to light as a result of an ill judged attempt to obtain either an admission or information from him by subterfuge. A female police officer set out to befriend the defendant and gain his confidence. It failed, but the defendant did tell her about the football match he had attended at Stamford Bridge on what, it turns out, was the night of the murder. Mr Alsopp, perfectly properly, wishes to read out, as part of his case, that alibi notice, then we will hear the evidence of the interviews in the police station. We take the view that the jury should hear the evidence of the WPC at this stage, otherwise they would be left with the impression that the first time the question of this alibi was raised was this weekend, when, in fact, the police were aware in November.'

Judge Crabtree intervened by asking Howard Alsopp why he objected to the evidence of the meeting between the defendant and the police officer, 'Should it not be before the jury?' he asked. 'I understand the prosecution does not accept the truth of the statement, but when and where it was made cannot be objectionable, can it?'

'Quite, but the police do not want the nature of the recording device disclosed. The identity of the police officer also needs to be protected.'

'Why, Mr Alsopp?'

'I have instructions that she has been engaged in undercover work in the area on a major drugs case.'

'Aren't the jury entitled to know how Barker came to say he was at a football match on the night of the murder? It would be unjust to the defendant and

mislead the jury if they did not hear this evidence. No.'
Judge Crabtree shook his head, 'If the defendant had
made an admission you would call the evidence. Either
agree some further admissions to give to the jury or
call the officer. I'll have the jury back, please.' Cassie
smiled broadly; she thought the jury would probably
think the circumstances in which Lenny's alibi had
been revealed added to his credibility, even if the judge
told them it did not.

As the usher made her way towards the door,
Stephen Burnett walked through it. Judge Crabtree
called the usher back and told her that he thought the
jury should go to lunch as it seemed the bail
application he had adjourned earlier was ready to go
ahead. Stephen nodded at the judge.

'Two o'clock for the case of Barker. Now, Mr
Burnett, your bail application.'

Cassie went up to the ladies' robing room and
turned on her mobile phone. Amongst the various
messages and texts one read 'Try Jackie at The
Jugglers. Sammy.'

Chapter 19

When the court reassembled that afternoon, Howard Alsopp read the Notice of Alibi that Cassie had prepared. 'This was served at the beginning of the trial and reads, "On the night of eighteenth September last the defendant, Lenny Barker, went to a football match at the Stamford Bridge ground, Chelsea. He arrived at the stadium at approximately seven pm and left after the match finished at approximately nine thirty pm. It took some twenty minutes to leave the ground and reach the southerly end of Warwick Road. He walked north to Holland Road and then to Ladbroke Grove, arriving at his home at around eleven pm. He attended the match with Edwin Walker, known as Hinds, whose address is unknown at the time of this notice."'

While he was reading, Cassie had time to observe the jury again. On the back row was a large man in his late fifties wearing a grey sweater. From her notes Cassie knew he was called Brian Claxton. His hands were clasped across his chest and his eyes were closed. He was sat to one side of Colin Heap, who realised that Cassie was looking at his neighbour. He smiled at Cassie, then leant over towards Mr Claxton and spoke to him. Brian Claxton nodded. He wasn't taking an afternoon nap after all.

Howard put the notice down and called Colin Dean. As he came into court he handed a sheaf of paper to the usher before stepping into the witness box. She stood still holding them in her hands as he took the oath in a steady voice, dusted lightly with some regional accent Cassie couldn't identify, while he looked straight at the jury. They appeared to be totally focused on the man in the witness box.

Cassie turned to the files in front of her and searched for the transcripts of the interviews. She had just found the first page when she realised that David Jennings had come over to her and was offering her two of the pieces of paper he had been handed by the usher. Cassie leant over, gave one to Marcus and then read the remaining copy. It was statement by an employee of Transport for London and confirmed that Lenny's Oyster Card had been used on 18th September for a journey from Notting Hill Gate station to Fulham Broadway by bus, arriving at 7pm. The journey had used the last of the credit on his card. The bus route was number 28, which according to the statement ran every ten minutes in the evening. The journey time from the stadium to the junction of Kensington High Street and Earls Court Road was thirty-five minutes, including six minutes on foot, and a further fifteen minutes to Ladbroke Grove.

She wasn't sure what they were trying to prove. The alibi notice had given the time Barker arrived at the Stamford Bridge as 7pm and this statement said he had arrived at Fulham Broadway at 7, but it was such a minor discrepancy, no judge would allow the prosecution to say the defendant had lied. If Barker had got the bus back immediately he could have been in Holland Walk any time from eight or thereabouts, but that didn't explain the events the taxi driver described.

Colin Dean spoke firmly, looking at the jurors, but making his replies to the judge. He described how he, with other officers, had gone to 26 Lancaster Grove on the morning of 27th October. He told the court the door was opened by Mrs Barker, and Lenny had come out into the hallway of the flat dressed in boxer shorts and a T-shirt. After Lenny had been arrested and cautioned, he and other officers had taken all the clothing they could find in Lenny Barker's room. They had decided to remove everything because of the length of time that had elapsed between the murder and the arrest.

'We knew it was unlikely there would be visible blood stains, but forensics can pick up marks even after things have been washed. There was the possibility that small specks of blood might be found on clothing and on the bedding the defendant had slept in.'

Cassie's mind was still working on the statement about the bus route, but she was impressed by the quiet authority of the officer as he explained how thoroughly the search had taken place. He acknowledged that, in their enthusiasm, they had forgotten to bring a paper suit for Barker, leaving the defendant stood naked, handcuffed to a uniformed officer, while they completed their search. The defendant's mother and sister were crying and shouting at the officers. The Sergeant had tried to calm them down and asked them to sit in the kitchen until they had finished, but they continued interrupting. After about ten minutes a paper jumpsuit was brought to the flat, Barker put it on and was escorted from the property. Dean told Mrs Barker that her son was going to Kensington Police Station and she should organise a solicitor for him.

Howard Alsopp continued by asking Sergeant Dean about the interviews.

'We interviewed Barker on two occasions; both times in the presence of his solicitor, Mr Durrant.' Dean nodded in the direction of Tim, and all eyes turned towards where he was sitting behind Cassie.

'Who conducted the interviews?'

'I did, My Lord. In addition to Mr Durrant, Detective Chief Superintendent O'Connor was present.'

'He's the officer in charge of this investigation?'

'Yes. The officer in overall control of the operation.'

'When were the interviews held?'

'The day of his arrest, twenty-seventh October.'

'Were the interviews recorded?'

'Yes, My Lord, and transcripts have been prepared from the tapes.'

'Have you any objection to the transcripts being given to the jury, Mr Pike?' the judge asked.

Marcus rose half way out of his seat, 'No, My Lord.'

Once the sheaves of paper were on their benches, the jurors shuffled in their seats, some of them producing spectacles, before they turned the pages. Mrs Nadswallah put on her round, gold-rimmed glasses, transforming her into a schoolmistress, stern and uncompromising. Cassie felt distinctly uneasy.

When they were all settled, Howard said to Colin Dean, 'Now I'm going to read the questions you asked, and can you read out the replies.' The witness nodded and they began to read the transcripts.

Cassie relaxed, Howard and the officer would simply read the interview record she had in front of her, there was no need to take notes. The jury too were following the questions and answers; she watched them and wondered how they imagined the scene. Did they picture a mean grubby room, painted in whatever tedious colour some official at Scotland Yard deemed to be suitable, lit by un-shaded bulbs, with four men round a small table, on which a tape recorder was sat, or something more like an office in a bank, brightly lit and painted in relaxing pastel shades?

After reading out the initial introductions, Howard Alsopp asked if the next few questions were put by DCS O'Connor.

'Yes, they were,' said Dean.

'Was Mr O'Connor's first question, "What did you think about her?'

The transcript showed a pause; Cassie underlined it. Colin Dean read the answer Lenny had given, 'She was very beautiful.'

Howard Alsopp read out the next question, 'That all? Just beautiful? Quite sexy, wasn't she?' and then added, 'Was there then another pause before Mr O'Connor continued by saying "She wore tight clothing; showing off her figure. Didn't you fancy her?"'

Sergeant Dean agreed Barker had not replied to O'Connor's original question but had said, 'She was beautiful. Yes,' in answer to the second.

'So you did fancy her?'

'Yes, but…'

Howard then said 'Did Mr Connor begin the next question with "You wanted .." but was interrupted by Mr Durrant asking him to let Barker finish his answer.'

'Yes, and Barker said, "but she wouldn't be interested in me."'

'Is that why you forced yourself on her?'

'I didn't.'

'Did you continue the questioning by asking "Where were you on the night of 18th September?" '

'Yes, and Barker replied "I don't know"'

'Just think about it?'

'It's weeks ago.'

Cassie saw Amanda Conrad pick up a pencil from the bench in front of her, and underline something in the transcript, and then pat her lips with the same pencil.

'You knew Shelley? Do you remember hearing she'd been killed?'

'Mm. Yes. I think Sammy told me but it might have been Mr Boxall.'

'Mr Boxall, he's your employer? Who's Sammy?'

'He has a stall, just by the flyover.'

Cassie smiled as she thought of the text message she had received.

'Did whoever it was say where she had been killed?'

'I knew it was in Holland Park.'

'You asked "Had you been to the park recently?" and did Mr Durrant intervene again and ask you to clarify the question, and you then said, "just before you were told of Shelley's death?"'

'Yes, that's right and Barker said, "I think so. I went to watch the football."'

'What time did you leave?'

'About eight, I think, when it got dark.'

'Did you go straight home?'

'"Perhaps." I noted Barker paused before adding, that he might have wandered round for a bit.'

'Where? Round the park?'

'Sometimes I go and look in the shops on the High Street, the sports shops.'

'Anywhere else?'

'Round school.'

'Holland Park?'

'Mm.'

'On your own?'

145

'Not always. I know other lads who hang around the school.'

'Why do they do that?'

Sergeant Dean replied, 'There was another long pause before Barker said, "You know, they use it as a pick up place."'

'They? You mean men cruising?'

'Yes.'

'Did you do that on this night we are talking about?'

'No. I was on my own.'

'Did you go to the school?'

'Not sure.'

'You would walk up Holland Walk after you left the sports pitch.'

'Yes, I guess so. The park would be closing.'

A movement amongst the juror's caught Cassie's eye and she turned to see Brian Claxton jabbing at the transcript with a finger, trying to draw Colin Heap's attention. Colin nodded at his neighbour, but didn't look at whatever passage of the transcript had excited Brian Claxton.

'You saw Shelley in the Walk.'

'No I didn't.'

'Didn't you see her and approach her?'

'No.'

'You went up to her and when she told you to go away, you argued?'

'No, I didn't.'

'You grabbed her as she tried to push you away, you stabbed her?'

'No, no I didn't.'

Howard then asked if at that point Barker had become distraught and was the interview terminated?'

146

'Yes, My Lord.'

Cassie glimpsed Anna Fry draw a line down a page of the transcript and wondered what impression the evidence of the interviews had made on the jury. The transcripts were almost the worst part of the prosecution case against Lenny. These were his own words; there was no mistaking what he had said to the police. They couldn't cross-examine them away and his explanation for telling the police officers he was in the park seemed hardly credible in the cool analysis of the courtroom.

Sergeant Dean said, before they interrogated Barker again, he had been offered a meal, but had refused to eat. It had taken some time to organise the identity parade which had taken place in the afternoon. Barker had seen his solicitor in private after the parade and before the second interview two hours later.

There was a shuffle from the jury box as the jurors turned over their papers to find the transcript of the second interview. Anna Fry put her hand up and told the judge some of the pages were missing. Some of the other jurors held up their copies as well. Judge Crabtree asked the usher to collect the documents and the court adjourned whilst the lost pages were recopied.

Cassie went to the back of the court to speak to Lenny. He was looking down at his feet when she spoke to him, but he lifted his face and tried to smile. She leant over and patted his hand and, in a low, calm voice attempted to reassure him. 'We'll come and see you after court, if we don't rise too late. If we can't it'll be tomorrow morning.' He nodded and looked up at where his mother was sitting in the public gallery. Mrs Barker smiled and waved at him. Cassie nodded at her

147

before going out into the corridor to join Tim and Marcus.

Colin Dean had wandered off. Howard and David were checking through the bundles of transcripts to identify the missing pages. Cassie couldn't see Tim, but Marcus was looking out of the window onto a grey afternoon. She went over to join him, below her the streets were wet and the cobbles in Seacoal Lane reflected the cold light. To their left, towards Fleet Street, the white tiered steeple of St Brides rose above the former newspaper buildings. It was a view Cassie was never tired of seeing, a reminder she was living and working in the centre of a great city and at the heart of the legal profession.

Marcus was so absorbed in the scene that Cassie hesitated to speak, but after a second or so, she pulled the mugshots of Hinds from her jacket pocket. Marcus saw her looking at the photographs. 'So, that's our lost alibi witness,' he said. Cassie nodded. Marcus looked at the photographs again, 'He looks a bit of a lad. I wonder if they'll find him. Hinds, funny nickname. When I was doing pupillage there was a man called Alfie Hinds, a safebreaker, escaped from here, got caught of course, eventually.' She was about to put the photos back, when Tim suddenly appeared and asked her for them. 'Do you mind if I hang on to them. I should be able to run those DVDs tonight after the parents' evening. It's probably more entertaining than Big Brother.'

'Fine,' she replied, 'Have you got them?'

'They have just been brought to court by O'Connor and I think he's got the WPC with him. Attractive girl, looks a bit like Shelley Paulson.'

148

Marcus was suddenly diverted from his concentration on the outside world. 'Cassie, if they are going to call her, I want you to cross-examine her. A woman's touch, you know.'

She had not been expecting to get to her feet at all during this trial, and had not prepared any cross-examination as was her usual meticulous style. At the far end of the corridor she could see David Jennings approaching with the jury bundles in his hands. 'Ready to roll. Just the first two pages missing on five of the bundles. Want to see them?' He held out one of the sets of papers. Cassie took it and flipped through the pages, checking that nothing untoward had been placed there.

'Seems to be OK,' she said handing it back and following him into court.

When everyone was back in their places, the trial continued with the evidence of the second interview. Cassie followed the questions and answers in her copy of the transcript.

Q. I think you know the witness identified you as the person he saw attacking Miss Paulson. Can you explain that?

A. I didn't kill her. I never saw her.

Then after a number of questions about his workmates and who might have mentioned the murder of Shelley Paulson, Colin Dean produced a copy of the Evening Standard.

Q. This is the Standard for the nineteenth September. I want you to look at page three.

(Rustle of paper)

Cassie noticed Colin Heap lean forward and begin to write in his notebook, then he stopped and, from

149

where she was sat, appeared to draw a line through whatever he had written.

Again the transcript showed a pause and noted Barker had failed to reply, before the questions continued.

Q. There is a piece about this killing, isn't there?

A. Yes.

Q. Did you see that?

A. I don't remember. Somebody usually picks up a copy.

Q. Do you look at it?

A. The sports pages, sometimes.'

Q. Was the paper the reason Shelley was mentioned?

(Pause)

A. Yes, I think it was.

Q. Who mentioned it?'

A. I think it was Jimmy.

Q. Was that because he had seen the paper?'

A. Probably.

Q. Did you talk about where the murder had taken place?

A. Yes. I knew it was in the park.

Q. Did you say you had been in the park that same night?

A. I'm not sure.

Q. Surely you would have mentioned it? Said something like you'd been there earlier?

A. Yes, I probably did. But I hadn't seen anything.

Q. So you had been in the park the night of the murder.

A. Yes, I've said I was. You know I was.

Q. You were in Holland Walk when you saw Shelley and when she refused your advances you killed her didn't you?

A. No, no. I didn't. I didn't.

(Crying)

Cassie turned her attention to the jury. They were looking straight ahead, their faces solemn. Amanda Conrad started to fiddle with corners of the transcript; Deepa Nadswallah took off her glasses and rubbed them on her deep blue sari.

Howard Alsopp was still on his feet, 'The copy of the Standard you produced, what is there on the back page?'

Colin Dean picked it up and looked at the paper, 'A report of the Chelsea–Everton game.' He held it up so that everyone could see a photograph of a footballer in blue and white.

'Exhibit 10, My Lord,' Howard said.

'Do you want the jury to see it now? I'm sure they all know what the paper looks like.' He beamed towards the jurors and most of them nodded.

'No.' Howard replied and handed it to the usher.

For a moment Cassie's belief in Lenny's innocence faltered, she had been so delighted to discover he had been at Stamford Bridge on the night of the murder, she had forgotten the paper had been referred to in the interviews. Why, she asked herself, when he saw the newspaper had he not made the connection with the Chelsea game? She looked round at him, his face was white, his lips quivering as if he was about to burst into tears; of course he was innocent.

'Mr Pike, do you want to start cross-examination now or in the morning?'

'Tomorrow, My Lord. I don't think I will be long but there are a few matters I wish to take further instructions on.'

Chapter 20

Outside court, Marcus told Cassie he had an urgent appointment and she would have to see Lenny on her own. 'It's not looking good. That newspaper,' he pursed his lips. 'If I was Howard I'd put the fingerprint evidence in. Rely on the similarities and forget the conclusion. Have you seen Alison Pretty in action?'

'No,' said Cassie.

'No, well, she's a very good witness, totally convincing. If that went in we'd be a dead duck. Howard's being a bit tight-lipped about it; he's saying he thinks it's inadmissible. Of course we'd object if he tried to call her, but I'm not as sure as he is that the judge wouldn't agree to her giving evidence.'

'You haven't raised it with Barker?'

'No, it's not evidence against him and it's unlikely to be. If he was wavering about his plea I would bring it up, but, as it is, he'll just deny it's his print, so there's no point. You'd better go down and see him. I'll see you tomorrow.' They parted as Marcus went up to the robing rooms, and she went down to the cells.

When Lenny arrived in the interview room, his face was very white, his lips a thin line, his eyes wide and panic stricken.

'I didn't mean to say I'd been in the park that night for certain,' he blurted out as soon as he got into the room.

'I know,' Cassie said, 'We'll ask Mr Dean about the video, and what was said tomorrow. It always sounds worse when it's read out by the officer.'

'Where's Mr Pike?' Lenny demanded.

'He's had to go back to chambers, but he'll be here in the morning.'

Tim chipped in, 'We've got some DVDs taken at the football game. I'll look at them later this evening and see if there is some footage of you and Hinds.'

Lenny's eyes lit up, 'I didn't know they used cameras at the match.'

'Don't get your hopes up. They record them when they are looking for known trouble makers. You may not be on them, but that won't mean you weren't there,' Tim told him.

'But if I am?'

'As Mr Durrant has said, don't get your hopes up. It's a long shot,' Cassie said.

A prison officer tapped on the window before opening the door and telling them the van for Brixton was in the yard.

Once Cassie and Tim left the cells, she turned to him and told him she should fly as she had a conference in Chambers. 'Hope the parents' evening isn't too awful. See you tomorrow.' Tim never said very much about his family; she knew he had twin daughters and lived somewhere near Tunbridge Wells, but beyond that she knew nothing about him. She had heard his wife had left him with the children, and she had noticed he didn't refer to anyone who might have been a partner.

The conference took more time than she had anticipated, and it was after eight when she got home; it took her fifteen minutes to make her supper; leeks fried with cubes of pancetta and mixed with crème fraiche before being poured over pasta and topped with grated parmesan. She didn't have any wine with her meal; her plans for the evening would probably result

154

in her drinking beer and she didn't like mixing them. She had just sat down to eat it when her mobile rang.

'Have you got time to talk to me?' said Ben, his voice rather stiff. Cassie grimaced; she'd forgotten again.

'Ben, I'm really sorry. I've been very busy. I got your message about tomorrow night. It would be great; but,' she hesitated, 'I'm not sure I can make it. What about Friday?' She chatted for a while, hoping he wouldn't be angry, but he didn't respond and, in the end, she said that she had to go.

'Back to work is it?' his voice resigned.

She didn't want to tell him what she was going to do. She knew he would tell her not to go, setting out the objections she already knew, but had decided to ignore.

'Yes. The prosecution have served some fresh evidence and I need to look at it. Look, we can meet up on Friday.'

She waited for a reply but Ben stayed silent.

'Ben, Friday. OK?'

'I'll call you,' he said.

Cassie swore to herself, she didn't want to upset him, but neither was she ready to change her lifestyle for him. He would just have to wait until she was ready.

She changed into jeans and a sweater and put her yellow parka on. She didn't want anyone in The Jugglers to think she was either a policewoman or a social worker. She decided against taking a handbag and put her purse, mobile phone and keys into her pockets.

It didn't take long to reach the pub and she stood outside for a few moments peering through the glass windows at the brightly lit interior. Although it was, by now, just after nine, she could only see ten or so people in the room. She pushed open the glass panelled door and strolled in. She had walked past the pub before, but only on a Saturday lunchtime, when it had been very busy with tourists joining market traders and shoppers, but at this time of night it appeared only a few locals came for a drink.

Sitting at the bar was a black man in his fifties, leaning on one elbow, and holding his pint glass close to his chest with the other hand. He was in an animated conversation with the barmaid, who broke off as Cassie approached the bar.

'Yes, dear. What can I get you?'

Cassie asked for a half of bitter. The woman began to pull the beer and said 'It's a bit raw this evening.'

'Yes, it is.' Cassie replied, fumbling in her purse for some pound coins.

Having got her drink, Cassie sat on one of the high stools by the bar and looked round the room. In addition to four young men playing darts and the man at the bar, there were a few others scattered round. A couple were poring over the back pages of a newspaper, the man gulping at his beer whilst the woman sipped a large glass of red wine.

On another table a solitary male was staring at the half empty pint glass in front of him. Next to his drink was a packet of cigarettes and a small bright pink lighter, which he picked up and drummed on the bare wooden top, and then put down again, a frustrated smoker. Under the window, at a large rectangular table, were four girls, who hardly looked old enough to be drinking. They were all dressed alike in sweatshirts and jogging pants, the shirts carrying a logo and the words 'Westway Hockey'.

'....seen you in here before?' Cassie realised the man sat at the bar had spoken to her.

'I'm sorry?' she said.

'I've not seen you in here before?' the man said.

'No, I don't get round here much.'

'Hm, it's quiet tonight. Usually there's a bit more of a crowd.'

'Yes, it seems quiet.'

The barmaid came back from washing some glasses at the other end of the bar, as one of the men who were playing darts came over and ordered another round.

'Four pints of best, Jackie, and have one for yourself.'

'You're feeling flush,' the barmaid replied as she pulled the first pint.

'Yeah. Payday.'

After she had finished serving, Jackie said to the man sitting at the bar, 'I don't like it when it's this quiet either. Not enough to do. You can only polish the glasses once.' She wiped the bar top.

'One of the market traders told me it was quite lively,' Cassie interjected.

'Who was that, then?' Jackie asked. 'We get a lot of them in here. Mainly at lunchtime.'

'Sammy. He has a fruit and veg stall up by the flyover.'

'I know. He does pop in from time to time. Not a regular though.'

'He thought you might know someone, a friend of mine. He's moved recently. Hinds, he's known as Hinds.' Jackie looked at the man sitting alone at the table and then back at Cassie.

'Mm, I know who you mean, it's a couple of weeks since I last saw him. How about you, Bill?' she asked the male at the bar.

'Not sure I know him.'

'Yes, you do. Tall lad, good looking.'

'No, don't think so.'

'Didn't you buy some tickets for a football match from him?' Jackie persisted.

'No. You've got the wrong bloke.' He got down from the barstool and went to an empty table.

Cassie noticed the other man had gone, leaving his cigarettes and lighter. A couple of minutes later, he returned to the pub through the front door, slipping a mobile phone into his pocket.

She watched as he sat down again, and then she turned to Jackie and asked her if she knew where she might find Hinds. Jackie said she didn't, but he did come to the pub fairly regularly.

'I need to speak to him soon,' Cassie said.

'You could try The Mango in All Saints Road. I think he gets there.'

Cassie thanked her, finished her drink and walked towards the door.

'It doesn't open 'til ten thirty,' the barmaid shouted at her as she left the pub.

On the pavement, she stood for a moment before turning right to walk home. She had only walked a few paces when she heard the door of the pub open. She looked over her shoulder and saw the solitary white male come out. When he saw her, he stopped and facing away from her, took a cigarette out of a packet and flicked life into his lighter.

Cassie continued walking south along Portobello Road. The shop fronts were all dark but ahead she could see the lights of The Electric Cinema; behind her, she could hear the footsteps of the man keeping pace with her. She stopped by the cinema and looked at the film posters, the footsteps stopped as well and then she heard the low drone of a car engine coming from behind. She looked back, the man had vanished but, the car, a large BMW without lights, was coming to a halt close to where she stood. She could see a black male was driving but he seemed to be alone in the vehicle.

She didn't know why, but she was sure they were looking for her, and she considered running to get away, but instead just quickened her pace. Away from the cinema the street was dark again. She heard the car doors open and the sounds of someone getting out of it. She turned and saw two men, almost invisible, in long dark coats. The younger man came and stood in front of her blocking her path, the other man, considerably older than his companion stood on the other side. Cassie looked from one to the other determined not to show any fear. She could feel her heart thumping, and she clenched and unclenched her fists to try to calm herself.

'You've been asking questions about a friend of ours. We'd rather you didn't,' the younger man said.

'I'm not a police officer,' Cassie replied.

'It doesn't matter. Whatever you want, he doesn't want to know,' said the older man, grabbing her arm and pushing her towards the wall.

'Why do you say that? He won't be in any trouble,' Cassie replied. She regained her balance and stepped sideways out of reach.

'So, why do you want to see him?' the older man asked.

Cassie started to explain that Hinds was needed as an alibi witness for a friend of his charged with murder, but it was clear the two men were not interested in Lenny's plight; they simply wanted to keep her away from Hinds. The younger of the two men grabbed her by the arm and pushed her up against a shop door. His face was close to her and she could smell curry on his breath. She tried to push him away, but he was too strong for her. She began to wriggle and shout, 'Leave me alone. Get off.' As she raised her voice, the man let go and moved back towards the car.

'Look, Miss, we've told you to stop looking for him. If you continue, you just might end up hurt,' the elder man said.

The two men returned to the car, 'Just leave it,' one of them said. Cassie couldn't tell which one had spoken. She felt weak and leant against the window of a shop. She heard a door slam shut and the engine of the car roar, before it sped away. Cassie could feel the cold from the wall of glass behind her, and her arm hurt where she had been grabbed. She pulled the mobile from her pocket and thought about ringing the police, but she realised there was nothing they could do. She didn't think she could identify the men, and she didn't want to spend the rest of the evening in a police station making a witness statement. She put the phone back in her pocket and concentrated on walking, trying not to stumble, as she made her way home.

Cassie's mother would have insisted on a cup of tea, but, in the absence of something stronger, she poured a glass of wine and curled up on the sofa. The wine helped to steady her nerves, and she began to think about who the men were and why they were so determined she should not speak to Hinds.

160

The telephone disturbed her thoughts and it took a few moments for her to answer it. Tim apologised for ringing so late, but he had watched the DVDs and he was sure that he had identified Hinds. Lenny, however, was not to be seen. He suggested they meet at Chambers early the next morning and watch them again together. He finished by reminding her that she was to cross-examine Rose Cummings.

Cassie sank back onto the sofa too upset to prepare any cross-examination, and pondering what they would do if Hinds could not be found.

Chapter 21

Cassie was not the first person to arrive in Chambers, Zoe, the only female clerk, was on the early morning shift, in case a solicitor rang wanting a barrister to attend court that morning. Zoe, a cheerful seventeen year old, was always dressed in black trousers and a brightly coloured sweater. Today it was yellow.

'Good morning, Miss Hardman. Mr Durrant is already here. I've put him in the conference room and set up the telly for you. Hope that's OK?'

Cassie nodded and made her way upstairs to what Zoe had called the conference room. In reality it was a tiny room, where a portable television was kept, but was otherwise used as dumping ground for left-over documents, which were stacked in dusty, uneven piles round the walls. Tim was fiddling with the remote control of the television, which stood on a small table, trying to get it to work; eventually it stuttered into life. The bruising on Cassie's arm still hurt and she held it stiffly, afraid of banging it against the arm of the chair in which she was sitting. She concentrated on the screen, ready to watch the film as if it were a set of stills.

Tim fast-forwarded the DVD until he found a section which showed some sort of melee around what looked like a bulldozer. A group of five or six men were pushing and pulling, moving around each other very quickly, making it hard to follow. He pushed the pause button.

'I think this is the section where I can identify our missing witness. See what you think?' He pushed the play button again and the scene changed as the camera zoomed out. Two of the men were throwing punches at each other and the others were intervening, endeavouring to grab the arms of the two men fighting. Amongst the group trying to stop the fight was an Afro-Caribbean male. There was a clock in the top right hand corner of the screen which showed the time as being 21.46.34. After twenty seconds the group broke up and the camera zoomed in on the faces of the men, first the two who had been fighting, and then the face of the multi-ethnic male.

'Stop it,' said Cassie, at the same time as Tim pushed the pause button.

The two of them stared at the screen. Tim took from his file, the photographs of Hinds, handed them to Cassie who looked at them and then back at the face on the television.

'Yes. It's him. He was there,' Cassie whispered, 'But no Lenny.'

'I've played the two DVDs twice and I can't see Lenny at all. Mind you this is the only view of Hinds.' Tim pushed the play button and another unknown face came into view.

'Tim, I think we need more details from Lenny; like how they got to the ground, which part of it they were in, what exit did they use, did they get separated at all? I don't know what the ground's like, do you? Can you go and see him before we sit this morning? I'll tell Marcus and we'll leave you to it.'

Once at the Central Criminal Court, Cassie made her way to the Bar Mess where she found Marcus examining a large album of photographs. He waved the bundle in Cassie's direction. 'They don't really give us anything, except to show how the police stripped the place,' he said.

Cassie took the photographs from him and flicked open the pages, revealing a series of pictures of every room in the flat in Lancaster Close, shot as the police had taken the contents and placed them in black plastic bags. A series of shots showed Lenny's clothes being put on the bed, the pile getting higher, then one with the bedding on the floor and finally the walls both before and after the wallpaper had been stripped away. The final photographs showed a bare room, a chair tipped on its side, a bedside cabinet with the drawers hanging out and the mattress half on and half of the bed. It could have been in a war zone. The other bedrooms were only marginally better; they had left the two women's belongings in piles on the floor.

'I think we might get the jury to look at these, what is it, a picture's better than a thousand words or something like that?' Marcus said. Cassie agreed with him and then told him about the DVDs.

'That's a pity. I hope Tim gets a good proof from him. But after all this time,' he shook his head. 'Can you get David to have some copies of those photographs available for the jury? I'd like them before I cross examine Dean. Don't you think it would be good to start with the arrest rather than the interviews?'

Cassie said she thought it would. Hopefully it would make the jurors be more sympathetic to Lenny, and give them some understanding of his state of mind during his interviews. Once she had confirmed her point of view, Marcus wandered across the room to talk to another silk, and Cassie set off to find David Jennings, her hopes of a quiet cup of coffee and the opportunity to prepare some questions for the WPC gone. The bruising on her arm was a constant reminder of the previous night's incident. She pushed it to the

164

back of her mind; there was no time to worry about it now.

Because they needed the copies quickly, David had photocopied the ones she wanted, put them into bundles, and given them to her. When she arrived at the courtroom she discovered the normal usher had gone on holiday and been replaced by a woman she knew, Mrs Beswick.

'Miss Hardman, I looked at counsels' names on the list and saw yours. How are you?'

'I'm fine. And you?' Mrs Beswick, a small comfortable-looking lady, who reminded Cassie of one of her mother's aunts, said she was well, and how nice it was to see Cassie again. The warmth of Mrs Beswick's words pleased Cassie; it was confirmation of her regular appearances at the Central Criminal Court, that some of the staff knew her, and what was more, liked her. She made a point of being friendly and polite to the ushers, the list office staff and the security men. A kind word at the right moment could pay dividends, if she wanted something copied, a law report collected from the court library or a message passed on, because they approved of her they would always help.

'Please, can you give these an exhibit number? We'll need them when Mr Pike is cross-examining.'

'Of course,' Mrs Beswick beamed at her.

When the court had reassembled, and Colin Dean was back in the witness box, Marcus got to his feet, put his papers on the desk-top lectern and turned it round towards the witness box.

'Mr Dean, you've already told us that you were determined to take anything from the home of Mr Barker that might have a trace of blood on it.'

165

'There was a possibility we might be able to find traces of blood on clothing and bedding to enable forensics to make a match with Miss Paulson's blood. So we took anything we thought he might have come into contact with on the night of the murder.'

'Quite so, quite so. Would you agree the flat was in a complete mess.'

'I would. I think there were six officers searching and bagging items up. It wasn't a tidy operation.'

'Quite a sight wasn't it?'

'Not a pretty sight, Sir.'

'Can you take a look at Exhibit 11? These are photographs not included in the original bundle, My Lord. They show the state of the defendant's home as the police searched and seized the Barker family belongings.'

Mrs Beswick handed one set of the photocopies to Judge Crabtree and took the rest to the jury. Cassie watched as they flipped over the poor copies. Anna Fry pursed her lips at the scene portrayed, and even Deepa Nadswallah looked over the top of her spectacles at the police officer and then back at the pictures again.

Marcus continued, 'Not surprising that Mrs Barker and the defendant's sister were upset?'

'No, sir.'

'And the defendant as well?'

'I wouldn't say upset.'

'Wasn't he?'

'No, he was dazed, stunned.'

Sergeant Dean sounded so very reasonable; Cassie knew it would increase his credibility with the jurors.

'Dazed and stunned.' Marcus turned towards the jury box, and looked at the jurors. He repeated the phrase again as he held their attention. Cassie saw

Amanda Conrad look down at the photocopies. That was enough for Marcus, and he turned back to the witness.

'At the police station, after he was booked into the custody suite, he was put into a cell still wearing the paper jumpsuit?'

'Yes.'

'Lenny Barker has never been convicted of any offence has he?'

'No. This is the first time he has been arrested.'

'That's very fair, officer. This would have been a completely new experience for him?'

'Yes, sir.'

'Not a pleasant one either?'

'No, it isn't. We did offer him tea and something to eat if he wanted, he hadn't had any breakfast, but he didn't at that stage.'

'Can we just go back to the point when you are in the custody suite with him, who else was there? Can you remember?'

'Certainly, the custody sergeant. His name will be on the custody sheet. I think it was Sergeant Bloom. DC Andy Vernon and I think the governor was there as well. That's Detective Superintendent O'Connor.'

'You were concerned with booking Mr Barker in, weren't you?'

'Yes. I was.' Colin Dean looked down at the edge of the witness box; Marcus paused before asking his next question.

'Mr O'Connor and Mr Vernon were talking about a video taken from a camera on the walls of Aubrey House?'

'Possibly. We had seized a video.' Cassie was puzzled as to why Sergeant Dean, who had been very fair so far, was prevaricating about where the information about the video had come from. Lenny had told them he had heard about it when he was in the custody suite, and had been thinking about it as he sat in a cell waiting for Tim to arrive and the interviews to begin.

'Mr Barker was in a position to hear that conversation, wasn't he?'

'Yes, he couldn't miss it.'

'Had you said anything about a video to him?'

'No, there was no point. There was nothing on it.'

'Yet Barker asked you about it, didn't he?'

'Yes, he did.'

'Mr O'Connor and Mr Vernon were talking about the video when Barker was in the custody suite. Even though it revealed nothing?'

Dean didn't reply.

'So, Mr Barker is put into a cell, dazed and stunned, knowing the police had a video? Wouldn't he think he had been arrested because of the video and that he was on it?'

Howard Alsopp got to his feet and objected to the question. Cassie smiled to herself; of course the officer couldn't say what Lenny was thinking but the point had been made for the jury. Colin Heap was nodding and clearly understood the relevance. Marcus was gracious, saying of course it was a matter to be dealt with by his client. He continued to ask Sergeant Dean if he could explain why the two other officers were talking about the video so long after it had been seized and viewed. Colin Dean replied he didn't know. Howard didn't object to that question although he could have done.

Marcus proceeded to ask Colin Dean about Tim arriving at the police station, and being given the opportunity to see his client before the interviews commenced.

'It was Mr Durrant who raised the videos, wasn't it?'

'Yes. He asked me about it before the first interview and I told him there was nothing of interest on it.'

'Did he have the opportunity to speak to Mr Barker before the interview started?'

'No, but he did before the second interview. Mr Barker would have known by the time of the second interview that the video did not show him in Holland Walk.'

Cassie underlined the answer in the notes she was making. Colin Dean had seen the point too, and was doing his best to counteract the inference that Lenny had admitted being in the Walk because he thought the police had him on video.

'But of course by that time, the eyewitness had identified him?' Marcus asked.

'Yes, My Lord.'

'Tell me, when was the video taken from Aubrey House?'

Colin Dean smiled, 'We had a bit of trouble contacting the owner and getting permission so it wasn't immediately. There should be a note of the day we did get hold of it and when someone, I think Mr Vernon, watched it.' He looked towards David Jennings, who was flicking through the pages of a file. David soon found what he was looking for and pulled out a sheet of paper, which he handed over to the usher, who passed it to the witness. 'Twenty-sixth of September, and Mr Vernon viewed it the same day.'

'Some five weeks before Barker was arrested?'

'Yes.'

'And there was nothing relevant to the arrest? Can you explain why Mr Vernon and Mr O'Connor were discussing it in the custody suite, just as you arrived with Barker?'

Howard started to get to his feet again to object, but Colin Dean answered that it was a matter Marcus should ask Mr O'Connor about.

Marcus swung round to the jury, beamed at them and said, rather emphatically, 'I intend to. Thank you, Mr Dean,' then gathering his gown into a bunch behind him, he sat down and turned to Cassie with a broad grin and said 'Have you got all that?' His voice was just loud enough for the jury to hear and they looked in their direction, although Howard Alsopp was about to begin his re-examination of his witness. She was curious about Howard's approach; there was a danger of adding emphasis to the points the defence had made.

'Just one question. Can you remember what you told Mr Durrant about the video?'

'Not the exact words, but I did tell him that we had viewed it and there was nothing on it that would assist the prosecution.'

Howard thanked Colin Dean and then told the judge they intended to call Detective Superintendent O'Connor next. Mrs Beswick left the court and came back without the detective. 'I've called twice and he doesn't appear to be here,' she told the court.

Colin Dean appeared at the door and beckoned to David Jennings, who hurried over to the officer. They whispered to each other and then David came back to counsel's row and addressed the judge, 'Unfortunately Mr O'Connor has been called back to Scotland Yard on an emergency and will not be available for some time. We will call WPC Cummings after the midday adjournment.'

'It's a good job you have another witness ready to give evidence. I don't like being kept waiting. Perhaps you can pass the message to Mr O'Connor.

Cassie had an hour to prepare her cross-examination.

Chapter 22

Alex picked up the phone and rang the police room at the Old Bailey. She asked for Sergeant Dean and told him she had been to the address in Willesden on two occasions, but had got no reply.

'I'm going to send you photos of the man we're looking for. Can you go back and ask in the vicinity whether this guy was living at that address. If he was, try and find out where he's gone to,' Dean said.

'OK. How quickly do you need know?'

'Yesterday. The case is going quickly, and our team think the judge may want to stop the case at half-time if we haven't got Walker.'

Chris Dundy looked up from his desk, 'What are we expected to do now?'

'Go back to that address in Willesden when we get some photos, and see if we can get a lead on where this guy Walker is.'

Two hours later, a large brown envelope arrived on Alex's desk. She opened it and removed a set of photographs showing Edwin Walker's face and both left and right profiles. She studied them for a moment, searching her memory for any previous encounter she might have had with the man, but decided she hadn't seen him before. They needed to get on with the search for him, but Chris had vanished. She decided to go alone; after all he wasn't a suspect in a case.

The address, Wellington House, Stringer Road, Willesden, was a block of flats, built of concrete and dark brick, about four storeys high with a flat on each side of a central stairwell. The double front doors were open. The flat she wanted was on the third floor. The stairs were well lit from a window on the rear wall and the doors of the flats were painted in bright red. On the second floor there was an enticing smell of spices, reminding her that she had not eaten since a hurried breakfast at six am. As she climbed the last flight of stairs, she could hear the sound of a violin being played, but wasn't sure if it was the radio or not. The sound was coming from flat number six; the music was familiar, but she couldn't put a name to it.

She pushed on the bell of Flat 5, but there was no reply. She bent down and looked through the letterbox. On the floor was a collection of envelopes, scattered as if they had been delivered on different days, indicating the flat was no longer occupied. Behind her the tune on the violin was being repeated; someone was practising. She tried the door but it was locked. The music stopped.

Alex remained standing outside the flat for a moment, weighing up her options and was just about to take her wallet from her pocket, when the door of number six opened and a young woman of about twenty-two put her head round the door. 'Can I help?' said the woman.

'Does anyone live here, or is it empty?' Alex asked.

'Well, yes.'

'Yes someone lives here, or yes it's empty?'

The woman looked at the door of number five. 'Someone lives there.'

'You don't seem very sure.'

The woman came out towards Alex, clutching a violin and bow in one hand. She took off her glasses and tried to perch them on her head, and then put them in the pocket of the long cardigan she was wearing.

'It was you playing the violin. I recognised the melody, but I can't place it.'

'It's the rondo from Mozart's Third Violin Concerto. Most people know it from the film Master and Commander. It's my exam piece. Anyway what do you want? Who are you?'

'I'm trying to find a family called Walker. Do you know them?'

The music student hesitated, and then said, 'They do live there, but Mrs Walker has gone to Jamaica.'

'Permanently?'

'No, I think just for a holiday, seeing her relatives, I think. Anyway who are you?'

'Detective Constable Seymour.' Alex produced her warrant card and showed it to the young woman, and then said, 'Was she living here on her own?'

'No, the children have gone with her.'

'Miss, I don't think you told me your name?'

'No. Claire Desmond.'

Alex put her warrant card away and produced the photographs of Edwin Walker.

'I'm looking for this man. He's an important witness in a murder case. He's not in any trouble. Do you know him?'

Claire Desmond replaced her glasses and peered at the pictures.

'Yes. It's Eddy.'

'Edwin Walker?'

'I don't know what Eddy's short for.'

'Does he live here, or has he gone to the West Indies as well?'

'No, he didn't go, and he does live here,' she paused, 'but he's away a lot.'

'Do you know where? It's really important.'

174

The young woman hesitated, and then said, 'He gave me a telephone number in case anything happened. It's a mobile. I'll just get it.'

She went back into her flat and vanished from sight. Alex started to follow but Claire Desmond came back almost immediately, and handed her a piece of paper with an eleven figure number on it.

Alex wrote the number in her pocket book and gave Claire one of her business cards.

'If he comes back, can you ask him to give me a call. It's about a friend of his, a Lenny Barker. You can tell him, he's not in any trouble.'

Alex thought Claire was wary of her, but it seemed sensible to tell her why she wanted to contact Walker. If she tried to call him on his mobile he would cut her off before she could explain, and, if he thought the police wanted to arrest him, there was a good chance he would abandon the phone. Walker's itinerant lifestyle suggested to Alex that he was probably involved in some illegal activity. With a mobile number they may be able to trace him using the mobile network, but that would take time. Claire would be able to tell him he wasn't a suspect, and he was simply required to be a witness in his friend's trial.

A few hours later, Alex's mobile phone rang, but when she pushed the call button, there was silence.

'Who's that?' she said.

'Eddy Walker. You're looking for me?'

'Yes. Thanks for ringing. Your friend Lenny Barker, is being tried for murder.'

'Yes, I know, bloody ridiculous. Wouldn't say boo to a goose.'

'He says he was with you at a football match.'

'I don't play now.'

'No, you went to a game at Stamford Bridge.'

'Yes, we did. Chelsea versus Everton.'

'That's it. His brief wants you to give evidence about it at court.'

'Can't do that.'

'Any reason?' Alex said.

There was no reply and Alex realised he had cut her off.

Chapter 23

Outside the courtroom, Marcus turned to Tim and Cassie, 'We're getting near the end of the prosecution case, we'll have to decide if we call him, or not. Tim, have we got a full proof about this football match?' Cassie's heart sank as she realized she wasn't going to get much time to prepare for the afternoon session.

'I've taken another statement from Lenny. My handwriting's not wonderful, so I'll get it typed up tonight,' Tim said as he handed over three sheets of paper torn from a counsel's notebook.

'Right, Cassie, let's go to the Bar Mess, read these and then we'll meet at quarter to two here, and discuss the next step.'

'I assume you agree we have to call him?' Marcus asked, although she knew he didn't care if she agreed or not, he'd made his mind up. 'We've served the alibi and we don't have the witness so I don't see any alternative but to throw him to the lions.'

Cassie knew he was right; she believed jurors thought if they were the one in the dock and they were innocent, they would want to give evidence. 'What about a submission of no case?' Cassie asked.

'Yes. Yes, of course, but it won't succeed,' Marcus said. 'Now this video taken at the football match; what does it show?' he asked. Cassie told him about the fight and the shot of the man, who both she and Tim thought was the missing alibi witness, but he was not with Lenny at that stage. 'It doesn't help us, but it doesn't exclude him being at the game. And if that is Hinds, and they left together, it was about quarter to ten, and that would make it impossible for him to have got to Holland Walk by nine minutes past, even if he took the bus rather than walked.'

'This statement,' Marcus waved the sheets of paper covered with sprawling writing, 'says the two got separated as they left the stand and he didn't see Hinds again until he was outside the ground. He was not aware his mate had been in a fight and it wasn't mentioned. Do we know how the police are getting on trying to find this lad?'

'No, I'll ask David again. I don't know if they are just hoping someone sees him; time is running out.' Cassie didn't tell Marcus about her visit to The Jugglers, acting like a private investigator was very unprofessional, nor did she mention anything about her encounter with the two men, and the threats they had made. Even with the evidence from Transport for London confirming that Lenny used his Oyster Card to travel to Fulham Broadway on the night of the murder, she was certain that without Hinds, the prosecution would say he had not gone to the game but made his way back to the park and was the one who had killed Shelley Paulson. The risk of Lenny's being convicted was high, the eyewitness had been so believable, and there were the forensics as well. Both Marcus and Tim thought he was guilty; she was the only one really fighting on his behalf.

After the court had reassembled, Howard Alsopp asked for Rose Cummings to be called to the witness box. A tall graceful young woman walked into court. Her resemblance to Shelley Paulson was uncanny. Cassie noticed all the men in the courtroom sitting a bit straighter in their seats.

After Rose Cummings had given her name, she told the jury that she was a police officer employed on special duties, and one of those had been to meet Mr Barker and strike up a friendship with him. The aim was to obtain information that might assist the prosecution case against him. She agreed it would have been a great success if he had admitted the offence, but she did not expect that, just details about his relationship with the deceased and other young women. There had been three meetings in the pub, The Rose and Crown, on 7[th,] 14th and 22nd November. It had been very difficult to get him to talk, indeed on the 14th they had spent most of the time playing pool. He had not spoken about Miss Paulson even when she had raised the subject, other than to say he knew her from the market and how awful it was she had been murdered. When he did talk about football, he was clearly enthusiastic about the game, and the Chelsea team. He had told her he had been to a football match recently at Stamford Bridge, when they had played Everton.

Judge Crabtree interrupted and asked if there was a copy of that part of the recording for the jury to hear. Howard said he was sure it could be arranged. David Jennings went off to obtain a copy of the CD and a player.

Whilst they waited for the equipment to be brought into the court, Marcus asked Cassie if she had heard the recording and scowled when she said no. 'I hope it's all right. It's too late now to object to it, even if it isn't.'

She knew she should have listened to them, but there had been so little time between getting the transcripts and the start of the trial, and much of that she had spent trying to trace 'Hinds'. She hadn't anticipated the judge would want to play the tapes, although she knew judges could be unpredictable and often had their own agenda. Along with the judge and jury, she and prosecuting counsel had once been dragged to a council flat in Finchley, not because the photographs were inadequate but because the judge wanted to leave court early to get to the races.

It took over half an hour to find both the recording and the player, but eventually the machine was set up and the jury could hear the voice of Rose Cummings asking Lenny how long he had supported Chelsea.

'Most of my life. I used to go with my Dad when I was a kid. Now he's in Australia.'

'Oh, I'd love to go there, all that sunshine. You could go and visit your Dad. Pack me in your suitcase will you?' Rose said.

'It's a bit of a long way, just on holiday,' Lenny said. In the background there was the sound of cues smacking balls, and then them hitting the side of the pool table, followed by pauses as the next shot was lined up. Cassie could picture the scene in the pub; Lenny leaning over the pool-table, Rose chalking the end of her cue. She looked at the jury, Colin Heap and Amanda Fry were looking upwards; did they have a similar picture in their minds?

'Be quite a journey back for the football, you being so keen. Bet you get to every game,' Rose said.

'Chance would be a fine thing. Last time was when a mate had a spare ticket.'

'Nice friend to have. Good game, was it?'

'Yeah, against Everton.'

'You went with your mate, did you?'

'Yes, we both went.'

'That's enough,' said Judge Crabtree and then to the jury, 'I thought you should have the opportunity to

180

hear that because you have been told that the alibi notice was only served at the beginning of this week, but of course he had told the policewoman in November last year he was at the football match with this man Hinds. It's a pity no one realized the game he refers to, if that was the match he was at, was on the night of the murder.'

Marcus got to his feet, 'My Lord, the defence were not told of these recordings until Thursday of last week. It gave very little time for us to investigate and establish that the Chelsea–Everton game was the same evening.'

'Yes, yes, Mr Pike,' the judge said, 'I'm sure the jury understand that.' He smiled and nodded at them.

Howard Alsopp said, 'I have no more questions for this witness.'

Cassie was usually confident in court, but she had not had sufficient time to prepare for this cross-examination and for once she felt nervous as she got to her feet. Judge Crabtree looked at her, 'Yes, Miss Hardman.'

'My Lord, just a few questions,' she turned to the witness, 'Your aim was to try and get him to confide in you about any girlfriends he had?'

'Yes, it was.'

'To that end, you were, I'll use the expression, chatting him up.'

'You could say that. I wanted him to feel comfortable with me. At ease.'

'You told him that you didn't have a boyfriend?'

'Yes, that's right.'

'The implication being that you were free to form a relationship with him?'

'I wanted him to see me as a friend. Someone he could talk to.'

'You wore a low cut blouse for these meetings?'

'I usually wore a denim jacket.'

'Which you took off because it was too warm in the pub?'

'I might have done.'

'Shall we find that part of the CD?'

'No, I did take my jacket off.'

'Revealing a low cut blouse?'

'Yes, I wanted him to like me. That was my brief.'

'He didn't talk about girlfriends, did he?'

The officer laughed, 'No, he told me there wasn't one.'

'He didn't say Shelley Paulson had been a girlfriend, did he?'

'No, he simply expressed some sympathy at her death.'

Cassie didn't ask if WPC Cummings had noticed anything unusual about Lenny while they spoke about Shelley. She didn't want to give the officer the opportunity to slip in something that might suggest he was uneasy talking about the dead woman. She always tried to be economical with her questioning; some barristers became too fond of their own voices and ending up getting answers they didn't want; she didn't do that.

'As many people might, who didn't even know who she was?' Cassie asked.

'I suppose that's one way of looking at it.'

'You tried to get him to talk about her on a number of occasions?'

'Yes, Miss Paulson and any other relationships he might have had.'

'Instead he talked about football?'

'Yes, mainly.'

Cassie looked steadily at the witness. She was about to ask a question to which she did not know the answer; that would break one of the golden rules of advocacy, but she could see no alternative.

The purpose of Cassie's cross-examination was to show the jury that Lenny was not the sort of man who would make unwanted advances to a woman he didn't know, so she was prepared to take the chance.

'He was embarrassed by your interest in him, wasn't he?'

Rose Cummings shrugged, and Cassie went on, 'I don't suppose you're used to such a lack of interest in you? He was embarrassed and blushed when you tried to press him about any sexual relationships he had. Isn't that the truth?'

'Yes. He seemed rather young for his age. Not quite what I had been led to expect.'

Cassie said thank you and sat down. Marcus turned to her and mouthed the words 'Well done.' She looked up at the jury. The 'two As' and Colin Heap were smiling at her.

Howard said he had no re-examination and called Police Constable Maltby.

'My Lord, we've been asked to call this witness, who was the first officer on the scene in response to the 999 call made by Mr Compton.'

As the court waited for the police officer to come into court, Cassie located the copy of the officer's notebook. The lined pages of the pad took up a sixth of the A4 paper used to copy it. The notes were not easy to read. PC Maltby was a tall, well-built young officer with a pronounced Adam's apple on which he seemed

183

to choke as he stumbled through the oath. He began to read his notes, 'Arrived at Duchess of Bedford Walk at ten eleven pm and ran into Holland Walk. Some thirty feet to the north I could see a body of a woman at an angle across the path. Her legs were crumpled under her.'

His evidence was interrupted by the sound of sobbing at the side of the court. Mrs Paulson, who had sat impassively throughout the trial, was leaning over, her face buried in her hands, and the sound of her crying filled the court-room. The people in the public gallery, including Mrs Barker, leaned over the edge of the balcony to try to see what was going on. As they were asked to sit back in their seats, Mrs Beswick helped Mrs Paulson out of the double doors, watched closely by the jurors. Amanda Conrad bent down, pulled a tissue from her handbag and blew her nose. Once Mrs Paulson had left the courtroom, Judge Crabtree told PC Maltby to proceed.

'Closer to me was a man in a long coat, who I now know to be James Compton, leaning over the railings of the park. I walked over to the body, but before I could do anything I heard the sirens of an ambulance, and shortly after two paramedics arrived. They went to the woman and almost immediately informed me she was dead. I radioed my control to inform them of the murder and asked for a scenes of crime officer to attend. With the assistance of the ambulance men, I secured the area and redirected some of the pedestrians, who had gathered, away from the location. I then spoke to Mr Compton, who told me what he had seen and I circulated the description of the man he said had assaulted the victim.'

'Can you help us with the description he gave?' Howard asked.

The officer turned back a few pages and again read the entry, which Cassie followed in her copies, 'Male, IC1,'

'IC1, can you explain for the jury,' Judge Crabtree asked.

'White Caucasian, My Lord,' PC Maltby replied.

Judge Crabtree nodded at him to continue.

'White male with a dark mark on his chin, probably a beard, six foot two, taller than the woman, slim, dressed in a dark track suit. He was unable to give the colour of the man's clothing, or hair.'

Before Howard sat down, Marcus turned round to Cassie and with a broad grin on his face said, 'You cross-examine him.' Cassie looked at him, her eyes wide open, got to her feet with the bundle of photographs in her hand and asked the officer to look at the pictures of Holland Walk.

'Of course, at night with the trees still in leaf, it would be quite dark?' she asked.

'Yes. My recollection is that it was dark and shadowy.'

'Your notes make no mention of the shape of the man's face, do they?'

'No, ma'am.'

'Did Mr Compton describe the man in the Walk as having a square face?'

'No, he didn't. I would have put it in if he had.'

'The only description he gave is the one you have recorded and told us about?'

'Yes, it is.'

'When you first saw him you say he was leaning over the railings, hanging on to them to support himself?'

The officer smiled, 'I think he'd vomited. He was very distressed.'

The next witness was Detective Chief Superintendent O'Connor. His hands as he held the bible were large, the fingers stubby and smoke-stained. He thundered the words of the oath swaying slightly, backwards and forwards on his toes as he did so. He was totally confident that his judgement was as good, if not better, than any jury's.

Howard asked him to confirm he was the officer in charge of the investigation to find the killer of Shelley Paulson. He said he was, and then described how difficult the inquiry had been. Despite an extensive investigation they had got nowhere, until they received an anonymous telephone call after the murder had been on Crimewatch.

Marcus began cross-examination, asking him why he had enlisted Miss Cummings to befriend Barker.

'The Crown Prosecution were suggesting the identification was weak. That's why he was granted bail. I wanted to plug any holes so to speak.'

'Instead it gave Mr Barker an alibi?'

'So he says.'

'The killer vanished after Mr Compton had yelled at him?'

'I wouldn't expect him to hang around,' the officer replied with grim satisfaction.

'How long after the murder had taken place did you discover there was a camera on the wall of Aubrey House?'

'One of my officers noticed it during the search of the scene.'

'It turned out to be useless?'

'Yes. It's a waste of money apart from as a deterrent.'

'The day Mr Barker was arrested you were in the custody suite when he arrived at the station?'

'Of course, I wanted to see the man who had killed Miss Paulson.'

'Another officer was there, a Detective Constable Vernon?'

O'Connor drew himself to his full height, paused and then said in a surprised voice, 'I think that's right.'

Cassie noticed one of the jurors waving a piece of paper at Judge Crabtree. 'Just a minute, it looks like the jury have a question,' the judge said. Once the note was in his hand, he read out the question on it: 'Was Mr Barker fingerprinted? If he was, were his fingerprints compared with any found on the silver bracelet?'

Both Marcus and Howard Alsopp were on their feet before the judge had finished reading out the note.

'Mr Alsopp, do you have an answer?'

'I think it is a matter we should discuss in the absence of the jury, if Your Lordship is agreeable.'

'Of course,' the judge replied and then he asked the jury to retire to their room.

'Now, you'd better tell me, what's this about?' Judge Crabtree.

'My Lord, of course Barker was fingerprinted and the prints compared with those found on a silver bracelet Miss Paulson was wearing the night she was killed. The prints on the bracelet were very indistinct, smudged and overlaid.'

187

'So more than one person's fingerprints on them?' asked the Judge.

'Yes. There was one print of the right hand second index finger that appeared to match Mr Barker's print. In her initial report Dr Pretty thought the prints matched, although she hesitated to come to any firm conclusion. She asked for a further set of prints to be taken from Mr Barker and when she re-examined the two, she found a very thin line across the new print of Mr Barker's right hand index finger, consistent with a cut across the finger-pad. She also thought that the scar was unlikely to have been the result of an injury inflicted after the murder had taken place. She could not find an identical line in the fingerprint on the bracelet.'

'If I understand what you are saying, she was unable to draw any firm conclusion as to a match between the prints.'

'Exactly; she can't say it is Barker's print on the bracelet, but she can't say it isn't, and we take the view, in those circumstances, the evidence should not go before the jury.'

'I think that's right. Have you anything to say, Mr Pike?'

'My Lord, I think the jury should be told fingerprints were taken, but there were no prints on any of Miss Paulson's belongings with which an adequate comparison could be made.'

'That seems sensible. Do you agree, Mr Alsopp?'

Howard indicated that he did and he would tell the jury.

While they waited for the jury to be brought back into court, Cassie asked Tim if he knew a second set of fingerprints had been taken from Lenny.

'Yes. I was told the first set had got smudged and they needed to do it again. I thought no more about it. Shouldn't the Crown have disclosed the further report from Dr Pretty? We might have wanted to instruct an expert ourselves in case they came to the conclusion the fingerprint was not Lenny's.'

'I wouldn't have advised that; it would have opened up a can of worms. The two sets of prints would have been given to the jury. They'd have done their own comparison, and probably come to the same conclusion I did. If they thought it was Lenny's fingerprint that would have been that,' Cassie said.

'I suppose you're right. What shall I say to Lenny? I should just go back and tell him what this is about.'

'Tell him not to worry; we'll talk about it after court rises today.'

Tim went to the rear of the court, into the dock and through the door that led to stairs going down to the cells, where Lenny was being held by the prison staff.

Cassie turned back to Marcus, who said, 'At last we got an explanation. I would also think that's what the argument between O'Connor and the CPS was about; that's why he got Miss Cummings to chat up our lad, and why he's so confident he's got his man.'

Before she could reply, the jury filed back into their box, Judge Crabtree returned to the bench and the trial resumed, with Marcus picking up his cross-examination where he had left off.

'Did you talk about the video with him whilst Mr Barker was being booked in?'

'With Barker?' There was a hint of derision in O'Connor's voice.

'No, of course not. DC Vernon. Did you talk to DC Vernon about the video?'

O'Connor opened his eyes wide and half turned towards Marcus. 'I can't remember. We might have been discussing it.'

'Why would you have been talking about a worthless tape some five weeks or so after it had been seized?'

'I'm not sure. It may have been that we had just got it back from the labs. We had it enhanced, just in case.' O'Connor was clearly bored with being questioned.

'You were quite desperate to make an arrest, weren't you?'

'I always like to catch a killer.'

'You talked about the video in the hope that Barker would think he had been recorded in Holland Walk?'

'His solicitor was told that the tapes were of no assistance to the inquiry at all.' He nodded towards Tim.

'Do you know when Mr Durrant was told that the video was irrelevant?'

'No, I don't.'

'Would it surprise you that Mr Durrant had to ask about it, before the situation was explained?'

'Sergeant Dean is a very competent officer. I trust him to get things right.'

'I'm sure you do,' said Marcus sitting down, 'I'm sure you do.'

Howard Alsopp had no re-examination, and told the court that Mr O'Connor was the prosecution's final witness but, if the judge was minded to adjourn, he would close his case the next day.

Judge Crabtree asked Marcus if they were calling their client, and when he was told they were intending to make a submission of no case to answer, he sent the jury home for the day. After they had left the courtroom, he turned to Howard and enquired if the Crown had made any progress in trying to find the missing witness. Howard replied that he had been identified, but despite police calling at his last known address, they had failed to find him. His mother and siblings had left the country. The police believed Walker had not, but his whereabouts were unknown.

'I don't really want to stop the trial at this late stage. I assumed the young man would have been located by now. Mr Pike, will you take instructions about continuing the trial. I will hear your submission but I am not minded at this stage to order an acquittal; however, I may be more sympathetic to an application to discharge the jury and order a new trial.'

Outside the courtroom, Marcus asked Cassie what she thought about applying for the jury to be discharged. 'I'm not sure. We may never find Walker, and Compton was difficult enough to cross-examine this time,' she said.

'Yes, this would just be a rehearsal. Next time the cracks would be papered over. But if we start again and get a hung jury, the prosecution would probably not have another bite at the cherry. And we may have found this witness. We'll have to take instructions.'

Immediately Lenny was inside the interview room and the door closed he declared he did not want the trial to start again. 'I've been inside for over a week and I just want it over with.' Marcus told him to think carefully about it. 'Look, the judge is worried; he would probably discharge this jury and give the police more time to find your friend. If we don't apply for the jury to be discharged then it may prejudice any chances of appeal if he turns up.'

'I just want it over with. I am telling the truth. I'm sure they'll believe me.'

'Don't be so sure. You may think differently after you've been cross-examined.' Marcus said, his voice betraying signs of irritation. 'Let's work on the basis we will continue with the trial.'

'What's this fingerprint stuff?' Lenny asked, without replying to Marcus's question.

'Miss Hardman will explain in a few minutes, after I've gone. Sorry, Tim, but I have a conference in my next case. Now, Lenny, the Crown will close their case formally tomorrow, that is they will say there are no more witnesses they wish to call or evidence they want to place in front of the jury. I will make a submission of no case to answer, which, well you heard what the judge said, he'll reject. You will then go into the witness box. You've got a copy of your proof.' Marcus paused until Lenny said he had. 'Read through it carefully tonight and try to make sure you can tell the story clearly and concisely. Have you got that?'

There was a faint yes from Lenny. Marcus got up and said, 'Right. I'll leave you with Miss Hardman. She'll explain about the fingerprints. I really do want you to think carefully about whether we apply for a discharge of the jury.'

Chapter 24

The results of the forensic examination lay on Alex Seymour's desk, the knife in a plastic exhibit bag beside it. She was right about the fingerprints; they were the same as those on the pizza box, so the knife must belong to a drug dealer. The blade had traces of cannabis, cocaine and human blood on it, and the report asked her if she wanted a search to be made against any previous samples. She wasn't aware of any unresolved crimes that the knife might be linked to, so she placed both the report and the knife back in the drawer of her desk.

Chris Dundy, the officer she normally worked with, was on leave for a few days, and some of the paperwork that had been on his desk had been put on hers. She began reading through the file on the street robbery, which had been returned from the Crown Prosecution Service with a list of further enquires they wished carried out. The defendant had entered a plea of not guilty despite being identified by the victim of the robbery, Janice Rigby, and the witness, Mrs Bampton. The Crown prosecutor who had dealt with the case at West London Magistrates Court wanted the victim to be interviewed again about the degree of force the defendant had used. Alex was sure the defendant was just wasting time and would eventually plead, but she would have to see Miss Rigby.

She sighed and pulled the telephone towards her, as she looked through the file for Miss Rigby's contact numbers, but before she found them, Mel Haskins put his head round the door and said he had something to tell her.

'Well, don't keep me waiting,' Alex said.

'Gives me an excuse to throw admiring glances at you, even if they're not reciprocated.'

'Come on, tell me this exciting piece of news.'

'It's your man from Cotburn Square. He was spotted leaving the sports centre by the Lancaster Estate. The guys who saw him are sure it's the same man from June last year. They thought about stopping him, but couldn't think of a good enough reason before he got on a bike and rode away.'

'What sort of bike?'

'Just a pedal cycle.'

'I thought you were going to say a Norton or a Ducati.'

'I'd heard you were a bit of a bike fanatic.'

'Reason I joined the force.'

Mel laughed, 'I bet that didn't go down too well.'

'No, it didn't, I got put in the CID instead. But our man on a pedal cycle…makes him a bit unusual for a drug dealer.'

'I'd say unlikely. They do it for the money, flash around the cash, buy an expensive motor, fancy watch. No, I think the man who left the pizza box is someone different.'

'Pity, I quite like the idea of ordering your pizza and your dope in the same box. Have you asked whoever saw the man leaving the sports centre to look at the DVD?'

'I did, and the two who saw him go to the Nightjar last year, as well. They thought it could be the same bloke, but not one hundred per cent.'

Chapter 25

It was about eleven and dark when Cassie walked into the All Saints Road. She could still feel the bruising on her arm from the attack the previous night, but she was determined to make one last effort to find the alibi witness, and to do that she had to come to this street, which in the past had a reputation as a centre for criminal behaviour, the front line in the war against drugs. But now, there was nothing to distinguish the street from any other.

The Mango Club was down a narrow alley protected by a barred iron gate, and stood back out of the light, immediately inside the gate, were two heavies dressed in black suits and black roll-neck jumpers. Cassie smiled at the two men, being on her own was non-threatening, and said to them, 'I've heard there is some really great music here, is that right?'

One of the men said she'd heard it right and let her walk into the club. The room was a large oblong, with a raised platform in the middle, where the disc jockey was sitting. He was a skinny black man of about fifty with dreadlocks, round spectacles perched on his nose and a cigarette hanging out of his mouth. Round him, on the edge of the dance floor were about twenty young women, black, white and mixed race, dressed in almost identical clothing, tight black trousers and white off the shoulder tops that glowed blue in the low ultra-violet lighting. Cassie didn't recognise the music ricocheting around the room, but the beat hit her ribcage, taking her breath away.

Along one of the narrower sides was a bar, with a couple of women dressed in black. One, aged about forty, was serving a man with a pint of beer, and the other was idly wiping a wine glass with a brightly coloured towel. There were benches against the other three walls, with small tables placed casually in front, a number of low stools scattered around them. It was too dark to identify the colour of either the walls or the upholstery, if indeed they had not faded beyond recognition. In addition to the women round the disc jockey, more were dancing on the small oval polished floor. The men, mostly in their twenties, were sitting on the benches, leaning back against the walls. Cassie was aware of their eyes measuring up the various young women, including herself, assessing their availability and vulnerability. She walked to the bar and ordered a coke, before sitting at an unoccupied table from where she could watch the entrance.

After a few moments, she leant back against the wall and watched the women on the dance floor; they danced with a rhythm she knew she could not emulate. When her eyes had become better adjusted to the light, she looked round the room, but she couldn't see Hinds. Was she on a wild goose chase? She pushed the thought to the back of her mind, it was still early, the evening had not yet begun, but there was an air of expectancy as if they were all waiting for someone to arrive, or something to happen. Cassie sipped slowly at her drink and tried to decide how long to wait. It was already eleven thirty and she wasn't very good at late nights.

There was a steady trickle of young people coming into the club and soon the room began to fill up. More and more youngsters moved onto the dance floor, which became a heaving mass of arms and legs as the dancers gyrated in time to the throbbing music. The room got warmer and, as it did, the smell of stale beer mingled with that of cheap perfume. A young couple sat down at her table. They were totally engrossed in each other and for a moment her attention was diverted away from the entrance.

Suddenly she heard a loud bang from the direction of the alley way, followed by a lot of shouting. She couldn't identify the words. She stood up and turned towards the door. There were two men hurling themselves through the opening, followed by a melange of arms and legs pushing and shoving, a crush of dark blue, topped by white faces, blocking the doorway as a group of men catapulted themselves into the room. The two men leading the group pulled baseball caps out of their pockets and put them on. The caps had the word 'Police' emblazoned across the front. They were followed by men and women in, what now became clear, were uniforms.

For a moment the scene was frozen. The music stopped. Those dancing were caught, bodies half turned, mouths open, a foot off the floor or an arm held aloft. A fraction of a second later, the men who had been sitting around the room leapt up. Then from pockets and handbags a shower of folds of paper and small plastic bags hit the floor. Cassie looked down and saw the wooden boards around her littered with them. 'Oh shit,' she muttered.

'Everyone stay still,' a voice commanded. The lights were thrown on, revealing clusters of girls huddling together; groups of men, mainly of Afro-Caribbean origin, stood tensely, their eyes antagonistic, watching the police officers.

Cassie's first instinct was to try to leave the club, but immediately she realised that was impossible. She swore under her breath. Around her the police began to pick up the paper folds and place them in exhibit bags. She moved forward a step and someone barked at her to stand still.

An officer was making notes of the exhibits and taking the name of the man or woman nearest to the item he was recording. Once the name was taken the men were asked to line up on one side of the room and the women on the opposite side. The officers produced handcuffs and after cuffing each of the men, they were handed out of the club, as if the police were playing passing the parcel. There was shouting and scuffles but no real fighting.

Cassie began to think the police would not bother with her, but after a few minutes a uniformed policewoman came up to her together with a man in plain clothes. 'Just about to buy something were we?' said the man. She started to protest but he interrupted her and told her to tell that to the custody sergeant. The female officer took her arm, 'I think you'd better come with me.' As she was led away, Cassie thought again about trying to explain who she was, but decided there was no point. She would go to the police station and explain there, tell them she was a lawyer and why she was there, then they would let her go, wouldn't they?

Cassie, along with another woman, was pushed into the back of a police car with a policewoman between them, and taken to Notting Hill Police Station. From the yard she was taken into the custody suite, where she was told to sit on a bench along one side of the room, with the young woman who had been in the police car with her.

She waited quietly and watched as a number of men were brought to the counter, where the custody officer took the details. He wrote their names, dates of birth and address laboriously on large sheets of paper. Each one was asked to empty their pockets and the contents were duly recorded. As soon as he had signed the list of his possessions he was led off to the cells.

After processing the men, the young woman sitting next to her was called up to the desk. She was an attractive black girl, about twenty-three or so. Her long, obviously-straightened, black hair fell over her face and she was continually pushing it back. She was asked by the police officer to tell him her full name. She told him it was Anastasia Devine. The officer had to ask her to spell both names. As he was writing them down, the female officer who had been sitting between them in the car came in with a small plastic bag containing what Cassie assumed were Ecstasy tablets. 'Just found these in the back of the car. She came here in that vehicle.'

'I wasn't the only one,' Anastasia screamed and pointed at Cassie. 'She was in the car as well.' Anastasia moved up to the policewoman and peered into her face stabbing with her forefinger. 'Or you planted it there. It ain't mine.'

Both police officers looked at Cassie. 'I know nothing about the tablets,' she said. They ignored her and the custody officer returned to documenting Anastasia Devine and the policewoman placed the tablets in a police exhibit bag and wrote on the label.

'They're not anything to do with me,' Cassie repeated.

'You'll get your opportunity to explain in due course,' said the policewoman.

Cassie was furious, but realized she would have to wait until the sergeant started to take her details before she could tell them who she was and what she had been doing in the club.

After the sergeant had finished with the black girl and she returned to the bench, he beckoned Cassie over to the counter, told her to empty her pockets and demanded to know her name.

'Cassandra Jane Hardman.'

'Address?'

'Flat D, 12 Chepstow Villas, Notting Hill.'

'Right, now this bag of tablets, probably Ecstasy. Yes?'

'I don't know anything about them. I'm a lawyer and I was searching for a witness who will be needed at the Old Bailey tomorrow.' Cassie sounded very pompous even to herself. At least she would be fulfilling their expectations.

'Oh, really. It's the first time I've heard that one.' The custody sergeant said with a smirk.

'Look, it's the truth. I really was looking for a witness. The trial is at the Old Bailey, in front of Judge Crabtree.'

'Now, now. Just calm down. The stories people come up with.'

'Are you going to detain me?' Cassie asked.

'I am indeed,' the officer replied.

'Can I make a telephone call?'

'In good time.'

He began to list the bits and pieces she had removed from her pockets and her handbag. She looked at them as he itemized them on the custody sheet, a mobile phone, a wallet with six credit cards, seventeen pounds in notes and thirty four pence in coins, a tube of moisturizer, a lipstick, a packet of Polo mints and some of the pink tape used to secure briefs. He asked her to remove a bracelet, which he listed as gold-coloured metal, her watch and a necklace with a pearl drop. It was like going through security at an airport, only much worse; there was no holiday to make the process worthwhile.

After completing the rest of the formalities Cassie and Anastasia were placed in a small detention room.

'Are you really a lawyer?' Anastasia asked.

'Yes. And I didn't have any drugs on me.'

'I know that. I just don't want to be charged, not with my record.'

Cassie didn't reply. They sat in silence for what seemed like two or three hours but must have been much shorter. Cassie spent the time mulling over in her mind what to do. Who should she call; Ben would be furious with her, Tim was miles away and Jack, she sighed, Jack would make her life a misery. Her career was in the balance, she would be unable to practice if they charged her with possession of drugs and disbarred if she was convicted. She needed somebody who would have enough influence to get her out of the police station, someone who could vouch for her. Alex Seymour, of course, but could she really ask someone she had only just met. She couldn't think of anyone better. Alex knew Cassie was a barrister and that Barker's case had started, and, just as importantly, this was where she was stationed. She could explain to the officers. It was a long shot, but she couldn't think of anyone else.

A young blonde haired policewoman put her head round the door and asked them if they wanted a cup of tea. They both said they did. When she came back with the drinks, Cassie asked if she could make a telephone call.

'I'll just check,' replied the officer.

She came back a few minutes later and said, 'Sarge says yes,' and held the door open for Cassie. Back in the custody suite, the sergeant, a tall portly man, handed her the phone and a telephone directory.

'If I could just have my mobile phone the number I want is there.'

The sergeant let her have the phone reluctantly, but insisted she use the telephone on the custody desk. As she listened to the phone ringing, she looked at the clock on the wall. The time was ten past three. The phone rang and at first no one answered. Then a sleepy voice said, 'Who's that?'

'Alex, it's Cassie Hardman. I need a bit of help. I'm at Notting Hill Police Station. Could you come and see me please?'

'What the hell…Cassie, what are you doing at the police station at this time of night?'

'I've been arrested in a drugs raid and I may be charged with possessing drugs. I am entitled to a solicitor.'

'Well, get one.'

Cassie looked at the sergeant to check if he could hear Alex, but he wasn't paying a lot of attention to her.

'Alex, I really would like you to come.'

'It's three in the morning and I'm on duty at seven. You know the law better than I do. Goodnight.' Cassie heard the receiver being replaced.

Chapter 26

Alex punched some shape back into the pillow and pulled the red-covered duvet up under her chin, but her desire to get some more sleep before going back on duty at seven was thwarted by the thought of Cassie Hardman arrested for possession of drugs. Of course, all sorts of people took drugs but Cassie hadn't seemed to be the type to risk her career. She turned over and closed her eyes, and then opened them. She wouldn't be able to sleep again. She threw back the bedclothes and turned on the light. It was three thirty am.

It didn't take long to get dressed and she soon left the warmth of her flat, a gift from her father, to walk the short distance along the lamp-lit streets to Notting Hill Police Station. Alex walked quickly, with elegant strides, her blonde hair swinging. She was alert, for anything untoward. She heard the faint rustle of a cat on the prowl, before she saw the ginger tabby cross the pavement in front of her. And then she caught the noise of a car approaching from behind, slowing down. She didn't alter her pace and kept looking ahead, until it had passed.

Once at the station she showed her warrant card at the front desk, and after she went through the security doors that kept the public at bay, she made her way into the custody suite. The sergeant on duty, who, she knew, was only interested in counting the days to his retirement, was just putting a cup of tea down on the counter when she walked in. He looked up at the clock on the wall behind him. 'You're a bit early for the morning shift.'

'Someone told me there's been a raid tonight.'

'Yes, at the Mango. We've a lot of bodies in here.'

Alex pulled the custody records towards her and scanned down the list of persons detained, until she found Cassie's name.

'Sarge,' she turned the book back towards him, and pointed at an entry. 'This woman here, Cassie Hardman. I think I know her.'

The officer looked at her over his spectacles, 'She says she's a brief.'

'That's right. Where is she?'

'We've put her and another girl in the detention room.'

'Can I go and see her?'

'Can't see any reason why not.'

Alex undid the top button of her navy coat, and peered through the window in the door of the detention room. Cassie was sitting on one chair with her back to the door, and facing her was a woman Alex knew. Anastasia saw her looking in, and as the door opened said, 'Miss Seymour, what yo' doin' here?'

Cassie spun round, 'Thank goodness you've come.'

Alex walked into the room and closed the door behind her. 'Cassie, what's this about?'

Cassie looked at her and then at Anastasia. Alex assured her that the girl, whom she called Annie, was all right, and anyway there was no option but for Cassie to explain why she had been at the club when it was raided.

'I'm in this case at the Old Bailey, a murder trial. We spoke about it on Friday. The defendant has an alibi, but the witness is missing. I was told he was a regular at that club. So I went to see if I could find him.'

'Bit bloody stupid, wasn't it? Why didn't you tell the police?'

'Because I don't think they'd do anything. Would they hang around in a nightclub in the hope a witness for the defence would turn up? I don't think so.'

Alex shrugged her shoulders.

'Then there's this drugs raid and everyone was arrested. There were drugs all over the floor,' Cassie went on.

'So I gather. Did you have anything?' Alex asked.

'Of course not. Some tablets of Ecstasy were found down the back of the seat in the car, but I assume they were hers.' Cassie pointed at Annie.

Alex turned to Annie and said, 'Still dealing a bit, then, are we?'

'There's only four tablets, just enough for the weekend for me,' Annie squeaked.

'OK, OK but they were yours? Not Miss Hardman's?'

'Yes, I wouldn't let her take the rap for me.' She shook her head, 'I wouldn't do that, honest.'

'Right, they may not charge you so I'll keep quiet until we know what's happening,' Alex said, and then turned to Cassie, 'Now, I'll see if I can get you out of here.'

Back at the counter, Alex said, 'Sarge, this morning there was a notice about some guy that's wanted as a witness at the Bailey; have you got a copy?'

'Should be in that pile there. Haven't had time to look through them myself. All this bloody paperwork, and then this lot arrive with a van load of punters.'

Alex made soothing noises as he went on complaining about his work load, and she searched through the papers he had indicated. He was still whingeing when she found the notice she was looking for.

'I've been tearing around the manor looking for this guy.' She held up the notice with Walker's face on it. 'And Cassie Hardman is the brief in that trial.'

'You know who she is then?'

'Sure, she was defending in one of the Kings Cross drugs trials. Did a good job too. Made a couple of our lot look real idiots.'

'Really. Well, looks like your friend's been caught with something she shouldn't have.'

He picked up his cup of tea and turned away from her and went back to his paperwork. She wasn't going to get Cassie out by talking to him.

'Thanks,' she said, and then made her way to the CID room where she found one of the night duty officers sitting at his desk writing a report. He was a soft spoken Scot, with whom she worked frequently. 'This drugs raid; not from this nick?'

'No, they're from Streatham, I think. They've lodged the punters here as the nearest place. Not sure they got what they were looking for. It's all low level supply.'

'Where are they now?'

'Where d'you think?'

Alex knew exactly what he meant and headed for the canteen. She pushed open the door and heard a wall of sound; the voices of many men talking. The conversation was interspersed with laughter and shouts of disapproval from Lizzie Talbot, the canteen assistant, who was detained after her clocking off time because of them. 'Why can't you get off home?' 'It's too late.' 'I want to get home even if you don't.' Lizzie was a small, skinny dark-haired woman of indeterminate age who treated all police officers as if they were about five. When she saw Alex she smiled with relief as if she was about to be saved from this unruly pack of men. 'Miss Seymour, can't you get this lot to go home. They're working me to the bone. I'm running out of things. There'll be nothing left after they've gone,' she whined.

A uniformed officer leant over and pinched Lizzie on the backside, 'You're skin and bones now, been worn out already.'

Lizzie slapped his face. 'Cheeky,' she said looking at Alex, her eyes begging Alex to intervene.

'I can't do anything about them, Lizzie. Sorry,' and then to the officer, 'Who's in charge here?'

'DI Tolland. Over there.' He pointed at a small fresh-faced man in a black bomber jacket sitting at the other side of the room. Alex pushed her way between the tables, conscious of the men eyeing her up and down, mentally taking off her clothes. 'What you doing later love.' 'Quite fancy that.' 'Give us a kiss.' She gritted her teeth and ignored them.

'Mr Tolland, can I have a word?'

The Detective Inspector looked up at her, and asked her to sit down, motioning the officer sitting opposite him to move. 'What can I do for you?' he asked as she took the vacated seat. He was a similar age to her and spoke in a creamy West Country accent. Alex thought he was young to be a Detective Inspector; the sort determined to climb the promotion ladder as fast as he could. He wouldn't want mistakes on his beat.

'You've arrested somebody I know. I've just had a word with her. She's a lawyer, and she tells me she was in the club looking for a witness in a murder case she's working on. We've been trying to find the same guy as well. Did she have any drugs on her?'

DI Tolland shouted out, 'Anyone arrested some pesky lawyer, a woman?'

'She's called Cassie Hardman,' Alex told him.

'Cassie Hardman's the name.'

Over the other side of the room a stocky woman stood up and began to walk towards them. She was rather short and the trousers of her uniform hardly contained her bulk, but her white shirt was clean and well pressed. Her light brown hair had come loose and flopped over her unmade-up suet coloured face. Alex sighed inwardly, a WPC who tried to be more macho than a man; she would be determined to hold on to her prisoner.

When the WPC was stood by them, DI Tolland asked her if Cassie Hardman had been found in possession of any drugs. She told him nothing had been found on her, but some Ecstasy tablets had been pushed down behind the car seat on the journey to the police station.

'There was another girl in the car, Anastasia Devine. We know her as a small time dealer,' Alex added.

'Is that right?' Mr Tolland asked the WPC.

'Yes, there was another woman.'

'Give me your notebook,' he demanded. The woman handed him the buff coloured notebook she was clutching. He flipped through it, and then read aloud the entry relating to the arrest of both Cassie and Annie. 'You've written "I returned to Notting Hill Police Station by police car in the company of Miss Cassandra Hardman and Miss Anastasia Devine. I was sat between the two prisoners. On arriving at the station they were taken into the custody suite and I remained in the yard in order to search the vehicle registration number TR 51 WTG. On the back seat pushed between the seat squab and the back rest, I found a small plastic bag containing tablets which I believe to be Ecstasy." Great,' said Inspector Tolland, 'Which side of you was Hardman sat? Which side of the car were the drugs found? Bloody useless.' He threw the book towards her. 'We'll have to let them both go.'

'I think Devine was on my left, the side the drugs were found. I think,' the WPC suggested.

'Too bloody late, now,' he said, 'You can't go altering your notes now. Any half-decent lawyer would wipe the walls of the court with you.' The woman backed away from him, before turning and heading out of the room. 'Go and snivel in the loo,' he shouted after her, then he turned to Alex, 'Now, you can tell the custody sergeant to let your mate go, and I suppose the other woman as well.'

Chapter 27

Annie was the first of the three women down the steps at the entrance to the police station. As she reached the footpath, she turned to face Cassie and Alex, 'Next time I need a lawyer, I'll ask for you. Imagine being locked up with a brief.' She almost skipped away from them as she headed off towards Ladbroke Grove.

'I'll walk home with you,' Alex told Cassie. 'You were lucky tonight. The policewoman was young and not very bright. It would have been very easy to fit you up with those drugs.'

'I know. I'm sorry I've dragged you into this. I wouldn't have done for myself, but I'm sure my client is innocent, and we really need to call this guy, Walker. He's the alibi.' Anxiety made her voice tremble.

'Walker is a convicted thief and a drug dealer. Not the best of witnesses. And what if you're wrong? You could have screwed up your life with this...' Alex didn't know what to say but continued with, 'this foolish escapade. Your client has been fingered, not fitted up for the offence. That doesn't happen on a murder. He's been positively identified.'

Cassie realised Alex was very angry and she wanted to explain, but even though Alex had arranged her release, she was still a police officer and on the other side.

'I know you think I've been stupid. I should have given the information about where Walker might be found to the police. I know that, but nobody else is really fighting Barker's corner, and what if he is innocent?'

'Yes, you have been foolish, very foolish. I've been trying to find your damn witness for three days now. So have other officers. Now we know where he lives and we have a mobile number for him.'

'So, why hasn't he been brought to court?'

'He's being very elusive. We'll go back to his address and we'll try to track him by his phone, but it will take a little time.'

'I didn't know you had an address for him. Nobody's said that, and, well, time is running out.'

'Why are you so sure he'll help you? Your client may be lying about the football match. Look, Cassie, a woman has died. Someone killed her and the evidence points to your guy. You want to call a young man who's as bent as a corkscrew to try and get him off.'

Cassie ignored her, 'I think the interviews with him were unfair, suggesting he was caught at the scene on a video recording.'

Alex wasn't going to tell Cassie she had spoken to Walker and he was unwilling to give evidence.

Neither spoke as they continued walking towards Cassie's flat. Alex was the first to break the silence, 'The court will be told tomorrow the information we have about Walker.'

They had reached one end of Chepstow Villas not far from the house where Cassie's flat took up the top floor. Alex stopped, no longer angry. She said, 'You might want to suggest getting a warrant for his arrest, that's the correct procedure, isn't it?' She pointed along Pembridge Road, 'I'm going this way. And the next time you get arrested, make it daytime will you. See you.' As Alex walked away, Cassie shouted, 'Thanks. See you.'

211

Inside the dark and empty flat, Cassie threw herself onto her bed. She knew she should not have gone looking for Walker, and certainly not gone to the Mango Club, the sort of place she would normally not set foot in, nor should she have gone alone. She had thought of asking Ben to go with her, but she knew he would have talked her out of visiting the club. Had she been charged with possession of drugs and convicted she would have lost everything she had worked so hard to achieve.

Chapter 28

Although she had slept only fitfully Cassie still arrived at the Old Bailey early. After getting her robes on she made her way to the Bar Mess, looking for David. He would surely have some further information about the search for Walker, but instead she saw Eleanor Hesketh, who waved at her, and called out that she had been hoping to see her. Cassie hesitated, she really didn't want to get involved with talking about Chambers now, but before she could think of an excuse, Eleanor was standing next to her.

'I wanted to talk about the tenancy. I know you're keen to have another woman taken on, and I think you're right, although the men don't like it,' Eleanor said.

Cassie nodded, although she was wondering what Eleanor's motive was for this sudden change of heart.

'Do you know Alison Cheshire?' Eleanor didn't wait for Cassie's reply, 'I think she would make a very good addition to Chambers, don't you?'

'And the Tenancy Committee?'

Cassie was well aware that Alison Cheshire's husband was a partner in a successful firm of solicitors, and that Eleanor's new found enthusiasm for selecting a female for the vacancy was in the hope of more work coming to her. Success and the money that followed was the driving force behind most barristers, particularly the more senior members of the bar, even if they had begun their careers with a strong belief in justice. She hated the continual arguments about tenancies, as everyone looked to their own interests. No. 3 Burke Court seemed to be prone to this kind of dispute, and she had been tempted from time to time to accept invitations to join other Chambers but she found it difficult to judge whether they were any better.

Eleanor went on, 'Of course that's fine for the babies, but there are other considerations, particularly if they are more senior. They don't want their current set to find out they're seeking pastures new until it's all settled. At that level we want someone who will fit in with us and we want someone with solicitors of their own.'

'Well, Alison certainly has that,' Cassie said as she spotted David Jennings coming through the library doors, 'Sorry, Eleanor, I have to go.'

'I'll tell Richard you're in favour then,' Eleanor said as Cassie turned away.

Cassie shook her head as she walked towards David. He told her he had not seen Sergeant Dean that morning and had no news about Walker.

Cassie suppressed any element of surprise at the absence of information on the search for the missing witness; she needed to keep her contact with Alex Seymour secret. 'I think we will apply for a warrant for his arrest. It will speed up the procedure if the police are able to arrest him and bring him to court.'

'As you will,' he replied.

Cassie went downstairs into the courtroom, and picked up her copy of Archbold to look for the passage on reluctant witnesses. There was real danger in calling someone who was unwilling; if Walker didn't come up to proof it would damage their case. She realised she was not in a position to ask the judge for a warrant, as Walker had not refused to give evidence, he just hadn't been found. They would have to wait.

The jury had been told they would not be needed until eleven o'clock, giving time for Marcus to make his submission to the judge that the case should be stopped. As he started, Colin Dean came to the door and beckoned to David.

'We do not say there is no evidence but that no jury properly directed could convict. In particular we rely on the case of Turner.'

Marcus outlined his argument in a measured tone, the difficult circumstances of the observation and the inconsistency in the description given by the witness. Judge Crabtree listened without interrupting, but didn't even call on Howard Alsopp to respond, before he ruled that there was a case to answer. Then, he asked Howard if there was any information on the search for Walker.

'I haven't heard anything this morning, but...' He looked towards the usher, who was pointing towards the door, and then came towards him and whispered something.

'I think Sergeant Dean is at this moment bringing my junior up to date.'

'I'll give you some time to find out what's happening,' Judge Crabtree said as he walked out of the court.

Outside in the hall, Cassie could see David, his chin tucked against his chest listening to Colin Dean. He looked up and waved Cassie, Marcus and Howard to come over to him. Once they were standing in a cluster, he asked the police officer to repeat what he had just said.

'We have a confirmed address for him now, and a mobile number. One of my officers spoke to him on the phone, and he told her he couldn't help, or wouldn't help. I understand he did say they went to the Chelsea–Everton game, so he may be able to support the defendant's alibi. But we have to locate him, and we would want to interview him as well.'

Cassie realised Alex had not told her the whole truth about the search for Walker, although she had suggested Cassie should apply for a warrant. Now she knew he was refusing to assist she had grounds for making the application, so she asked Dean if that would help. When he confirmed it would, she said, 'Right we'll do that, and meanwhile, you'll keep looking for him?'

Chapter 29

Alex too had spent the remainder of the night tossing and turning. She was deeply troubled by the knowledge she had about the trial of Lenny Barker. As she had reminded Cassie, a young woman was dead, Barker had been identified by an eyewitness, and Detective Superintendent O'Connor had a good reputation for finding murderers. On the other hand, Cassie was a talented barrister, and she was so convinced her client was innocent she had risked her career by going to that awful club in the All Saints Road. And Walker had said he and Barker had gone to the match at Stamford Bridge. In addition there was that knife with the bloodstains on it, and the man who had sat in the gardens of the square where Shelley had lived. She had suggested to Cassie they should apply for a warrant for Walker's arrest. She hoped Cassie would do so. But what was she to do? If Walker could be found and persuaded to go to court then at least Barker would get a fair trial. She would go back to Walker's address and hope he turned up while she was there.

She went out without breakfast and stopped at a sandwich shop to pick up a coffee and some porridge. She parked on the other side of the road from the block of flats, and settled down to watch the front door, which, she was fairly sure, was the only way in and out of the building. It was seven thirty. She looked up at the block; the curtains of number 6 were closed, Claire Desmond was still in bed, but at number 5 they were open. Was that an indication Walker had got up already or, more likely, he had not spent the night there?

Being on observation was a variation of sitting in a café and people-watching, one saw such a variety, young and old, rich and poor, some shabby, others smartly dressed. A lad in his early teens came out of the block, dressed in the uniform of St Paul's School, starting his journey to school and, sometime in the future, out of these flats. Ten minutes later, a twenty-five year old Afro-Caribbean woman left the block and walked along the street in a pair of high heeled shoes and a pale pink coat, off to work in an office somewhere in the City. A few minutes later a white people-carrier drove up and parked outside; a woman dressed in jeans, a dirty white cardigan and a well-worn pair of trainers, got out, said something to the driver, before going into the block. She looked like she had been working all night, probably cleaning.

A double-decker bus came past Alex, and pulled up at the stop in front of the flats, obscuring her view of the door. She hadn't seen anyone waiting at the bus stop, so she surmised it had stopped for somebody to alight. When it moved away, there was nobody on the pavement. Whoever had got off had gone into the block of flats.

She looked up at the building and saw a face at one of the windows in Flat 5. She was too far away to identify the person. She got out of her car and crossed the road, looking up at the figure in the window. A car narrowly missed her and hooted to attract her attention. She ignored it. The person at the window vanished. As she reached the pavement, the curtains in Flat 6 were drawn back. The door to the block was open and Alex burst through and ran up the stairs. The door of Flat 5 was ajar. Alex lost no time in entering the hall of the Walker family's property, and then headed into the sitting room. It looked uninhabited, a beige sofa and a black leather easy chair were placed facing a large television. Her heels tapped on the wooden floors. She turned back and opened the other doors off the hallway. A set of bunk beds in one of the bedrooms had been stripped. In the second bedroom, the bedding had been pulled back and on a small bedside table was an open can of Red Bull. She picked the can up and shook it, there was the sound of a small amount of liquid sloshing around, but it was the only sign the flat was occupied.

Alex had gone back into the sitting room when she heard the sound of a door opening somewhere. Although she hadn't closed the door of the Walkers' flat, she couldn't see the entrance to Flat 6 from where she was standing. She walked forward towards the landing when a lock clicked softly into place. It could only have been Claire Desmond's.

She moved as silently as possible to the outside of number 6, then stood and listened for a moment. There was no music today. Alex pushed the white plastic doorbell attached to the post, and waited. After a few moments, she heard the sound of feet crossing a wooden floor, and then the door opened.

'It is you,' said Claire Desmond.

'Have you just been in next door?' Alex asked.

'Yes, so what if I have?'

'You didn't say you had a key.'

'I didn't think it was important.'

'You've left the door open. Were you going back in for something.'

'No, no. I didn't realise I'd left it open.'

'Perhaps you'd better close it.'

219

Claire stepped forward, holding her door, preventing it swinging open. There was a rustle from inside.

'I think you need a key,' Alex said.

Claire stared at Alex, her face immobile, her eyes wide, doe like. Alex pushed past her and flung the door open. She saw a music stand in the centre of the room, but before she could look around, a young man jumped up from a sofa.

'Edwin Walker, isn't it?'

Chapter 30

Cassie watched the jury as they trooped in. They were more relaxed with each other than they had been on the first day, more animated, more talkative, more a group, no longer individuals maintaining their own space. They separated and formed a single file, to walk across the back of the court, between the lawyers' benches and the front of the dock. The 'two As' and Colin Heap looked at Lenny as they passed him, while Brian Claxton and Deepa Nadswallah kept their eyes firmly fixed on the jury box.

It took several minutes before all the jury were in their places, and had made themselves as comfortable as possible in the confined space. Marcus got to his feet again and told the judge they were ready to begin the defence case. They would call the defendant, Leonard Barker.

As Lenny walked from the dock to the witness box, flanked by prison officers, Cassie thought he looked very vulnerable. This was his trial, suddenly he was visible, at the centre of it. This was the time when the jury were able to make some assessment of the man, in the words the judge would undoubtedly use, to judge his character and demeanour as he was examined-in-chief and then cross-examined. Marcus would guide him through his evidence as he began his account, but once the prosecution began their questions, he would have to fend for himself. She didn't feel confident he would cope with Howard Alsopp, who would wrap difficult questions in smooth language, take apart the answers given, and twist words to make Lenny appear to lie, or to conceal the truth.

Cassie had impressed on Lenny how important it was for the jury to form a favourable first impression and he had taken her advice, and had chosen jeans, with a white shirt and grey sweater. He looked very young, much younger than his twenty two years. As he took the oath she could see the card with the words on quiver in his hands and he was gripping the bible tightly. She turned to the jury box, hoping to see if their faces revealed their initial thoughts. Twenty-four eyes were watching, concentrating on Lenny, beginning to think, she assumed, about what kind of young man he was and asking themselves if he really was capable of murder.

Marcus began by asking Lenny his full name and address and then, to give him a bit of time to settle, a few questions about his family and where he worked. The purpose was to provide the jury with a snapshot of Lenny's life, living at home with his mother and sister, working in a local store. A glance at the jurors confirmed they were listening attentively and a number were making notes, including the 'two As', Colin Heap and Deepa Nadswallah, but one of the older men was slumped in his seat, a sceptical look on his face. Cassie took a mint from the tube she kept in her pencil case.

'Now,' said Marcus swivelling round so that he could see the jury, 'have you been convicted of any offences at all?'

'No, Sir.'

'Have you been arrested for any offences?'

'Only for this.'

Cassie saw Amanda Conrad nod, as if her first impression of Lenny was correct. Colin Heap had leant back in his seat, the end of a pencil in his mouth. He looked at Marcus and then smiled at Cassie. She smiled back.

'You've told us you've worked at the hardware shop for just over a year. What did you do before?'

'I couldn't get work when I left school but I used to help out on the market, moving boxes, running errands, you know, just helping out.'

'Did you get paid?'

'No, Sir. Sometimes I got some left over fruit or vegetables. It was better working than doing nothing.'

'Quite so.' Marcus beamed at the jurors, a smile that said isn't he a nice young man.

As Cassie listened to Marcus drawing Lenny's account from him, she saw Sergeant Dean come into the courtroom and speak to David Jennings, and then sit down next to Mrs Paulson. He spoke to her, and she nodded in reply to whatever comment he had made.

David passed a note to Cassie, she opened it and when she read the contents had to purse her lips together to stop herself crying out with delight. Walker had been found. She turned to Tim and showed him the note, he rose and made his way round the back of the court and left the room with Sergeant Dean. Cassie leant forward and carefully placed the slip of paper on the edge of Marcus's lectern. He paused before continuing with his questions.

Before finishing his examination-in-chief, Marcus asked Judge Crabtree if he could make an application in the absence of the jury. When they had left the court, Marcus told the Judge Walker had been found and was being brought to court, and he would prefer not to continue with Barker's evidence until they had the opportunity of taking a statement from Walker.

Judge Crabtree was only too happy to agree. Now Walker had been located his refusal to grant an adjournment could not be criticised.

Down in the cells, Cassie told Lenny, 'The police have located Hinds, and they'll bring him to court soon.' A broad grin spread across his face. 'He'll tell them I was at the football match, then they'll let me go.'

'Hang on. The trial will not stop because of Hinds. It'll still be up to the jury to decide.'

His face dropped. 'But it will improve the prospect of an acquittal,' Cassie added quickly.

When Tim and Cassie returned to the courtroom, they found the list office had taken the opportunity of putting a guilty plea in front of Judge Crabtree. The defence barrister was addressing the judge in mitigation, while his client, a black male with dreadlocks, scowled at a police officer sat behind prosecuting counsel.

Cassie waited between the two sets of doors into the court until she was able to catch Mrs Beswick's eye. The usher came towards her and whispered to Cassie that Mr Pike was upstairs in the Bar Mess waiting for her.

Marcus was sitting on one of the large green leather sofas at the library end of the refectory. There was a cup of coffee on the low table in front of him and he was idly flipping through a copy of Country Life.

'When this Hinds individual arrives I think you should be present as Tim takes a statement from him. See what you make of him. We need to know about any previous, and what information he had about the girl. I'm not convinced by this alibi. Why would our guy want the trial to proceed, rather than an application for the jury to be discharged, if he was with this man? Well, it's all water under the bridge now, he's turned up.'

It was almost midday before David Jennings appeared in the Bar Mess and told her that Walker was in the cells. She leapt up and went to look for Tim.

When Edwin Walker came into the interview room he frowned at the sight of them and in a belligerent voice asked Tim who he was, and if he was another police officer. Tim explained that he was the solicitor representing Lenny Barker, 'We believe you and Lenny went to a football match at Stamford Bridge on the eighteenth of September, when Chelsea played Everton. If that's right then Lenny couldn't have been in Holland Park when Miss Paulson was murdered.'

'I told that policewoman, I'm not giving evidence. Anyway it's the most ridiculous thing I've heard. Lenny wouldn't hurt a fly.'

'Did you go to the match together?' Tim persisted.

'Yes, we did, but I don't want to go in the box.'

'Not even to get your mate off?'

'They can't convict him. No one in their right mind would think Lenny killed that girl.'

'Unfortunately the police do, and they have made a good job of trying to persuade the jury. He's been identified by an eyewitness to the murder who says Lenny is the killer. Lenny needs you to give evidence to confirm he was at the match that night,' Tim said.

Walker didn't say anything.

'Why don't you tell us about how you came to go to the game?' Tim asked.

'I'm not telling you where the tickets came from.'

'OK, OK. But you had two tickets and you went to Stamford Bridge?'

225

'Yea, I asked him if he wanted to go a couple of days before and we agreed to meet at the Coach and Horses on Portobello. We caught the bus to Fulham Broadway, went into the ground and watched the match. Had to walk home because he didn't have any money left on his Oyster.'

'You could have got home on the tube or the bus?'

'I guess so. I think there was still some cash on my card.'

'Was Lenny with you throughout the match?'

'Yes. It was a good game; we were glued to our seats.'

'And when you left? Did you stay together?'

'We walked home together, at least up to Holland Park Road, then he went up Ladbroke Grove on his way home. I went onto Shepherd's Bush and got the train from there to Willesden.'

'Any trouble as you left the ground?'

'There was a bit of a scuffle in front of me,' Walker paused, 'Yea, I've just remembered. There are building works going on, and Lenny got the other side of some of the gear. Then there was this bit of a fight and I pulled the big guy off. Got past the JCB and Lenny was there waiting for me. We left the ground and walked home as I've said.'

'Let's get this right. At the time you were involved in this scuffle.'

Walker interrupted Tim, 'I wasn't involved. I pulled the bigger guy off, stopping the fight.'

'OK. When you intervened in this fight, Lenny was just the other side of a JCB?'

'Well, some big machinery or something.'

Cassie tried to recollect the video she had seen, but couldn't remember the details. If she had time, she

226

would look at it again to check if Walker's account could be confirmed. Tim went on with his questions.

'Did you know Shelley Paulson?'

'Yea, you bet.' He made an hourglass shape with his hands. 'She was real good looking. Wicked.'

'When did you first meet her?'

'No, don't get me wrong. I just knew who she was. She was a hooker, you know, classy, but a hooker. Not that she worked the streets. It was all upmarket stuff. She had this minder; like, he made sure of that.' Cassie was astonished at the remark about a minder. This was the first time anyone had mentioned knowing Shelley Paulson had one. She didn't want to interrupt Tim so she said nothing.

'But you knew who she was?'

'That's right. She did the market. Bought old clothes, vintage ain't it, and bits of jewellery, you know. Fruit and veg sometimes. Everybody knew her. Well, all the blokes anyway.' He smiled at Tim as if the two shared an experience.

'What about Lenny?'

'Just the same. Lenny helped out on the market, like me.' Course then he went to work for Mr Boxall just round the corner.'

'Did he ever say anything about her?'

'No. Never.'

'Didn't say he fancied her? Anything like that?'

'No. No, not him. Bit of an innocent, you know. Likes his football, a game of pool and a pint now and again. That's it. Bit of a mummy's boy.' Walker looked across at Cassie and asked her if the police really thought Lenny had killed Shelley.

'Yes, they do,' she said, 'they think he tried to force himself on her, and when she refused, he killed her.

And they have an eyewitness who's picked him out on an ID parade.' Walker was shaking his head as she talked. 'If he's convicted he'll get life imprisonment. You know Sammy on the market?'

'Yea, I do. Lenny helped him out a lot. Got bad hands.' He twisted his own hands to demonstrate.

'Sammy said nobody deserves to go to prison for something he didn't do. That's right isn't it?'

'What happened to her minder? She had a minder.'

Cassie and Tim looked at each other. This was the second time he had mentioned a minder and the police had said that Shelley had worked without one. Cassie chose to ignore the comment; it was something to discuss later. She pressed on, 'You know he was at that match with you. Can you live with yourself if he gets life imprisonment?'

Walker took a deep breath and looked from one to the other. Neither Cassie nor Tim spoke. After what to Cassie seemed like minutes he whispered, 'No, no, I couldn't. Not life, not for murder.'

'So you'll give evidence?'

'Will I be asked about the tickets? Where I got them from?'

'We can object to the question, but you can also tell the judge you don't want to answer as it may incriminate you,' Cassie said.

'What does that mean?'

'That you'll be admitting you committed an offence,' Tim replied.

'It's not really relevant. The prosecution will be satisfied by a refusal to answer,' Cassie added.

'One last thing,' Tim said 'Previous. How many and what for?'

'A few for possession, a Twoc and a couple of assaults?'

'You've served some time?' Tim wanted to know.

'Yea. Got six months for abh plus my bender and did six in the Scrubs.' He shuddered at the memory. 'When will I be in the box?'

'Probably Monday now. After Lenny.'

'They'll not keep me in until then? Will they?'

'I don't know,' Cassie said, 'It's up to the judge.' It wasn't her concern, it would be better if he was in custody, he couldn't go missing again, but as she had told him, it was a matter for the judge.

Walker thought for a moment, then relaxed, and Cassie took the opportunity to ask him about Shelley Paulson's minder. 'You've mentioned Shelley had a minder, do you know who that was?'

'Not really. I don't know his name or anything, like. He supplies drugs, the snowy. He's a bit of a loner. Rides round on a bike, you know, a cycle.'

'What's he look like?'

'White guy with a purple mark on his face. Birthmark isn't it?' He put his hand up to the left hand side of his face.

Chapter 31

The public cafeteria on the third floor of the Central Criminal Court resembled an over–used motorway service station littered with people and paper cups. An intolerable mix of witnesses, defendants' families and solicitors were talking, arguing, gossiping. Voices rose and fell above the hiss of coffee-making machines, the clatter of spoons on saucers and the banging of trays; Cassie could hardly think never mind have any reasonable conversation, but it was the only place where she could get a cup of coffee and talk to her solicitor; only barristers were allowed in the fifth floor Bar Mess.

Tim told Cassie that he had asked the police about Shelley Paulson's having either a minder or a pimp when he had attended Kensington Police Station for the interviews, and they had told him there was no trace of one.

'But we know she took drugs?' Cassie said.

'Yes, some stuff was found in the flat. Cocaine. And there's the blood analysis.'

'She must have got it from somewhere.'

'Dean said they couldn't trace her supplier, even after offering immunity and a reward. No one came forward with any information.'

'But if Walker is right, there is this guy with a birthmark on his left cheek. Who is he? I'd better go and find Marcus,' Cassie said, 'See what he's getting up to.' She got up and ran up the two flights of steps to the robing rooms. She put her foot on the bottom step of the flight up to the Bar Mess, then stopped, turned round and walked back to the dimly lit hall by the lifts.

She opened her handbag and searched around for her mobile phone; as usual it had slipped to the bottom. Her hand closed round the small oblong shape and she pulled it out, switched it on, scrolled through her contacts and pushed the call button. The call was answered by a voice saying. 'Notting Hill Police Station, CID, can I help?'

'I'd like to speak to Alex Seymour, please.'

'Who's calling?'

'Miss Hardman.' Cassie heard the same voice shout, 'Is Alex in?' and then someone said, 'Yes, in the fingerprint room.'

The man on the telephone repeated the information and then added he expected her back soon. Could he get her to call?

'Please, if you could. She knows my number.' The telephone call was ended abruptly.

Cassie went up to the Bar Mess, where she found Marcus in the middle of telling an anecdote to an attentive audience. She heard him finish the story by saying, 'The word the interpreter translated as grunting, actually meant snoring. The complainant admitted the defendant had been snoring. "In the middle of raping you?" I asked. End of case.' There was an explosion of raucous laughter from the group of male barristers he was entertaining with the story. Cassie went up to him and he looked at her face, 'Cassie, don't be starchy. Just a little fun. You women, always so serious.'

'Walker is here, and Tim has taken a statement but,' she paused when she realised that Howard and David were sitting within earshot, 'I think there is something we should discuss.'

Marcus pulled a face at his audience, 'Looks like I'm in trouble,' he said to them, but he got up and walked with her to the door of the library. Cassie told him what Walker had said about Shelley Paulson having a minder.

Marcus didn't reply immediately, 'Do we know if the police did try and find a minder?'

'Tim said he asked, and they told him they couldn't find anyone despite offering a reward.'

Marcus thought for a few moments, then said he didn't see how they could use the information. Cassie was about to argue with him, but he walked away from her. She went into the library and sat down at one of the tables. She didn't want to talk to anyone else for a minute or two. She knew he was right; in this trial, whether or not Shelley Paulson had a minder was irrelevant in the absence of any evidence suggesting someone other than Barker was the killer.

A young man in shirt sleeves, but still wearing his bands tied round his stiff collar, came into the room and stretched across her to reach one of the law reports. He sat down at the table next to her, opened the book, searching through the pages for the authority he wanted, and began to read. When Cassie's telephone rang, he looked up and said, 'It is a library, you know.' Cassie made her way out of the room, pulling faces at the man, who had turned his back on her, and into the Bar Mess as she answered the phone.

'Cassie, it's Alex. What is it now?'

'Alex, just hang on a minute. It's noisy here and I can hardly hear.'

Cassie went down a flight of stairs to the hallway. 'Alex, something has come up. We've got Walker here and he's going to give evidence, but he's told us that the girl had a pimp or minder.'

'Not unusual.'

'No, but the police inquiry didn't find one, despite offering a reward. And Walker says the guy supplied drugs, mainly cocaine. He also said he has a birthmark on the left side of his chin. That might look like a beard.'

'A beard?'

'The description of the killer was that he had a beard. Lenny doesn't, but this man does have a birthmark. He must be the killer.'

'That's a big step, Cassie. You're grabbing at straws. Anyway what do you expect me to do?'

'He's the killer, Alex, find him of course.' The tannoy went, calling all parties in the case of Lenny Barker to court. 'Alex, I have to go. Ring me later.'

She turned the phone off and dashed down the spiral staircase to the next floor where Court 12 was situated. Judge Crabtree was just walking onto the bench when she pushed open the door. She waited until he had sat down before making her way in front of the dock, to her seat behind Marcus. Examination-in-chief continued with Marcus asking Lenny about Shelley Paulson.

'Now Miss Paulson. She was a regular visitor to the market.'

'Yes. She came most Saturdays to shop.'

'How did you learn her name?'

'I can't really remember.'

'Can you remember when you learnt her name?'

Lenny shook his head. Cassie looked up and held her breath, worried the silence would be interpreted as a sign Lenny was trying to hide something.

Marcus repeated the question and Lenny said he couldn't remember. Cassie glanced at the jury, who were still absorbed by Lenny, but she could not detect any change in their attitudes towards him.

'When did you learn she had been killed?'

'I don't know, I'm not sure. I think someone at work mentioned it. I think it was in the Evening Standard.'

'So the next day, or the day after that?'

'Yes, I would have thought so.'

'Do you remember seeing the report of the Chelsea game in the same paper?'

'Don't know. I knew the result so I didn't need to look.'

'Did you read the piece about the murder?'

'Not sure. I might have done.'

Cassie and Tim had asked him to try to remember if he had looked at the report on the game, but he couldn't. She hoped the jury would think his lack of memory was simply due to the lapse of time and not anything more sinister.

'What was your reaction to the news of her death?' Marcus said.

'Dunno really. It's not like I really knew her, not like she was a friend or nothing. Just thought it was sad she'd been killed.'

'Not a friend, but someone you recognised. What did you think of her?'

'She was lovely, but. I didn't know her, not to say anything about her, really. My mother says you can't tell a sweet by its wrapper.'

There was a tiny ripple of laughter around the courtroom. Even Judge Crabtree smiled before looking sternly around the room. Lenny had said the same to

234

Cassie, when she had asked him about girlfriends. He was secretive about sexual relationships, and Cassie had wondered if he was gay and was hiding it, or whether his mother was too controlling, interfering in his life, because she wanted him to remain at home as the man of the house. She looked up at the public gallery, where Mrs Barker was anxiously watching her son, but not joining in the laughter.

'Did you ever try to talk to her?'

'No. She was too, well, up-town, you know what I mean.'

'Do you know where you were the night of the murder?'

'I do now. I went to a football match at Stamford Bridge with a friend, Hinds.'

'That's Chelsea's ground?' Marcus asked, 'Close to Fulham Broadway is it not?'

'Yes. Not far.'

'Can you remember who was playing?'

'Everton were playing.'

'What time did you leave the ground?'

'Not sure. There was injury time so it was nearer nine thirty, I'd say, when we left. It takes a while to get out of the ground.'

'I'm told about, about fifteen or so minutes? Does that seem about right?'

Lenny shrugged his shoulders, and then said, 'I guess so.'

'Did you and Walker leave together?'

'Yes, we walked home.'

'What route did you take?'

'Up Earls Court Road, Warwick Avenue. That's where we separated. I went along Ladbroke Grove to home.'

'Mr Pike,' Judge Crabtree interrupted, 'We'll leave it there. I'm going to send the jury away so we can discuss some administrative matters. Members of the jury, there are some routine matters that don't concern you at this stage, so you can go now and be back promptly on Monday morning.'

As the jurors walked past Cassie to leave the court, Colin Heap grinned at her and Anna Fry nodded. She felt encouraged into believing at least some of the jury would be willing to listen to the arguments the defence would make.

After they were all out of the courtroom, Judge Crabtree addressed both counsel, 'I understand the warrant has been executed and the young man is here.' He didn't wait for a reply. 'Mr Pike, has your solicitor had the opportunity of taking a statement from him?'

'Yes, My Lord.'

'Do you intend to call him?'

'Yes, we do.'

'Right, I'll have him brought up to court.'

While they all waited, the judge asked about the timetable for the rest of the trial. Once Edwin Walker appeared in the dock, Judge Crabtree directed that he be released and asked him to come into the witness box.

'Mr Walker, I understand that you will be called as a witness in this case, probably on Monday afternoon. Are you prepared to give evidence?'

Walker nodded.

'You are, good. I don't want to keep you in custody over the weekend, but I do need your assurance that you will attend on Monday. I will release you on condition you stay at the address you've already given, and you are here by twelve noon. If you are not you will be arrested again, and I will deal with you for contempt. Now you can go.'

Judge Crabtree got up, 'Monday morning, gentlemen.'

Outside court Walker was nowhere to be seen.

Chapter 32

Alex was taken aback by Cassie's call. She wasn't sure why she had given her the information, then, suddenly, she thought of the man Mel Haskins had told her about, the man she believed had hidden the drugs and the knife in Cotburn Square Gardens. He too had a birthmark, and how many men with the same description were selling drugs in the area? If this man had been Shelley Paulson's minder then it was possible the knife in her desk was the murder weapon. She took out the exhibit bag containing the knife, and looked at the report from forensics attached to it, before replacing it in her desk. She went back to the papers she had been reading, but couldn't concentrate. She leant back in her chair, twisting the pen she was holding round in her hands, then she grabbed her coat and, said she was going out and would be back later, to no one in particular.

Once out of the police station she walked towards the tree lined Holland Park Road, crossed the road by the tube station. The newsvendor's stall, she noticed, was selling a variety of foreign newspapers, now the Metro and the Evening Standard were free. On the south pavement she turned left and then right into Holland Walk. She was still uncertain what steps she could or should take, but she headed towards the scene of the murder, in the hope she would get some inspiration.

She must have walked along the lane many times before, but now she looked carefully at the backs of the houses as she climbed towards the top of the hill. These terraces were home to the wealthy, their

238

windows reflecting the afternoon sun, and the woodwork painted in expensive, old fashioned colours. She tried to identify Mrs Bampton's house, but couldn't. When she came alongside the garden wall of Aubrey House, she spotted the security cameras. Now the Walk began to descend, and on her right was Holland Park, where, behind the sentry of iron railings, the green spears of the daffodils were poking through.

As she got level with the secondary school, crowds of teenagers emerged from the walkway under an enclosed bridge. The youngsters, dressed in a grey-coloured uniform, swarmed passed her, chattering to each other and into their mobiles. Alex stopped just before the entrance to the park by Duchess of Bedford Walk, the place where Shelley Paulson had been murdered. There was nothing to mark the point where Shelley had lost her life. At first, the area would have been cordoned off and the chalk marks where the body had fallen would have been visible on the tarmacked surface, but now there was nothing. She watched the animated school-children walk over the site, unaware they were trampling over the death bed of a young woman.

She still wasn't sure what she wanted to do; it seemed possible the wrong man was in the dock, and, even worse, a killer was at large. She searched in her pockets and found her mobile, then scrolled through the contacts, until she found the name, Mike Kemp. He had been in the same class at the police training school. She pushed the dial button. The call was answered quickly. After exchanging a few pleasantries with him, Alex asked him if he was still stationed at Kensington Police Station. When he confirmed he was, she inquired if he knew anything about the Paulson murder investigation.

'The Governor's sure they have the right man but I've heard whispers that some of the team are not as convinced. O'Connor is not the man to cross. Not if you want to keep your job,' he told her.

'Can we meet? I've got some information about it from…well, I'd rather not say,' Alex said.

'OK, when do you suggest?'

'How about now? The café in Holland Park?'

'Be there in ten minutes.'

Alex liked the café, it was unpretentious despite its location, and today in the spring sunshine the tables outside were full. Most of the customers were women; she had almost forgotten there were so many. There was a group of young mums escaping the isolation of their homes, the babies in pushchairs and the toddlers running around the garden furniture on the enclosed terrace. Dotted around the tables were older women, speaking languages she didn't understand even if she recognised some of the words. She imagined these women had spent their youth in similar cafes in the various capitals of Europe, and now, exiled in London, they were trying to recapture their earlier lives.

She found a table in one of the remaining archways of the covered walk that had led from Holland House to the Orangery. She was so engrossed in her surroundings that she didn't notice Mike Kemp until he was stood in front of her. He was a handsome man, his blond hair cut short and brushed forward. For a few days in the hot-house of the residential training school at Hendon, they had flirted with a more intimate relationship, but it had come to nothing. He wasn't interested in a woman who wanted a career, and Alex came to the conclusion she preferred him as a friend rather than a lover. A calm but undemanding friendship had developed; a friendship which had waned when they left Hendon, and now they met infrequently.

He leant over and kissed her on the cheek. 'What's this all about?'

'What about a cup of tea first? I'm buying.'

When she returned with the tray, she told him she had learnt that a man who had been seen in the garden square where Shelley Paulson had lived fitted the description of Shelley's drug supplier. 'And in the gardens there was a pizza box full of drugs and a knife hidden in a compost heap.' She pulled the plastic bag containing the knife out of her handbag, looked round to see if they were being observed, and then placed it on the table between them, the forensic report, which was stapled to the outside, facing towards him. Mike read the report, whistled gently, 'What are you saying, this is the murder weapon?'

'I don't know, but it may be, and if it is, the kid standing trial is the wrong one.' She pulled the knife towards her and replaced it.

Mike looked nervous. 'I'm not involved in the investigation so I don't know any of the details. What are you going to do?'

'What would you do? It seems to me that this is evidence that may undermine the prosecution case and should be disclosed to the defence lawyers, shouldn't it?'

'But you can't be sure that it is the same man.'

'Not unless I can get forensics to compare the DNA of the bloodstain on the knife against Shelley Paulson's. I need to get into the incident room at Kensington.'

241

'There isn't anyone in there at the moment. The Sarge, Colin Dean, and the Governor are up the Bailey.'

'Could I get in there?'

'I don't know. I assume it's locked.'

'I need to get hold of the copy of Paulson's DNA profile from the files. I'd like to look at some of the statements as well, the original description given for one, and perhaps house to house enquiries. It depends where the investigation went. Can I come back with you and try to get in?'

'I'm not getting into it. Why don't you just contact Colin Dean, he's a decent bloke, he'll sort it out?'

'Because I can't. There's an informant and I don't want to tell him who it is. Come on. I won't mention your name. Just take me back to the station, then go back to whatever you were doing when I called.'

'Alex, you'll be in trouble if you get caught. Colin Dean would accept you wanted to keep an informant secret. At least to begin with.'

'I can't risk it. I need to get that profile for myself, before I tell anyone else. Please, Mike, if my information is right, the real killer will be arrested, as well as an innocent man acquitted. All I need is you to point me in the right direction.'

After some hesitation he agreed to show her where the major incident room was, but stressed she was on her own after that. She needed him to vouch for her, she didn't want to produce her warrant card, or identify herself to the station sergeant.

'That's OK. I won't drag you into anything.'

They walked to Kensington Police Station in silence. Once inside Mike took Alex thorough a labyrinth of corridors, past the main CID office to the door behind which the major incidents were investigated. Alex tried the door, but as she had expected, it was locked. 'If I've learnt anything in this job, it's how to slip a lock,' she said as she removed a credit card from her handbag. As she pushed it between the door jamb and the catch, Mike walked away.

At first the door didn't open. Before she could try again, a policewoman came along the corridor. Alex groaned inwardly but the woman simply nodded at her, and went through a door on the opposite side of the corridor. Alex saw it was marked 'Ladies'. She had a few minutes to open the door before the woman emerged. She slipped her card into the lock again, and gently pushed to force the catch back. This time it worked and Alex was able to open the door and quickly slip inside.

Along two walls of the room was a long work top with a number of computer monitors ranged along it, a chair in front of each. The drawers in the ranks of filing cabinets were all closed but there were also files along the worktops, some half open giving the impression they had been abandoned hurriedly. Alex turned on one of the computers, hoping she wouldn't need a password to access the files. She was in luck – the computer she was using had not been closed down securely and the screen came to life displaying a list of documents. Each folder showed clearly the type of information it contained: identification, house to house, forensic, interviews.

She opened the file named 'Forensic', but apart from a list of the items sent to the Forensic Science Service, there wasn't a copy of Shelley Paulson's DNA profile. She clicked on the exhibit list, but it wasn't there either. Of course, if there was no evidence of DNA in the trial, the profile would be amongst the unused material. When she opened that file and scrolled down the items she found it listed with a number indicating where it was located in the filing cabinets. She checked her watch; it was just after two thirty; she wasn't sure how long she would have before someone came back, probably till well after the court rose about four. That would give her over an hour, but she needed to work quickly.

It didn't take her long to find the drawer where the copy DNA profile was supposed to be stored, and she rifled through until she found a folder with the reference she had noted from the computer, but it was empty. She swore under her breath, and then searched through the contents of that drawer, in case it had been misfiled. She could find no trace of the document. Just as she was about to leave, the door opened and a voice said, 'Who are you?'

She looked round and saw a middle aged man dressed in a dark blue suit and a brightly coloured tie.

She didn't really want to give her name, but decided it was better than provoking more questions. 'Detective Constable Alex Seymour, Sir.'

'Are you supposed to be here?' he enquired.

'I'm doing some research. On major enquiries. This seemed a good place to start.'

'OK. It's been cleared with DCS O'Connor, I assume?'

'I understand so.' Alex hoped he wouldn't ask her who she was working for, but the man seemed satisfied and closed the door, leaving her alone again.

She didn't want to leave the room immediately; if she ran into him before she could get out of the station

244

he might start questioning her again. Instead, she would wait and look at some of the other files on the computer. She began by opening the identification file; amongst the documents stored there was one labelled 'Notebook'. She double clicked on the icon. The document was the note made by the police constable who had spoken to the eyewitness at the scene of the murder. It read, 'Description of offender; tall, taller than victim, about 6' 2", IC1 male, dark shadow on left cheek, possibly beard?' It was so similar to the man who had been seen leaving the sports centre last June, it had to be the same man.

Alex moved on to the file containing the notes made by the officers who had conducted the house to house inquiry. There was very little of interest. Most of the local residents had seen or heard nothing until the urgent whine of the police sirens and the ambulance had disturbed their evening television. One or two had pulled aside their curtains, but when they realised whatever incident had resulted in the police and ambulance speeding along Campden Hill Road was not in their sight they had gone back to their evening's entertainment. She was beginning to despair of finding anything of interest when she opened a notebook that contained an account of a conversation with a Mrs Muriel Haldane.

She had told the officer who had asked her if she had seen anything unusual that for the last six months she had lived alone in a ground floor flat in Campden Hill Mansions. She was in the habit of taking her dog out just before the ten o'clock news. She remembered hearing the sirens and saw both the police car and the ambulance as they drove along Campden Hill Road. She put the time she left home as about nine forty. Her route took her north towards the Windsor Castle public house, down Peel Street and then she would return by way of Bedford Gardens.

Alex smiled, Mrs Haldane liked to talk. The officer must have been very patient, taking down everything she said, although she had very little of importance to tell him. It was part of the job, listening to people's stories, hoping they would give you some piece of information that, put together with others, gave a picture of the crime you were investigating.

She must have told him about having to pick up after her dog, who was called Hazlitt, and that may have lengthened her walk, and then about the man she had seen cycling towards Notting Hill Gate. He was riding so furiously she thought he would hit her, and she had stepped back from the pavement. Then a police car, travelling in the other direction, towards the High Street drove past her at speed. Otherwise, she hadn't seen anything else unusual or noticed anyone acting suspiciously that night.

A man on a pedal cycle, another similarity to the drug dealer, Alex thought, and she made a note of Mrs Haldane's full address, before continuing with the remaining statements. She returned to the screen displaying all the different files made during the inquiry, and was looking at their names, when the telephone by the computer she was using rang. Instinctively she reached out to pick up the receiver, but then remembering where she was, let it ring, hoping nobody would come into the room to answer it. While she listened for the sound of footsteps, she scanned the screen to see if there was anything else that might provide a lead to Shelley Paulson's drug supplier.

When the telephone had stopped ringing, she opened the file containing the exhibits taken from the deceased's flat in Cotburn Square, and scrolled down it, amongst them was an address book. Would Shelley Paulson have kept the phone number of her drug supplier or minder in an address book? She went back to the main screen and looked for a file of statements taken from people whose names and numbers were in the book. She soon found it. There was a long list of documents, each with the name of some individual. She went back to the list of property removed from Shelley Paulson's flat, and checked that the document number of the address book had been given. There was a mobile listed as well.

Alex knew where the mobile and the address book were in the cabinets from her previous search. She quickly located them and was closing the drawer when the door opened and a young male officer with short dark hair put his head round the door. 'I'm looking for Sergeant Dean,' he said questioningly.

'He's at the Bailey,' Alex replied.

'I don't remember seeing you before. Are you new?'

'I'm doing some research on major enquires,' she said, thinking please go away.

'Interesting, is it?'

'Yes, but I don't have a lot of time and I really do need to get on.' She turned away from him, and stared at the screen, waiting for him to go.

'Sorry to interrupt.'

Once he had closed the door behind him, she turned off the computer, and then waited, listening to the sound of his footsteps getting fainter as he walked along the corridor. The clock on the wall caught her eye; it was nearly four o'clock. She had been there for almost two hours and the officers would be back soon from court. She didn't want to give up, but she had to leave, so although she knew she should put the book and mobile back, she placed them in her pocket. She would return them later. She went to the door, listened carefully for any sound of movement, and when she was sure there was no one in the vicinity, moved quickly out into the corridor.

Chapter 33

Alex's flat was in a mansion block in Ledbury Road. It was, in estate agent's jargon, large and spacious, but sometimes she felt she didn't really live there. When her father had purchased it, he had, without consulting her, retained an interior designer to furnish it. It was decorated in shades of beige and ivory, with no personal touches that would make it home. She never seemed to find the time to search for the cushions, rugs and decorative pieces of furniture that would make it hers. Nor were there any pictures on the walls, just two photographs on a console table, one of her in police uniform taken at her passing out parade, and the other with her parents and brother from a skiing holiday about two years before.

She cleared the coffee table of last Sunday's newspapers and pushed the remotes for the TV and the stereo to one side, before placing the address book, Shelley's mobile and the knife in the space she had created. She picked up the book first, then put it back and tried to turn the phone on. The battery was flat. Somewhere she had what had been described as a universal charger. She began looking for it, her frustration increasing as she searched the cupboard in the hallway and the chest of drawers in her bedroom. Eventually she discovered it in a kitchen drawer along with boxes of matches, tea lights, spare light bulbs, a hammer and a pair of scissors. Fortunately it fitted and she put the phone on charge.

Then she picked up the address book and began to read the entries under each letter of the alphabet, looking for something that might be a pseudonym, a code or disguise. She kept glancing at the exhibit bag containing the knife, which reminded her she had failed to find the DNA profile. She tried to think where it could have gone. She hadn't searched anywhere else apart from the unused material. The unused material, of course, Cassie would have copies of everything that was in the unused. But if she called Cassie to ask about the profile, Cassie would want to know why she needed to see it, and that would mean telling her about the knife. Alex wasn't sure what the rules were, but she thought it likely that once Cassie knew there was a knife, she would want to call the evidence about it in Barker's trial.

She went back to the address book. It was small and battered, the handwriting had changed, the letters becoming more even and regularly spaced, as if written over a number of years, perhaps even since Shelley's schooldays. A number of the entries had been deleted or altered; many of them would be out of date. Probably the list of contacts on the mobile would be the ones she still used regularly. Alex put the book down and looked at the mobile, checking to see if it was sufficiently charged for her to see the numbers on it.

The contact list on the mobile was even longer than the number of names and addresses in the book. Alex knew that the inquiry team had obtained the numbers Shelley had called in the weeks preceding her death, and had contacted as many as they could. Really she needed the information her colleagues had uncovered when they had telephoned or spoken to the various individuals. Those documents would be amongst the unused material served on Cassie, as well as the details of Shelley's telephone calls. There was no other solution, she would have to contact Cassie and hope they could work something out, so that her involvement would remain hidden, at least for the time being.

When her mobile rang Cassie answered straight away. She was surprised the caller was Alex, and puzzled when Alex asked her if she had Shelley's DNA profile. Cassie confirmed she had been sent the profile, but hadn't paid too much attention to it as there was no link with Barker.

'Why do you want to see them?' Cassie asked.

'Can we meet later this evening and I'll tell you then. I promise you, you'll find it very interesting.'

Cassie agreed, and then remembered, despite telling Ben she would see him that evening, she had not contacted him to make any arrangements, nor had he called her. She considered whether she should just leave things as they were and hope he wouldn't turn up without telephoning, or should she call him and put him off until the next day. She didn't want Ben to be there when Alex turned up. Alex might be reluctant to share whatever information she had in his presence, but neither did Cassie want to lie to him. Until she knew what was going on and had decided what to do about it, she wanted her meeting with Alex to be a secret. In the end she did nothing – if he turned up she would sort things out then; there was no point in anticipating a problem that might not arise, she had enough to worry about.

When the doorbell of her flat rang, Cassie pushed the intercom button, and after Alex said her name, Cassie said 'Come straight up. I'm on the third floor.' Cassie waited in the hallway at the top of a further flight of stairs, while Alex climbed up.

251

'Do you need oxygen to live here?' Alex asked.

'It's my only real exercise,' Cassie retorted, laughing at the same time.

Cassie was uneasy about Alex's presence in her flat, she found it difficult to think of Alex as anything other than a police officer, and police officers were not friends to be invited into one's home. On the other hand she was grateful for Alex's help and anxious to learn what she had to tell her.

Cassie was conscious of Alex looking round the brightly lit living room. She thought it must look very cluttered; there were the papers dumped on the dining table, as well as on the desk and coffee table, and books and CDs lay amongst the briefs. She was impatient to hear what Alex had to tell her, but she tidied the piles of paper on the coffee table, and then went to close the curtains, which were open, revealing the city lights towards the east.

'Good view,' said Alex, as the city vanished behind dark folds of cloth.

'Yes, it is. I understand you were the one who found Walker.'

'I went to the address his mother rented. She and her younger children have gone back to Jamaica, but we were told Eddy Walker still lived there. I went back in the morning before my shift started, and just waited until he turned up.'

'That must have been tedious.'

'Fortunately I didn't have to keep observation for too long. I don't think he had spent the night there, but he arrived soon after I got there.'

'It's a relief. He's told the judge he will come to court on Monday, and, hopefully, his evidence will provide an alibi for my client. That should raise sufficient doubt in the minds of the jury, and he'll be acquitted.'

'If he's not the murderer, the real killer is still at large and that's who I'm interested in. I think I may know who that person is.'

Cassie's eyes opened wide. 'What, you think you know who killed Shelley? Was it her minder?'

'I don't know about her minder, but certainly her drug supplier.'

'So, who is he?'

'I don't have a name yet, but...' Alex went on to explain about the pizza box full of cocaine being found in the gardens of Cotburn Square.

'Where Shelley Paulson lived,' Cassie said. She began to pace around the room, as she listened to Alex's account of the knife being found in the same place, and then about the DVD showing a man who fitted the description of the killer.

'Why hasn't all this been disclosed to the defence? The police do have a duty to let us have any information that may help us, and this clearly would.'

'Because they are so sure they have the right man, the investigation has stopped, so no one has made the link between the two, until now. I'm telling you, because I think you have a copy of Shelley's DNA profile and I want to have it compared with the blood on the knife.'

'If it matches, then the man who left the drugs and the knife in the garden is the man who murdered her.'

'That would be logical. Have you got a copy of the profile?'

'Isn't there one in the police files?'

'No. It appears to have gone missing. Look, I broke into the investigation room to try and find it, but it wasn't there.'

Cassie went to a box of papers sitting on her desk and began to search through them. 'I think it's amongst the papers I left here, and not at court.'

As she searched she asked Alex why she hadn't told Sergeant Dean about her suspicions.

'They're sure they've got the right man. After I saw you the other night in the police station, I thought it was worth making some further enquiries. And, well, it's rather difficult to say you're consorting with the enemy.'

Cassie went through the bundles of paper slowly and methodically, making sure she didn't miss the document they wanted.

'This is it, isn't it? It's on a piece of celluloid. It must be the original.'

Cassie considered what she should do; could she really trust Alex? She was a police officer – on the other side – but then Alex had rescued her from the police station, and gone to considerable trouble to locate Walker.

'I assume you want to take this and send it with the knife for comparison.'

'Yes, that's what I had in mind. I can send it off tomorrow and we should have the result back in the early part of next week.'

Cassie placed the profile on the platen of her printer and pushed the Copy button.

'Just in case it gets lost. Always better to have a copy.'

'Sure,' said Alex.

'If you don't get a result before the judge sums up, I will have to tell the court about the knife. You do realise that?'

'I thought you'd say that. I'm gambling on the DNA profiles matching, otherwise I'm for the high jump. I want to be in a position to arrest the killer, and I need as much time as possible.'

'I think you've got till Wednesday.'

'Now, there is something else. I took Shelley's mobile and address book to see if there is a number there that might be this supplier. I'd like to see the statements taken from the people on the contact list in her mobile. Do you have them?'

Cassie pulled one of the files of papers from the table and handed it to Alex. 'There's an index of the names with a page number, but I think the papers are filed in chronological order.' Alex nodded and opened the file. 'What are you looking for? I've been through them already, but that was before we'd spoken to Hinds,' Cassie said.

'Let's go through them again,' Alex said as she pulled out the book and the phone. As they read the papers they checked off each name in the index against those in the address book. Some were friends who knew nothing about Shelley's life as a prostitute. They had told the police she worked for an employment agency that specialised in highly paid secretaries and personal assistants. Some men had simply denied knowing her, and, only when they had been pushed, admitted they had used her services. All the men had been asked to provide details of where they were at the time of the murder, and all had satisfied the police they had water-tight alibis and could not have killed Shelley.

The police had been unable to find any connections between Shelley's family, friends or clients. She had kept them in separate compartments, each part of her life unconnected to any other. It was probably the only way she was able to keep her secrets. There were three girls she had been at college with whom she had met regularly, usually for lunch at a fashionable restaurant. Those three had been interviewed at length but had made no mention of any male friends, or even a boyfriend.

'What did they say about drugs?' Alex asked Cassie.

'They didn't seem to know she took drugs. Well, two of them didn't. The third, Charlotte, um, I've forgotten her surname, said she thought she smelt cannabis once, but it wasn't repeated.'

Alex laughed, 'But she knew what cannabis smelt like?'

'Clearly,' Cassie smiled as well. 'What about the mobile?'

Alex turned the phone on and they began to go through the contacts listed on it. There were rather more than in the address book; most had been interviewed and discarded as suspects.

When they had finished, Cassie said, 'Where now?'

'I don't know. I really don't know,' Alex replied.

'Would you like a glass of wine or something?' Cassie asked.

'Wine would be fine.'

'I hope white is OK.'

When Cassie came back with a bottle and two glasses, she said, 'I think I have the telephone records of all the numbers Shelley called in the week before she was killed. I'll get the list.'

She poured wine into the glasses, and handed one to Alex, and then went to her desk. After another search she pulled a squashed roll of paper out from the middle of a bundle still held together by pink tape. She showed Alex the documents, which had a tick and a name written in pencil against each telephone number.

'I think someone took the numbers from her mobile. That would be the easy way to do it; put the number in and it would show the name of the contact. And...' Cassie paused as she checked the numbers, running her finger down the lists, 'if I'm not mistaken...' She smiled as she handed the roll to Alex, 'She had a pizza for supper three times that week.'

Cassie pointed out to Alex the three telephone calls.

'Two of the numbers are the same and it's a mobile. The other is a landline. Are there any statements taken from the pizza restaurants?' Alex said.

'Who bothers about fast food places? Nobody notices pizza delivery boys in this area. You see two or three every night.'

Alex tapped in the mobile number and pushed the dial button. The phone at the other end rang and eventually an answering service came on and asked the caller to leave a number.

'I'll have to do a trace on that one,' Alex said, 'but it will have to wait until Monday'.

'Why not now?'

'I don't have the authority. The phone companies can be very difficult. I will have to go through the proper channels, so it will have to wait.'

'I think there is one more thing you should know. Scrapings were taken from Shelley Paulson's fingernails but they don't match either the profile taken from my client or her own. It may help if you can arrest the man.'

'That's if I can find him.'

Chapter 34

Saturday morning and Cassie felt a sense of freedom for the first time in days. She had been disappointed that Lenny had not finished giving his evidence, but at least Hinds had been found, and promised to come back to court. It might have been better if Judge Crabtree had kept him in custody, rather than risk him vanishing again; she didn't want to think about the consequences if he went on the run.

Even if Lenny was still to be cross-examined the jury had gone home for the weekend with his account of the night of the murder in their minds, his evidence ringing in their ears. The prosecution would find it harder to change their minds after they had the weekend to dwell on his account.

She would try not to think about the trial or the possibilities opened up by Alex. Ben hadn't phoned her since Wednesday evening, and she had been so wrapped up in the case that she hadn't tried to contact him. Their relationship, if you could call it that, was such a stop-start affair. She was still wary of involvement, afraid her judgement was flawed. She enjoyed his company; he listened attentively when she told him about the trials she was conducting, and to her complaints about judges she thought were being unfair. She tried to be as interested in his research work, and he could be very funny about some of his students and his contacts with other researchers in the same field. Away from work Cassie enjoyed the theatre but they had never gone to a play together, although they had gone to the cinema a couple of times. Mainly when they got together either she would prepare a meal for them or sometimes they went out to eat; then they went to bed. There was very little time left for anything else.

Never mind, she would call him and, hopefully, he would agree to meet her. She would book a table at Kensington Place. For once she didn't want to cook or wash-up; she deserved a treat after the week's events. She would pay for the meal, the Barker brief would be reasonably well paid; of course she knew she was deceiving herself, it would be six months or so before she received any payment for it, and by then she would have forgotten about the cost of the meal out, and spend the money again. They both liked the restaurant, even though it was noisy with chairs scuttling on the bare floors and the sound of overloud, confident voices echoing on the hard surfaces, and eating there would, she hoped, make up for neglecting him. She called his mobile and asked if he would come and see her. He appeared to have forgotten about the broken promise of meeting the previous evening, and accepted her invitation straight away; she was both relieved and delighted, there was much to tell him.

The morning was cold, bright and sunny, large clouds scampered across a baby blue sky, just the sort of day for joining the crowds on the Portobello Market. She strolled through the crush of tourists, at the southern end of the street, their voices speaking in many languages, a modern day Tower of Babel. She listened to the twang of a couple of overweight elderly Americans looking at some silver, and the lilt of two Irish girls as they searched through boxes of plastic costume jewellery. Further on she noticed a tall dark-haired woman examining vintage handbags, talking in Italian to a man wearing a full length raincoat, with a suede collar.

Then the crowds thinned a little as the stalls changed from selling antiques to food. There were vans selling hotdogs and hamburgers, the smell of hot fat drowning that of flowers and fruit. In addition to the stalls selling vegetables, there were ones with bread, olives, sweets, packets of biscuits, tinned food and small kitchen utensils. Londoners mingled with the overseas visitors, continuing their hurried lives amongst the leisure of the holidaymakers.

She found herself near the Westway and stall 143, where Sammy was serving a large black woman wearing a flamboyant patterned dress, a purple scarf flung over her shoulders. He saw Cassie and winked at her. 'I won't be a minute, love,' he said to her, and then to his customer, 'Is that all, dearie?' The women said it was and paid him, the coins clinking into his broken hands.

Once she had gone, Cassie said, 'I want to thank you for your help.' Sammy shrugged his shoulders as if to say it wasn't important.

'Hinds has turned up, and is going to give evidence about where Lenny was on the night of the murder.'

'I'm glad about that. The kid deserves a fair trial, even if he did kill her.'

'That's for the jury to decide, but...' she tailed off, her own view was irrelevant.

A young man with a large shopping basket came to stand next to her and picked up some apples, Sammy turned his attention to the man and waved goodbye to Cassie.

'See you,' Cassie said as she moved away.

Once back at home, she sorted out the blue counsel's notebooks she had filled during the course of the trial, settled down at her desk, and began to read

261

through them, a yellow highlighter in her hand. If she had been doing the trial herself, she would have prepared an outline of her speech at the beginning and used that to plot her questions, as she endeavoured to provide the points she would make to the jury. She had just begun to read the notes she had made of James Compton's cross-examination, when the telephone rang. It was Stephen Burnett, the junior member of the Tenancy Committee.

'Cassie, the vacancy for a tenant. It's being mooted that Alison Cheshire wants a move from her current chambers and has approached Eleanor about coming to us.'

'I know; Eleanor has already spoken to me. Personally, I think we can do better, we should revisit the applicants we interviewed last month.'

'Alison has a lot of work and most of it she'd bring with her. We're in a highly competitive business. Her husband is a partner with Hubert and Mardon. They do a lot of big fraud work.'

'But what about the quality of her work? She's a nice woman, but not a really good advocate.'

'Sure, there are better, but not many have her connections. Look it's preferable to taking on a judge's son just to improve Peter's chance of silk. At least we'd all get something out of it.'

'I thought he'd gone elsewhere,' Cassie said, 'Anyway, it's just so unfair to advertise a vacancy and then take someone who didn't even apply.'

'I've said it before, Cassie, you overdo being fair. We don't want to keep wasting time interviewing. I thought you'd approve, another woman. Anyway Alison isn't a newly-qualified advocate and she won't want to go through an interview.'

'That's what Eleanor said. I just feel we ought to give someone else a chance. Alison has a tenancy.'

'Well, Richard is taking soundings about her, so you'll have to make up your mind.'

'I'll think about it. OK.'

'OK,' replied Stephen and put the phone down.

Cassie went back to her notebooks, but before too long was interrupted again by the telephone ringing. This time it was Peter Maynard.

'Cassie, how's things?' he began. When she said she was fine, he continued, 'Cassie, Alison Cheshire, you know she's applied to come to Chambers?' He paused between words, choosing them carefully.

'I understand so.' Cassie paused too, wondering what he was about to say.

'Cassie, I'm not very keen on her coming to Chambers. I know you want another woman, but I don't think she's right for us. I know her husband has lots of work, but it's not the only consideration, is it? I mean if someone's not our sort, then they're not, are they?'

'What do you mean, not our sort?'

'Well, I've heard some rumours about her having an affair with someone, well I don't want to mention names.' He was clearly struggling, and not being truthful.

'Really, Peter, you shouldn't listen to gossip. I've never heard anything like that. Anyway if adultery was a bar to Chambers quite a few would be ineligible. The only question we should be asking is, is she a good lawyer?'

There was silence at the other end of the line. Clearly he was thinking about what to say next.

263

'Look, Cassie, I'll be truthful. I had a skinful one night and made a pass at her. I just find it too embarrassing, the thought of having to meet her in Chambers, and what about Chambers parties and dinners, when Melissa's there?'

'Don't be ridiculous, Peter,' Cassie said, 'Just because you made a fool of yourself. Anyway, her husband would be at any functions, so she's not likely to say anything in front of him. I bet she's forgotten all about it.'

'Do you think so?'

'Yes, I do. It happens all the time, when there are these drinking sessions. The real issue for me is whether she's talented enough. Our Chambers has built a reputation by having really good people, so when work has to be moved from one of us to another, solicitors are confident they won't be getting a dud.'

'Right,' Peter's voice was more upbeat. 'I'll let you get on with your weekend. I don't know about you, but I've loads to do. Melissa says all I do is work and she wonders why I bothered getting married at all.'

She had only just finished that call when her mobile rang. Cassie didn't recognise the woman's voice. 'Cassie, it's Alex. I thought you ought to know Walker got beaten up last night.'

Cassie stood up and turned away from her desk. 'What? What do you mean beaten up?' She felt her stomach turn and her heart beat a little faster. Was he going to be able to give evidence on Monday was her first thought, before wondering if he was badly hurt.

'He was found staggering around in the Portobello Road late last night. At first the officers thought he was drunk, but when they got him back to the nick, they saw the bruising on his face and whisked him off to hospital. He's had a beating, but says he doesn't know who did it and won't prefer charges.'

'He will be able to give evidence, won't he?' She felt sick at the thought that Walker might vanish for good.

'I doubt he'll be going anywhere for a day or two. Hopefully he'll be fit enough to get to court on Monday.'

'He is all right though, isn't he?'

'As right as you can be with a collection of bruises on your body, one eye half closed, looking like you've just done three rounds with Mike Tyson. I suppose he won't look quite so good for a while, but he'll get over it.'

Cassie thanked Alex for letting her know about Walker before reminding herself that getting Lenny acquitted was her concern, not what happened to other people. But there were those men who had threatened her only three days before.

Chapter 35

The trial resumed after the weekend, starting where it had left off, with Lenny giving evidence. He walked from the dock at the back of the court to the witness box without looking around. He still looked very young, his clothes neat and tidy, and his hair carefully brushed away from his eyes. He stepped into the waist-high box, placed both hands on the pale wooden edge, and looked round as if searching for a friendly face. As his eyes lighted on Cassie, she smiled at him, hoping to give him confidence; it was all she could do to help before he continued with his account; he had to be believed.

'Just to recap, you told us you walked up Warwick Road with your friend, Hinds, and then separated to go to your own homes. Is that right?'

'Yes. I went home. I think Hinds did as well.'

'After you left the stadium were you always with Hinds?'

Lenny creased his forehead and looked puzzled, 'I'm not sure what you mean.'

'Did you walk out of the stadium side by side?'

Lenny relaxed, 'No, sir. We went either side of some vehicles, or something, and then met up again just before we left the ground. There's some building works going on.'

'Now, I want to go back to the day of your arrest. You were at home on the morning of Thursday twenty-seventh October when the police arrived.'

Under careful questioning by Marcus, Lenny told the jury about the circumstances of his arrest. How he had been dragged from bed, stripped and left naked in front of all the police officers, 'Including some women police, as well as my mum and sister.' His tone of voice demonstrated how distressed he had been, and still was. Cassie underlined that section of the notes she was making. It was difficult to write, keep an eye on Lenny and watch the jury, but she thought Amanda Conrad found his evidence upsetting. She hoped the others did too; it was important to their case for the jury to understand the effect of the stress induced in Lenny by the police. It was the only explanation for his statement in interview that he was in the park the night of the murder.

Then Marcus asked Lenny to tell the court about what had happened in the custody suite and how he had first heard about the video. Cassie could picture the scene, recognising the feelings, when the procedures are unfamiliar, the surroundings alien and everyone against you, from her own brush with the police the previous week.

'Were there any other officers connected with this case in the custody suite with you and the sergeant?'

'Um. There were two men in plain clothes. Mr Dean called one of them Guv.'

'What did Sergeant Dean say to them?'

Lenny looked at Marcus but didn't reply. Cassie looked up and willed him to say something. Lenny began to stutter, then managed to get out that he didn't remember what Dean had said.

'Do you remember what the other two men were talking about?'

'They said they had a video taken in the park and I was on it?'

'Did they say you were on the video?'

'Not sure if they said I was actually on the video. I took it I was.'

'Did you learn when the video had been taken?'

'The night Shelley was killed.'

'Is this a fair summary? When you were first in the police station, two officers talked about a video that you believed showed you in Holland Park on the night of the murder.'

'Yes.' Lenny said very firmly and, for once he looked straight at the jury. Cassie marked that exchange as well. If he had been hesitant before, now he sounded certain he believed the video showed him in Holland Walk. Of course he was wrong, but that didn't matter, as long as the jury believed at the time he was interviewed that idea was firmly in his mind.

'We've all heard the interviews read out in court. Do you agree that the officer has told the jury what you said?'

'Yes.'

'You told the officers you were in the park that night. Can you tell the jury why you said that?'

Marcus turned away so that Lenny wouldn't look at him, but at the jury. Cassie's pen was poised over her notebook; this answer had to be right. The jurors had to find him credible.

'I couldn't remember, I was very upset, it was a few weeks before,' Lenny stumbled over the words, 'I thought I must have been in the park that night as they had the video. Then that man said I was there. At the parade. I thought I was, so I said it.' Then as an afterthought he added, 'I do go there to watch the football. There's a pitch the schools use, and some other clubs.'

'Finally, Mr Barker, did you kill Shelley Paulson?'

268

Lenny could not have been more emphatic, 'No, Sir. I did not.'

Cassie took the packet of mints out of her pencil case. At least Lenny had not made any mistakes during examination-in-chief, but ahead was the most dangerous part of the case for him, the cross-examination.

As Howard Alsopp got to his feet, his eyes twinkling with anticipation, Judge Crabtree said, 'Before you begin, Mr Alsopp, we'll take a short break. Back in fifteen minutes, members of the jury.'

Outside the courtroom, Marcus walked quickly away from Cassie and Tim. 'Wasn't too bad,' Tim muttered.

'I didn't think so either. You think Marcus expected something better?' Cassie was surprised. Lenny had struck just the right note, not too confident not too hesitant. Surely the jury would have found him a convincing witness.

At the far end of the corridor, Howard and David Jennings were deep in conversation, no doubt discussing lines of cross-examination with which they hoped to trap Lenny.

Marcus returned and joined them, 'Sorry I dashed off, bit of a crisis in the clerk's room.'

'I thought you were disappointed in our client's performance,' Cassie said.

'No. He did quite well. It's how he handles Howard's questions that matters. Can they shake him into saying something silly?' The question was rhetorical. Marcus didn't wait for an answer, he swept back into court.

Cassie wasn't sure how Howard would conduct his cross-examination; how he would lay his traps. She expected him to begin gently, trying to lull Barker into a false sense of security. He would want to get Lenny into a position where whatever answer he gave would be wrong; penning him in like sheep.

'Mr Barker, you agree that you told the police on the day of your arrest that you were in Holland Park on the night Shelley Paulson was murdered.'

'Yes, I did.' The muscle in Lenny's left cheek began to quiver.

'You accept, however casually, you knew Miss Paulson.'

'I knew her name.'

'You knew her name, could recognise her if you saw her?'

'Yes, of course.'

'Would you also agree she was a very attractive young woman?'

'She was, yes.'

'Can you remember the last time you saw her before she was murdered?'

'No, she came into the shop from time to time, but I can't say when the last time was.'

'So you saw Miss Paulson for the last time when she came into the shop?'

Lenny pulled his eyebrows down and looked quizzically at Howard Alsopp. Cassie knew what was coming. There was a receipt for some picture hooks from Boxall's which had been found in Shelley Paulson's flat. She had been in the shop on the Friday before she was killed. When Cassie had asked Lenny about it, he couldn't remember if he'd seen her then or not, the date had meant nothing to him.

'Could you just look at this, Exhibit 13, My Lord.'
A small piece of white paper was handed to Lenny by
the usher. He looked at it and back at Howard.

'It's dated the fourteenth of September and it has a
number on it just under where the name Boxalls is
printed. Do you see that?'

'Yes.' Lenny paused before saying, 'It's my till
number but, but I don't remember serving her in the
shop at all. Not ever.'

'But do you agree that the receipt would indicate
you were the person who put the money in the till and
gave her that receipt?'

'It seems so.'

'You didn't tell the police you'd seen her on the
Friday before she was killed?'

'No.' He hesitated, 'I don't think so.'

'If you'd served her in the shop five days before she
was killed wouldn't you have said something like, "she
was only in here last week"?'

'I don't know. I don't remember serving her.'

'You didn't say anything did you because you knew
you'd killed her?'

'No, no, I didn't.' His voice reached a crescendo
before dying away into a whisper, 'I didn't kill her.'

Howard waited until Lenny had composed himself.
Cassie took the opportunity to look at the jury. What
were they thinking? Were they feeling sympathy for
Lenny or did they agree with the prosecution that he
was hiding his culpability? Anna Fry was biting her lip
and Colin Heap was gazing round the courtroom,
avoiding any eye contact as if embarrassed by the
outburst from Lenny. Deepa Nadswallah, her face set
in a grimace, looked at the witness box.

271

'Do you remember the police asking you when you found out she had been killed and you said probably the day it was in the newspaper. I think you said the Evening Standard?'

'Jimmy usually brings a copy in, when he comes back from lunch.' Lenny lifted his head up as if to say he had nothing to hide.

'We've managed to get hold of some copies of the Standard for Wednesday the nineteenth of September.' Howard handed a bundle of newspapers to the usher, who distributed them to the judge, Marcus and Cassie, and finally the jury. The front page showed a photograph of Holland Walk at night and inset was a picture of a smiling Shelley Paulson. Cassie turned the paper over; on the back was a large action photograph of a football player in blue and white, and next to it a report of the game played at Stamford Bridge.

'You told the police you usually looked at the sports pages?'

'Yes.'

'Did you that day?'

'I don't remember.'

'Let's look at the back page.'

There was a rustle as six of the jurors, the judge and Lenny turned the newspaper over. 'You saw that didn't you, and now, when you have been identified you have decided you were at that game?'

'I was at that game. I wouldn't forget.'

'But you did, didn't you? You told the police you were in Holland Park?'

Lenny began to sob. 'I didn't remember the day of the match.'

Howard paused and looked at the jury, demonstrating how fair-minded he was being. Mrs

272

Beswick handed Lenny a tissue. He blew his nose and rubbed at his eyes. The muscle in his left cheek was quivering again. Cassie struggled to avoid showing any feelings, and did succeed in keeping her face expressionless.

'I did go to the match with Hinds. I didn't know the day, but it was Everton playing Chelsea.'

'What do you wear for work? Any special clothes?'

'Not sure, just jeans and usually a T-shirt or a sweater. Nothing special. We have overalls we keep at work.'

'Does Mr Boxall expect you to be smartly dressed?'

Lenny was clearly puzzled by where this was leading. 'No. We have overalls, a kind of coat, tan coloured.'

'So he wouldn't mind if you didn't shave once in a while?'

'No, I don't suppose so.'

'Are there days when you don't shave?'

'Sometimes. When I'm late.'

'Did you shave on the morning of the eighteenth of September?'

Marcus jumped up. 'Really, My Lord. How can Mr Barker be expected to remember whether he shaved on a particular morning six months ago? A trial is not a memory test.'

'I'm inclined to agree. Haven't you got your point, Mr Alsopp? I'm sure the jury will see what you are getting at. If he didn't shave that morning he may well have a shadow that looked like a beard by ten in the evening.' Judge Crabtree looked along the jury benches, raising his eyebrows as if to say sometimes

273

counsel can be very silly. Cassie dropped her head to hide her amusement.

'As you please, My Lord. Mr Barker, you have been identified as the person who killed Shelley Paulson by a man who witnessed the incident?'

Lenny looked at Howard and then at the judge, but said nothing.

'That's right isn't it?' Howard went on.

'Yes.'

'And you knew Shelley Paulson?'

Lenny nodded and then mumbled, 'Sort of.'

'Did you wear this sweater, on the eighteenth of September?' Howard held up a grey sweatshirt and waved it around so that everyone could see.

'I really don't know,' Lenny whispered.

'Similar fibres to this on Miss Paulson's cardigan?'

Lenny shrugged his shoulders then said, 'I bought it on the market, there must be loads of them.'

'It's quite a coincidence, isn't it, that Mr Compton should pick out someone from a number of similar young men, who also knows the deceased?'

'He's wrong. It wasn't me.'

There was little evidence to support the prosecution's version of the events that had led to the murder of Shelley Paulson, but Howard Alsopp had to ask Lenny if they had occurred.

'You went to Holland Park on the night of September eighteenth, as you told the police, to watch the football game being played on the sports ground in the south of the park?' he asked.

'No, I went to the game at Chelsea.'

'When it got dark you left the park but stayed in the area of Holland Walk?'

'No. Why would I do that?'

274

'I'm the one asking the questions, Mr Barker. You went to the Walk by Holland Park School, just by the school's bridge didn't you?'

'I did some times.'

'Some of your school friends hang around that area to watch homosexual men cruising, I think that's the expression, along Holland Walk.'

'Some do.'

'You told the police that from time to time you joined them?'

Lenny was silent.

'Is that right?'

'Yes, but that night I was with Hinds.'

'Whatever you did, you were in Holland Walk when you saw Shelley Paulson walking south. You went up to her because you had served her the Friday before and that gave you an excuse to talk to her.'

'No. I didn't see her on the Friday.'

'When she didn't want to talk to you, you argued with her?' Lenny just shook his head. Cassie could see Mrs Paulson, still dressed in black, her face pale and her eyes, like two dark moons, staring at Lenny.

'Then you grabbed her by the arm and pulled her towards you?'

'No, no.'

'She continued to struggle away from you. You were upset by her rejection of you so you took out a knife and stabbed her?'

'No. I didn't. I didn't. I wasn't there.' Lenny's voice was getting louder and louder.

'When she fell, and Mr Compton shouted at you, you ran away through the grounds of the school you had attended?'

'I didn't kill her. I wouldn't do that.' Cassie looked at the jury. All twelve were concentrating on Lenny with such intensity that it was impossible to tell what they were thinking. She put her pen down, began to fidget with her notebook, and to stop herself betraying her emotions, took another sweet from the green and white packet lying on the bench, between her files.

Howard must have decided he didn't need to cross-examine anymore, because he thanked Lenny and sat down. Marcus stood up, leant over to Cassie and asked her if she thought they needed to re-examine their client. 'I can't think of anything we need to clarify,' she replied. Marcus told the judge they had no further questions for Lenny. Cassie watched him walk back to the dock with his head hung down. As he sat down again, she saw him look up at the public gallery towards his mother, who smiled encouragingly at him.

Chapter 36

Marcus asked for Edwin Walker to be called into court. Cassie heard Mrs Beswick call out his name once and then again. She suddenly feared he had not turned up, and she would have to confess about the telephone call from Alex telling her Walker had been assaulted.

Tim got up and hurried out, trying to move as silently as possible. Mrs Beswick came back into court and told the judge Mr Durrant had gone to see if he could find Walker. 'Like the infamous Alfie Hinds,' Marcus commented in a low voice.

'Have you got another witness you can call, Mr Pike?'

'Mr Boxall, My Lord.'

A few seconds later Cameron Boxall was taking the oath. Cassie had not met him before and was surprised to see a ginger-haired man in his early forties. She had expected him to be in his late fifties, possibly even sixty. He told the jury he had employed Lenny for just over a year at the time of his arrest. Lenny had been recommended by one of the market traders as a good worker, reliable and helpful. He had found that to be true, and he believed Lenny to be honest. Shelley Paulson came into the shop from time to time, buying small items like light-bulbs or batteries. He agreed she was a very attractive woman. Most men would notice her, he said. Marcus asked him to look at the receipt from his shop dated 14th September. He told the court that although it had Lenny's till key number on it, there were circumstances in which either he or one of the other sales staff might use it. He didn't remember her being in the shop just before she was killed. When he was asked about Lenny having a beard he said that he hadn't and although there may have been occasions when he didn't shave in the morning, it was never a regular occurrence.

'Did Lenny have girlfriends come to the shop at all?'

'No,' Mr Boxall laughed, 'He was very shy.'

Cassie leant forward, hissing 'Marcus. Time off.'

'Mr Boxall. I nearly forgot. Have you got the record of Mr Barker's employment with you that show any holidays he took?'

'Yes, I have. He had a week off in May but then worked through until he was arrested.'

'Was he late for work at all?'

'I don't remember him being late ever. He's usually at the door, waiting to be let in.'

'So no unusual behaviour in September last year?'

'No, Lenny's, well just Lenny.'

Amanda Conrad was smiling, Colin Heap picked up his pen and made a note and, even Deepa Nadswallah appeared to have sympathy with Mr Boxall.

In cross-examination Howard asked Mr Boxall if Lenny had talked about going to Stamford Bridge in September round the time Miss Paulson was murdered.

'He was always talking about football. He's passionate about the game,' Mr Boxall said.

As Mr Boxall left the witness box, Tim came back into the courtroom. He nodded at Marcus, who said, 'I think Mr Walker is here.' Tim nodded again and walked round the back of the room to his seat on the row behind Cassie. She turned to him and asked him what had happened. 'He decided he didn't like the look of the canteen so he went out to get a coffee from across the road.'

278

'Stupid man,' Cassie groaned as Edwin Walker sauntered into court and the witness box.

He was a handsome young man, the mixture of genes enhancing his features, or he would have been without a bruised left eye. His dark hair was closely cropped, his face the colour of caramel or milk chocolate, his eyes a dark liquid brown. Despite the black-eye he had a mischievous smile, a smile that embraced everyone in the courtroom. In Cassie's view, he showed no sign of being nervous as he stood in the witness box and took the oath. Of course it wasn't his first time in court.

'Can you give the court your full name and address, Mr Walker?' Marcus asked firmly. Cassie was anxious in case he played up in the witness box. Marcus needed to keep a tight rein on him, if he could.

'Edwin Coates Walker and I live at Wellington House, Stringer Road, Willesden. Most people call me Hinds.' He smiled at the judge and then at the jury. Cassie saw Amanda Conrad smile back at him. Colin Heap didn't look so impressed, and Brian Claxton was positively bristling with antagonism. Walker was clearly a ladies' man.

'You know Lenny Barker?'

'Yeah, we played for the same football team, Westbourne Wonders, until I…' Walker stopped.

'Before we go any further, do you have any convictions for any offences at all?'

'Yes, I've been in court a few times.'

'Was the last occasion two years ago, for two offences of assault on the same day?'

'I pleaded not guilty to those. I was attacked so I hit back, defending myself, like, but they came off worse

279

so I got convicted.' He shrugged his shoulders as if it was of no consequence.

'For those offences were you given a sentence of twelve months' imprisonment.'

'Yeah. I was in breach of a bender as well.'

'Yes, I see, you had breached a suspended sentence imposed for the possession of Ecstasy,' Marcus said as he checked the list of previous convictions.

'How did you meet Lenny?'

'We both did a bit of work on the market, before he started at that DIY place. Played a bit of football together, like I said. Westbourne Wonders, not that we were very wonderful.' Walker looked down trying to hide his smile, his amusement at his own joke. Cassie turned to see how the jury were reacting. A wry smile crossed Colin Heap's face, Brian Claxton seemed to find it mildly amusing, but she wasn't too sure about Deepa Nadswallah.

'How would you describe your relationship with Lenny?'

'We were friends, not best buddies or anything. We were both keen Chelsea fans. When we met, we talked about football.'

'Have you been to a game at Stamford Bridge this season?'

'I went with Lenny to the Chelsea–Everton game last year. Is that what you're getting at?'

'I don't suppose you can remember the date?'

'Naw. Evening game, needed the lights. Be on the fixture list.'

'Who suggested going to the game?'

'I did. A mate gave me a couple of tickets. Something had come up. Said he couldn't go. I bumped into Lenny, asked him if he fancied coming with me. He jumped at it.'

'Can you help us how long before the game you offered him the spare ticket?'

'Not sure. It was a midweek match and I think I saw Lenny on the Saturday.'

'How did you get to the ground?'

'Went by bus. We met at the Coach and Horses, or was it the Three Bells, and took the bus.'

'Once inside the ground did you stay together?'

'Yea, we had seats in the stand.'

'What time did the game finish?'

'I can't really remember. I think there was a bit of injury time so I would say nine thirty or thereabouts.'

'Did you leave the ground together?'

'We walked out of the stand together, but there was a scuffle, some sort of a fight going on, and I kind of got into that, trying to break it up, like. Lenny had gone the other side of some truck. I think he waited for me, then we walked home.'

'Can you tell us the route you took?'

'Naw. It's a long time since. It might have been Warwick Avenue or,' he paused trying to recollect, 'I really don't know, we parted at Shepherds Bush but I'm not sure how we got there.'

'Any idea what time it was?'

'Ten o'clock, ten fifteen at the earliest.'

'Mr Barker had been with you throughout the evening from six pm?'

'Yea, he had.'

'Miss Paulson, the deceased, did you know her?'

'She was a regular on the market. I knew her from there just like Lenny.'

'Did you ever see Mr Barker talking to her?'

Walker shook his head, 'No, no way. Not his type.'

'Did he ever talk about her?'

'He did say once he thought she was very pretty. But he was very respectful.'

Marcus thanked him and asked him to stay where he was as he would be asked a few more questions. Cassie was pleased, he was quitting whilst they were ahead.

Howard's first question picked up on the last answer Walker had given, 'Mr Barker was very respectful; was there any reason why he should not have been?'

'Well, she was a working girl, you know what I mean.'

'She was a prostitute. You knew that; did Mr Barker?'

Cassie saw Mrs Paulson shift uneasily in her seat, close her eyes and lean her head back against the panelled wall. Hearing the unsavoury details of her daughter's life must be very distressing.

'I don't know. I didn't tell him.'

'If he knew, he would have thought he could pay for sex with her, wouldn't he?'

'Lenny didn't have that kind of money. She was a high roller.' He looked at Howard with an air of incredulity.

'Let's turn to the football game, Chelsea against Everton. Yes?'

'Yeah.' Walker was suddenly wary, looking first at Tim, then at the judge.

'Sure it was that game?'

'Yes. I don't get tickets every day.'

'I don't suppose you do. How much did you charge Mr Barker for the ticket?'

282

'I didn't. He's a mate.'

There was the noise of something hitting the floor from the direction of the jury box causing Howard to pause. Mrs Beswick hurried across the room and picked up an exhibit file that had fallen and handed it back to Deepa Nadswallah, who blushed as everyone looked at her.

'Not best buddies though, yet you gave him a ticket which you could have sold?'

'I could have, but I didn't.'

'You weren't working, the money would have come in handy, wouldn't it?'

'I gave Lenny the ticket.' Walker's face showed how exasperating he found the questions.

'How did you get the tickets?'

'I've said, a friend gave them to me.'

'Can you tell us who the friend was, this friend who just happened to give you two tickets for the stand?'

Walker looked at the judge, 'Do I have to answer that?'

Judge Crabtree asked if there was a problem about the tickets, and was told by Walker that he didn't want to give the name of the person who gave them to him, as that might get them into trouble.

'Are you saying there was a criminal offence involved?' the judge queried.

'I don't know. I'd just rather not say who gave me the tickets.'

'Mr Alsopp, do you want to pursue this line? Is it really relevant to your case?'

'I won't take it any further, My Lord.'

He didn't need to, the damage had been done; he had succeeded in making Walker appear evasive. Howard then suggested the reason Walker couldn't remember which route they had taken was because they had not walked home from the ground. Walker insisted they had, but he hadn't paid much attention to the way they had gone, and anyway he emphasised it was six months ago and he just couldn't remember.

'You got separated, when you tried to break up the fight, didn't you?'

'Yes, I've said so.'

'You didn't see him again?'

Walker shook his head, 'I think we met up again. It's a long time since, I'm not sure.'

Cassie was shaken by his reply. Tim had been very careful taking the proof from Walker, and he had been sure that he and Lenny had walked home together. She didn't look up to see what jury thought as she didn't want to betray her feelings, and she was sure her disappointment was visible.

Howard then went on to question Walker about his previous convictions and in particular his plea of not guilty to the assault charges. 'Did you give evidence in that case?' he asked.

'Yes.'

'The jury didn't believe you?'

'They convicted me.'

'They did not believe you because you lied on oath?'

'I didn't.'

'You lied on oath, just as you are now?'

'I'm not lying. Why would I?'

'You've lied to protect your friend, the man you were such good friends with that you gave him ticket to a football match.'

'I am not lying. We went to that football game together.'

'And walked home together,' said Howard Alsopp, 'the jury will have to make their minds up about that.' He gathered his gown up into a bunch behind at his back, lifted it up like a duck's tail, and sat down with a dramatic flourish of his hands as he released the material.

Chapter 37

'It could have been worse,' said Marcus as he and Cassie left the courtroom, 'but not much.'

Cassie felt despondent at the failure of their witness to repeat what he had said to Tim; not coming up to proof made the case for whichever side called the witness, whether prosecution or the defence, appear less truthful. Walker had seemed so sure he and Lenny had walked back to Shepherds Bush together, but under pressure from Howard Alsopp had changed his mind.

She had hoped Alex would have the results of the DNA tests by this point, but when she had turned on her mobile there had not been any messages. Now all the evidence was before the jury, she would have to tell Marcus about the knife, and where the information had come from. She wasn't sure how Marcus would react to her disclosure. At the worst he would be angry with her, at best displeased.

'Marcus,' she began tentatively, 'before we close our case, we should ask Howard about the knife that was found in Cotburn Square Gardens.'

Marcus swung on his heels, 'What are you talking about?'

'I've learnt, a police officer told me, a knife had been found in a compost heap in the gardens of Cotburn Square.' She went on to tell him about the pizza box with drugs in it and the description Alex had given her of the man who had been in the gardens at about the time of the murder.

'When did you find all this out?' Marcus was clearly furious with her.

'Friday evening.'

'We'll have to get hold of Howard immediately and that officer, O'Connor.'

Fortunately Howard had not left the building, and it wasn't long before Cassie was repeating the information Alex had given her. She thought DCS O'Connor was going to explode when she admitted she had been told about the knife by a police officer friend. He demanded to know who the officer was. Cassie was reluctant at first, but when he asked her if by any chance it was a Detective Constable Seymour, she conceded it was.

'Right, I'll make some enquiries about it,' he said and stormed off. Cassie felt like a naughty school girl as Marcus and Howard walked off together, leaving her alone outside Court Number 12. As she began to follow them towards the lifts her mobile rang and she looked at the text which read, 'Sample contaminated. No result yet. Alex.' Cassie swore under her breath.

Alex and Chris Dundy had been out all day, continuing their inquiries about street robberies. As soon as they returned to the CID office Alex realised she was in trouble, when the duty sergeant told her a Detective Chief Superintendent called O'Connor was chasing her, and she was to go to Kensington Police Station immediately. 'Like now, my girl. I don't know what he wants but he's spitting fire. I'll ring and say you're on your way.'

She didn't wait, but instead of going directly to Earls Court Road, she went home and picked up the mobile and the address book she had taken from the Major Incident Room.

Detective Chief Superintendent Badger O'Connor had a reputation in the Metropolitan Police Force for being a difficult man, and a misogynist; he still thought all women police officers should be restricted to working with females and juveniles. The men who worked for him were intensely loyal; he was a good thief catcher. Even as a young man his black hair had a streak of white running through it, so that when he acquired a reputation for talking nonstop until, it was said, suspects confessed just to shut him up, he been given the nickname Badger.

Alex was ushered into an office next to the room she had broken into. O'Connor was sitting behind the desk, and another, younger, man was stood leaning against a filing cabinet.

'Detective Constable Alexis Seymour, sir. I understand you asked to see me.'

'I'll go,' said the younger man. He gave her a sympathetic smile as he turned and left the room.

O'Connor was a big man, but his face and hands seemed disproportionately large despite his size. His eyes were slightly hooded and his nose was flattened, like a rugby player's or a boxer's. He didn't invite her to take the empty chair in front of the desk, but let her stand while he studied her face and ran his eyes down her body before speaking, 'I've been told you are interested in this investigation, so interested that you somehow got yourself into the room next door. Don't tell me how, I think I'd rather not know. Can you tell me why?'

'The knife, Sir.'

'Ah yes, the knife. The defence lawyers told me about the knife this afternoon. Where did it come from?'

'I told you about it, Sir, when I reported the result of the enquiries we'd made to find this Walker. It was in Cotburn Square; where the girl lived.'

'OK, OK, but what's it got to do with this investigation?'

Alex could see his fingers drumming on the desk, and his gaze was so penetrating she began to feel very uncomfortable, but she was determined not to be intimidated by him.

'I understand the murder weapon's not been found, and this knife was in the gardens.'

'Who told you that?'

O'Connor was shouting at her, and his face was contorted with anger.

'That the murder weapon had not been found? I'd rather not say, Sir.'

'I'd rather not say, Sir.' He mimicked her voice. Then he lowered his tone, 'I'm ordering you to tell me.'

'I can't, Sir. There is an informant involved. I don't want to reveal the identity.'

'An informant, is there? Registered with your Chief Inspector?'

'No, Sir.'

'No, Sir. You know the rules. All informants should be registered. You know that, don't you, don't you?'

'Yes, Sir, but…'

'No, buts. Now why are you so interested in this case? I want an explanation, no excuses. The killer is standing trial now.'

'If the knife was used to kill Shelley Paulson, the same fingerprints are on a pizza box that contained drugs, cocaine, found in the same place. She was a user wasn't she? The killer is a drug dealer not some pathetic shop assistant.'

'Don't challenge me. Who do you think you are, Jane Tennison? Of course he's the killer. Snivelling little brat, only way he was going to get his leg over. He killed her when she wouldn't oblige.'

'I've information that Miss Paulson had a minder, who was probably her drug supplier.'

'And where has this information come from that we didn't manage to uncover?'

'I've said, Sir, I'm not prepared to disclose the identity of my informant.'

O'Connor picked up a bundle of letters from his desk and then threw them back down.

'I think I know where you've got this idea from – that pesky woman defence lawyer. I bet she didn't tell you there was a fingerprint match. Her client's fingerprint on the bracelet the girl was wearing.'

For a moment Alex was unable to say anything, as she tried to work out, why Cassie had not mentioned it; it seemed unlikely Cassie would be so sure Barker was innocent if she knew about the fingerprints.

'But, if there's a match, what's the difficulty with the case?' she asked.

'It's not good enough, too faint a print, too smudged. Some of the prints are overlaid as well, so the scientist isn't prepared to say it's his. Inadmissible, no value as evidence. Now I've got the barristers on my back wanting this knife examined for bloodstains. And the bloody DNA profile has gone missing. Did you take it, along with the other items you...' he paused, ' borrowed.'

'No, Sir. I think a mistake was made and the original sent to Miss Hardman. I got it back and sent it and the knife off for comparisons.'

O'Connor leant forward in his chair, 'When will we get the result?'

'The blood was contaminated and it's unlikely forensics will be able to make a comparison for some time. They're trying to enhance the specimen now.'

'Right, so no link with your drug dealer. And there won't be. We've got the murderer. I consider the case is closed. I won't be looking for anyone else if this lad is acquitted, so that's it. And I don't like my investigation being interfered with. Now I think you'd better return those items you took, now.'

Alex took the phone and the address book out of her pockets and placed them on the desk in front of him.

'Sir, the description of the man I think is the drug supplier is very similar to the description the eyewitness gave, and he was seen a few days ago sitting in the gardens for about twenty minutes.'

'Not that old one, the killer feeling remorse returns to the scene of the crime. Really.' He put his hand to his open mouth in a pretend yawn, then shook his head. 'Mr Compton identified Barker, and that's good enough for me. This case could be lost because of your interference. You know, they'll want to bring this knife and the drugs into the case, trying to make it look as if we didn't do our job properly; hiding things from them. I haven't made up my mind what to do about you. I could have you disciplined, but your Inspector says you've the makings of a decent copper. Not sure I believe it myself, but for the moment, I'll take no action. This won't be the last you'll hear about it.

You'd better be at the Bailey tomorrow. Tell the lawyers about this knife. Now get out.'

'Yes, Sir.' Alex left as quickly as she could.

Chapter 38

'I think Mr Alsopp should explain about the evidence the Crown failed to disclose until yesterday,' Marcus told Judge Crabtree.

Howard Alsopp got to his feet, his face immobile, and when he spoke his delivery was slow as if it pained him to speak.

'It appears that about a week ago a knife was found in the garden square where Miss Paulson lived and handed to a police officer. She sent it for examination, and the fingerprints found on it matched those on a pizza box containing cocaine, which had been discovered in the same garden about five months ago, close to the date of the murder. The blade had bloodstains on it, and an attempt is now being made to compare that blood with Miss Paulson's profile. I have spoken to the officer this morning, if you wish she could give evidence about it.'

Judge Crabtree waved his hand as if to say he didn't want to hear from her. Howard went on, 'Unfortunately the sample is contaminated; it was in a compost heap for some time, possibly many weeks...'

'In a compost heap?' Judge Crabtree interjected. 'Can it be analysed at all?'

'Possibly, there is no certainty, but if the sample can be enhanced then it may be possible.'

Judge Crabtree then asked Marcus what he had to say.

'We think the jury should be discharged. If the blood on this knife is from Shelley Paulson, then it is evidence pointing to someone else other than Barker being the killer.'

293

'We think it's a bit of a long shot,' Howard said. 'The trial is in its last stages, the eyewitness has returned to the States. The knife was found in a locked garden a mile or so from the murder scene. If the trial proceeds and Mr Barker is convicted, then if, by any chance, there is a match, my learned friend has his remedy in the Court of Appeal.'

It didn't take long for the judge to decide that the trial should continue with speeches, and then he would adjourn until the next day, but if there was no result from the scientists he would proceed to sum up the case and send the jury out. 'As Howard says, you can appeal, and in the circumstances I'm sure the Court would expedite the hearing.'

Cassie was disappointed Marcus hadn't been more forceful. It was easy for Judge Crabtree to say that if the profiles matched, then they could go to the Court of Appeal. He wouldn't have to spend time waiting to hear the results of the analysis in Wormwood Scrubs or Wandsworth Prison, but, she thought, no doubt Marcus and Howard were anxious to start their next trials.

Howard Alsopp placed his papers on his lectern and rose to address the jury, his voice level, calm and reasonable, without any trace of the annoyance he had demonstrated earlier. Cassie scanned the two rows of jurors as did Howard; no doubt searching for those he hoped would be amenable to his arguments; she hoped to see how they would react to his words.

'Members of the jury, Leonard Barker is charged with the murder of Shelley Paulson on eighteenth September last. In due course His Lordship will direct you on the law, but we want to place before you the issues that you have to decide. We say issues, but really there is only one. When Mr Compton picked out

294

Leonard Barker at the identification parade, was he right? Is he a reliable witness? The defence will, no doubt, point to the time that Mr Compton took on the parade as evidence that he was unsure if the killer was there. Is that right or did he hesitate, because, as he told you, he was trying to imagine the man he saw without a beard? Did he feel he had to make an identification to help the police? You may remember the phrase he used, "If I thought the man wasn't there, I would have said so." You saw him give evidence, he was a serious and thoughtful man; as he said to my learned friend when he was being questioned about the description of the man he gave to the police officer, who attended the scene of the murder, "I knew it was very important. A young woman was dead. I had seen the man who killed her."'

He paused, not to look down at his papers, but to search again the faces of the jury. Cassie saw Brian Claxton nodding; Deepa Nadswallah met his gaze, but then looked down before writing on the papers in front of her.

Howard Alsopp continued, 'Of course a truthful witness can be unreliable and in due course we anticipate the defence will say he was clearly wrong about his identification because he has got the height wrong. In that first description he said that the man was taller than Miss Paulson. She was five foot ten and was wearing four inch heels, which they say means that the man must have been over six feet tall, and Mr Barker is five nine. No one, they say, would describe him as taller than she was. You will have to decide whether that discrepancy is such that it makes the identification unreliable, or is it just the sort of mistake a witness might make in such distressing circumstances.'

Deepa Nadswallah was still writing and so too were Colin Heap and Anna Fry. Brian Claxton was leaning forward, his elbows on the desk in front of him, his hands supporting his chin and blocking Cassie's view of Amanda Conrad.

'Mr Compton has always maintained that the killer had a beard. The defendant and his employer have given evidence that he didn't. Mr Compton was not suggesting that it was a long Old Testament type beard, or like Richard Branson, but rather some shadow round his cheeks, which he thought was a beard. Could it have simply been a day-old stubble?'

It wasn't the prosecution's best point and Cassie thought the reference to Richard Branson by Howard Alsopp sounded rather stilted. He didn't do 'man of the people' very well.

'The case doesn't stop there, though, does it, because Mr Compton picked out a man who admitted he was in Holland Park on the night of the murder. Not only did Mr Barker say he was in the park, but he knew Miss Paulson. We say it was no coincidence that he was the man identified by Mr Compton. He was identified because he was there.'

Now he was dealing with the real crux of the Crown's case, this was the argument the prosecution had to win. Cassie concentrated again on the jury panel, attempting to assess their response to this analysis of the case. She found it impossible, so engrossed were they in Howard's words that their faces gave nothing away.

'Mr Barker says he told the police he was in the park because he believed they had a recording which showed him in the Walk. Yet now he tells you he went to a football match at Stamford Bridge, something he had forgotten when he was interviewed, keen Chelsea supporter that he is. Does that ring true or not? Particularly when his solicitor told him there was no video evidence.'

Howard paused, his eyes sweeping the jurors, until they lighted on Brian Claxton. He addressed the next part of his argument directly at him. 'He says that he couldn't remember the date of the Chelsea–Everton game at the time of the interview, but he also says that he learnt of her death when one of his fellow employees brought the Evening Standard back to the shop the next day. And as we know, that copy of the newspaper was produced during his interview and,' Howard paused, and picked up the paper, which he had placed by the side of his lectern, and waved it at the jury, showing them the front and back pages, 'and on the back of the same paper is the report of the game Barker says he went to. We suggest that the death of Shelley Paulson would be linked indelibly with that football match. Would he not remember where he was the night she was killed, when the game and the report of her murder were in the very newspaper from which he learnt of her death?'

Brian Claxton sat upright and nodded vigorously. He wasn't the only one who appeared to agree with that comment. However, Cassie could now see Amanda Conrad, and she was looking down, her head resting on the fist of her left hand.

'Then what of Edwin Walker, the man with the rather strange nickname, Hinds; he has given evidence in support of that alibi. A convicted thief and drug dealer, who has lied on oath before. Do you believe his account of giving an expensive ticket to a friend for nothing? Not his best buddy, was the way he described

297

the defendant. Mr Walker was certainly at that game but we say Leonard Barker was not. He did go to the vicinity of the ground, his Oyster Card shows that, but that doesn't mean he went to the game. Even if he did, he could have caught the bus back to Kensington High Street, just by the entrance to Holland Walk, in time for the fateful meeting with Shelley Paulson. Walker wasn't sure they had walked home together.'

Cassie grimaced, after the risks she had taken to locate Walker, he had let them down. It was a blow to their case, if the jury thought the alibi was concocted they would probably convict Lenny. She expected Howard to say more about the alibi but he didn't press home the point.

'Unlike so many television programmes there is little forensic evidence to assist you in this case. The Crown says that is really down to the lapse of time between the offence and Mr Barker's arrest, certainly as far as his clothes are concerned. There are a few fibres matching a T-shirt of Mr Barker's, but His Honour will direct you on how you must approach that. The fingernail scrapings from Miss Paulson have the DNA of some stranger in them. But there is no evidence of a struggle that would point to that being the DNA of her assailant, so we say it does not exonerate Mr Barker. The DNA may have had many sources particularly when one takes into account the victim's lifestyle. We say it's irrelevant to this case. Ignore it.'

Cassie had been curious about how he would deal with the lack of forensic evidence. Would he mention it at all, or as he had, tell the jury it was of no consequence? There was so little reaction from the jury, she was unable to form any view as to their reaction to Howard's observations.

Howard then moved to his final comments. 'We submit he approached her and when she rejected him, he grabbed hold of her. She tried to fight him off and in anger he stabbed her. The identification by Mr Compton is one you can rely on and you can return a verdict of guilty.'

Howard Alsopp turned towards David Jennings, who nodded, then Howard picked up his papers shuffled them, sat down and put them underneath the lectern.

Judge Crabtree picked up his notebook and rose, saying to the jury, 'We'll hear from the defence this afternoon.

Chapter 39

Alex left the Old Bailey and took the tube from Blackfriars to Kensington High Street. Throughout the train journey she mused about what to do next. DCS O'Connor would wait until after the verdict to decide whether or not she should be disciplined; if Barker was convicted he would forget about her misdemeanours, but if he was acquitted, she would be in real trouble, disciplined and probably demoted back to uniform, unless Shelley Paulson's drug dealer was the real killer. She really needed to find him. She ran through the various people who might know who he was and where he could be found. Annie Devine was the most likely candidate. Alex didn't know where Annie lived or worked, but probably she was on the Drug Squad's database.

Alex used her mobile to contact Mel Haskins and asked him if he had any information that might help her find Annie.

'Yes, our Annie. She does a bit of dealing, nothing too serious. Surprisingly, she manages to hold down a job, works as a hairdresser.'

'Do you know where?'

Mel asked her to hold on a minute and she heard him tapping on the keys of his computer, then he gave her the address and telephone number of a beauty salon.

The premises were in Kensington Church Street, just a short walk away. It didn't take long to find the hairdresser's, which was called 'Cut and Come Again', on the first floor above a shop selling last season's clothes. She went up the stairs into a waiting room.

The front of the receptionist's counter had pale pink imitation leather, pinned with studs across it, and a blonde haired girl, probably about seventeen years old, sitting behind it, filing her nails. There was a strong smell of shampoo, hair colouring and overheating hairdryers. Alex stood at the desk for a few seconds before the girl looked up and asked if she could help.

'I could do with my hair trimming, and I've been recommended an Annie Devine. Is she free at the moment?'

The young woman peered down at a diary, which from where Alex was stood appeared to be unmarked. 'Do you want a wash and blow dry as well?' the young woman asked.

'Yes, of course.'

The girl smiled, 'I think we can help you today. We are quiet.' She got up and walked through into a much bigger room, which had three hairdresser's chairs along one wall, and at the far end a row of sinks. Stood over one of them, and rubbing her hands energetically through the soapy hair of a woman leaning with her head back over the basin, was Annie Devine. Alex followed the teenage receptionist towards Annie, who looked up at her.

'This lady would like a cut, shampoo and blow dry,' the girl said.

'Really,' Annie replied.

'Sure,' Alex said quickly, 'Why not?' and she took off her jacket and handed it to the receptionist, who pointed her to one of the chairs. Through the large mirror in front of her, Alex watched Annie as she continuing washing the woman's hair. From time to time Annie looked towards Alex, her face anxious as she chatted to the customer.

301

As she wrapped a towel round the woman's head, she said, 'I'll just be a minute,' then she walked over to Alex, stood behind her and looked at her in the glass.

'What can I do for you today?' Annie asked, her voice quavering a little.

'I'd like my hair trimmed, and then I want some information from you.'

'I'll just need to finish off my client, then I'll be right with you.'

Alex scrutinised Annie, as she and the customer talked. She could hear their conversation from where she was sat, the usual topics of holidays, boyfriends and the latest events in East Enders. Annie appeared nervous, glancing towards Alex as she fashioned the woman's hair. That job over she turned towards Alex, placed a dark blue cotton cape over Alex's shoulders and took out the elastic band that held Alex's hair back.

'How much do you want cutting off?' Annie said.

'Not much. Can you just tidy it up?'

Annie ran her hands under the long blonde hair, spreading it out. 'You've nice hair, Miss Seymour. Are you sure you want it cut?'

When she said she did, Annie waved her over to the sink and washed Alex's hair. Once Alex was back sitting in front of the mirror, she asked Annie how long she had been working at the salon.

'About eighteen months.' Annie chewed her lower lip as she worked.

'Have you been to the Mango Club recently?' Alex asked.

'Not since that time, the one you know about.' Annie kept her voice low and looked round quickly to see if anyone was listening, but the only other person in the salon was the receptionist and she was still busy with a nail file.

'Annie, you remember that night, the other woman talked about the murder of Shelley Paulson? Did you know Shelley?'

'I would have recognised her if I'd seen her.'

'Nothing else? You don't know who supplied her with drugs?'

'I never did, Miss Seymour.' Annie had stopped wielding her scissors and was staring at Alex in the mirror.

'I'm not suggesting you did. But do you know who she got her drugs from?'

'No.' Annie tugged at Alex's hair, checked it was level and then began to move away to get a hairdryer. Alex grabbed her arm and held her close to the chair.

'I know there's a guy dealing around here, goes to the Nightjar and the Mango selling. Rides around on a push bike, like he's delivering pizzas. Tall with a birthmark on his left cheek.'

Annie pulled away, 'You're hurting me.' She rubbed her arm and went off. She returned a few moments later, plugged in the dryer and began to blow dry Alex's hair. The noise of the hairdryer made conversation impossible.

When her hair was dry and the dryer turned off, Alex asked her if she knew anyone who fitted that description. Annie flicked a comb through Alex's hair, removed the cape and asked her if she liked the hair cut.

Alex said it was fine and stood up. The two women stood face to face. 'You owe me a favour, Annie. I think you know who this man is and I want you to tell me, or...' Her voice was low and threatening.

'Or what?'

'I might decide a search of your flat would be a good idea. You never know what I might find there.' Alex forced a slow smile across her face, hoping Annie would believe the implicit threat.

'You'd plant something on me?' Annie spat the words out.

'I didn't say that, but I'm sure a visit to your place would get a result, eventually. As I said, you owe me a favour. What if my friend was right? This guy could be the real killer.'

Annie paused, looked up at the ceiling and then at Alex. 'Try Hugo Duff. He does a bit of supplying, but I can't help anymore.'

'Have you bought drugs from him?'

'Once or twice.'

'How did you contact him?'

'I rang a mobile number.'

'Always the same one?'

'No. He switches between several phones.' Alex's face dropped. Annie added, 'If you have a number, leave a message and he usually rings back within an hour or so.'

'OK. Thanks. Take care.'

Now, she decided she would go and see the witness who lived on Campden Hill Road, Mrs Haldane. It was a long shot she would remember anything about the man on the bike, but it was worth trying. It might help to put this man, Hugo Duff, if Annie was being truthful, near the scene of the murder.

Muriel Haldane lived in what the inhabitants like to call Garden Flats. Alex stepped lightly down the short flight of steps to the front door and rang the bell. She heard a dog barking. What was the animal's name?

Hazlitt, that was it. The door was opened by an elderly lady, dressed in black trousers and a yellow cardigan.

Alex smiled at the woman and said, 'Mrs Haldane, I'm Detective Constable Alex Seymour. Can I come in?' Mrs Haldane smiled back, got hold of the collar of a small terrier and told the animal to be quiet, before stepping back from the door and inviting Alex in.

Mrs Haldane led the way along a corridor to a sitting room flooded with light from floor to ceiling windows. The garden beyond was a green haven, with a display of daffodils and primroses brightening the borders of a small lawn. She pointed to a chair covered in pale green linen, and invited Alex to sit down.

'Now, how can I help you?' Mrs Haldane asked.

'I'd just like to run over the events of September eighteenth last year. The night the young woman was murdered in Holland Walk,' Alex said.

Muriel Haldane nodded. 'It's quite a while since. I'm not sure how much I can remember.' She looked worried. 'Is it important?' she asked.

'I'm not sure. It may depend on what you can tell me. When you spoke to a uniformed officer initially, you said you left the flat about nine forty-five.' Alex paused.

'That's right. I usually give myself about fifteen or twenty minutes to walk the dog round the block, before the ten o'clock news.'

'So you left here about nine forty, nine forty-five. What route did you take?'

'I turned left out of the door and across the road to the row of shops by the pub, the Windsor Castle. Do you know it? It's quite rowdy in the evenings.'

'From there?'

'I walked down Peel Street towards Kensington Church Street, then I turned right, walking towards the High Street, turned right again into Bedford Gardens, and walked back towards home.'

'You said at the time you had to wait to cross Campden Hill Road?'

'Yes. I think I'd heard the siren of the police car. It must have been turning from Holland Road into Campden Hill Road. I certainly looked towards Notting Hill. I couldn't see it, but I didn't want to risk crossing the road so I continued to wait. I find it very difficult to tell which way the cars are coming from the siren. I looked left towards Kensington and saw a man on a bike, pedal bike, coming up the hill towards me. He was pedalling furiously. Then the police car came past very fast. Isn't that what I told the other officer?'

'Yes,' said Alex, who had wanted her to repeat what she had seen to get her to picture the scene again, before she asked her next question. 'Can you remember what the man looked like?'

Mrs Haldane shut her eyes, trying to visualise the man. Alex waited. 'No, no I can't. Wait, there was something strange about his face, a dirty mark or something.'

Chapter 40

During the luncheon adjournment, Cassie tried to contact Alex, who she thought might be at the Bailey, but she was not answering her mobile and no one in the CID office at Notting Hill knew where she was.

When the court had reassembled for the afternoon, Marcus got to his feet, his face alight with enthusiasm. He turned to face the jury, relaxed, leaning against his lectern, where the notes they had prepared together were spread out. Cassie knew this to be one of the most important parts, if not the most important part, of their case; their opportunity to persuade these twelve men and women that the identification was wrong, and the alibi evidence may be true. The purpose behind every question both in chief- and in cross-examination had been to provide the content of this speech. She always listened carefully to jury speeches, knowing how different barristers could be in their approach; some lectured the jury, some made juries laugh, others sounded like they were preaching. She liked to think of it as a one-sided conversation, the sort one might have with a neighbour over the garden wall or sitting over a cup of tea. Marcus Pike had a reputation as a formidable jury advocate, and she had never been in a case with him before, so she was eager to listen to him.

He began in the time-honoured way, 'Members of the jury,' and then launched into the body of his speech, 'as you have already been told, the issue in this case is whether Mr Compton is correct when he said that he saw Lenny Barker, in Holland Walk, stab Shelley Paulson. Are you sure he was right when he selected Lenny at the identification parade? That is the question you have to ask yourselves. If you are certain he is right then you will convict, if you think he was wrong, or may be wrong.' Marcus emphasised the word 'may' and went on, 'if that is the conclusion you come to then you must acquit, because you would not be sure, you would have some doubt in your mind, and that allows you only one verdict, not guilty.'

Cassie scanned the jury, looking for reaction to this explanation of the law. Brian Claxton looked puzzled, Deepa Nadswallah was writing furiously, but the rest did not react in any visible way.

'What do we say about that identification? First, as the prosecution have already told you, you will look carefully at the circumstances in which Mr Compton saw the murderer. Look again at the photographs of the lane; try to imagine the same scene at night and with leaves on the trees, shadows falling across the couple as they argued.' Marcus spoke carefully, his voice gentle as if he was reading a bedtime story, then his voice strengthened.

Deepa Nadswallah stopped writing, opened the bundle of photographs, flicked through them, and then looked intently at the open page.

'There are two details of his initial description which we say should make you question his accuracy.' Marcus paused and asked for Exhibit 2 to be handed to him. Mrs Beswick searched on the exhibit table, found the brown bag marked in felt-tip pen with a large 2, and took it to Marcus, who carefully opened it and took out the pair of red high-heeled shoes. He took one of them in his hand by the toe, turning the heel towards the jury. He continued to hold it as he spoke, the jury's eyes fixed on the shoe as he held it steadily in his hands. 'Lenny Barker is five foot nine, Miss Paulson was five foot ten, but she was wearing these high heels when she was killed, making her over six feet tall. Mr Compton said in the first description to the police and later in a written statement that the murderer was taller than his victim.' Marcus waited for a second, allowing his words to be absorbed and then put the shoe down carefully on the bench next to the other one. The jurors' eyes followed his actions. The shoe, the colour of blood, stood defiantly upright, glowing like a jewel against the black of the silk's gown, and for a brief moment of time, Marcus allowed the jurors to gaze at it.

'He doesn't say the man he saw was over six feet tall. It's a comparison he makes between killer and deceased. We know precisely Miss Paulson's height and we know the height of these heels.' He pointed to the shoe. Cassie was impressed by the theatricality of his actions, which were intended to etch on the jurors' minds the image of those shoes.

'We say that discrepancy alone should make you doubt the accuracy of his identification.'

Colin Heap and the 'two As' nodded as if agreeing with the point Marcus had made. Brian Claxton continued to look perplexed and put his head down, avoiding Cassie's eyes.

'The Crown says it is too much of a coincidence that Mr Compton identified a man who admitted he was in the Holland Park on the night of the murder. Lenny Barker says he agreed he was there, because at the beginning of September, from time to time, he went to the park to watch football on the sports ground at the southern end, and he had heard the police talk about a recording made by cameras on the walls of Aubrey House. He believed he had been photographed. It seemed obvious to him that he must have been there. He wasn't asked, indeed there was no reason to do so, if he had been at the football match at Stamford Bridge. What he had forgotten was the date of the game against Everton, not the game itself.'

A look of disbelief crossed Brian Claxton's face. He was not going to be persuaded of Lenny Barker's innocence. Cassie picked up her packet of mints and carefully removed one, trying not to make a sound.

'You may think that he should have said he was not sure he was in the park, but consider the circumstances: arrested at dawn, made to stand naked, taken to the police station; all very distressing, particularly for someone who had never been arrested before. As Sergeant Dean told you, Barker was dazed and stunned; he overheard the conversation between Mr O'Connor and some other detective about this tape. The evidence on that is not contested. What was he expected to think?' Marcus had dropped his voice again, sounding conspiratorial.

'We suggest he was meant to believe there was evidence on the recording linking him to the murder, or at least, showing he was in the vicinity. That was why he said he was in the park.'

He paused again and surveyed the jurors' faces; the 'two As' were wide-eyed, clearly drinking in his every word. Deepa Nadswallah was scribbling furiously.

'We say that the most compelling fact that calls into question the identification of Lenny Barker is the lack of forensic evidence to link him with Shelley Paulson, or the scene of the murder.' Marcus stressed the words 'lack of forensic evidence' and then, raising his voice slightly, repeated the idea. 'Despite extensive searches, nothing significant has been found. A few fibres that could have come from any one of thousands of sweat-shirts is the best the Crown can come up with. Nothing on his clothes or bedding, nothing at the scene; all tests were negative.' Marcus paused and looked up and down the two rows of jurors. Some met his gaze, others looked down at their papers or turned towards the judge.

'There was one negative test,' Marcus said, with some emphasis, 'one negative test, that should have been positive. The DNA of the scrapings from Miss Paulson's fingernails did not match Lenny Barker's DNA. She had DNA from some other person under her nails, and we suggest it was that of the killer. Remember Mr Compton's evidence, Shelley Paulson scratching like a cat at the face of her assailant.'

He took a moment or two to let that idea take hold with the jury and then continued, 'One of the curious features of this case is the meetings between Rose Cummings, that undercover police officer, and Lenny. She was instructed to try and get further information that may assist the case against him. Instead he talked about football, and told her he went to the Chelsea–Everton game. Later research done by my very able junior…' Marcus turned towards her and waved a hand in her direction; all the jurors looked at her and she met their gaze, her face open and without any doubt.

He continued, '…established the match was the same night as the murder.'

'The prosecution suggest that even if he was at the game, he could have got back to Holland Walk in time to kill Shelley Paulson. We say that is nonsense; it relies on him leaving the ground very quickly and catching a bus immediately. Knowing London

311

Transport, when did a bus ever turn up so conveniently?'

Quite a number smiled at that comment, as it coincided with their own experiences. Cassie had in the past used the same technique, making arguments with which the jury could identify; the ordinary events they would all have encountered.

'If Mr Barker walked back home, as he says, and as Mr Walker confirms, then he has an alibi. Whatever the prosecution suggest about Mr Walker's truthfulness, yes, he is a convicted thief and drug supplier, we submit he is telling the truth, confirming the spontaneous account given to the undercover policewoman.'

Cassie caught Colin Heap's eye and smiled at him, but instead of smiling back, he gazed around the room, until he focused on the red shoes by Marcus's right hand.

'If you come to the conclusion that the account of going to the match at Stamford Bridge is true, you will acquit, or if you think it may be true then you will also acquit. Members of the jury, that is what we invite you to do. Thank-you.'

Marcus sat down and turned to Cassie, 'OK, I didn't leave anything out, did I?'

'No, it was fine.' She looked up at the public gallery, where Mrs Barker and Jane were leaning forward, and nodded at them. Mrs Paulson, sitting almost directly underneath them, whatever she was thinking, was as inscrutable as she had been for most of the trial.

Chapter 41

Alex held the phone close to her ear, whilst it rang and rang. After a few seconds that seemed like minutes, the answering service kicked in. A male voice invited her to leave a message. She had rehearsed what she was going to say if her call was answered, whether by Duff or by a machine.

Keeping her voice level she said, 'Hi Hugo, I'm Alex, I've been given your name by a friend from the Nightjar. He says you may be able to supply a packet for me. Can you give me a bell?' She gave her mobile number before pressing the button to cut off the line.

Now she would wait and hope Duff returned the call. It was just after seven pm. Annie said he normally called back after an hour or so. She didn't like waiting, and didn't know what to do. She checked the TV listing for the day, but nothing grabbed her attention. She wandered into the kitchen and opened the fridge, perhaps having something to eat would help pass the time, but the shelves were virtually empty. There was a pack of beer, some rather mouldy cheese, a limp lettuce and a half full can of baked beans. In one of the cupboards she found a tin of tuna; she took it out and opened it. There was a baguette in the freezer; she looked at its use by date. Hopefully it was still edible.

While she waited for the oven to heat up, she took the last but one bottle of wine from the wine rack and poured a glass. Just as she took her first sip, the telephone rang. She picked it up and said, 'Hello. Who's that?'

'Alex, it's Chris. I've been looking for you. What're you doing?'

'Chris, I can't talk at the moment. I'm waiting for a call.'

'Alex, what have you done?'

She put the phone down, and went back to the kitchen, put the bread in the oven and set the timer. She found some mayonnaise, past its use by date, and mixed it with the tuna. Returning to the lounge she sat down with the Evening Standard and her glass of wine, waiting for the baguette to cook. She found it difficult to concentrate on the paper, so she got up and went to the window. Of all the crazy things she had done this was probably the most absurd and dangerous, but if she was right, or rather if Cassie was right, then Detective Chief Superintendent O'Connor would not have her disciplined. She noticed something moving in the street below her, a car manoeuvred into a parking space and Chris Dundy got out, looked up towards her flat before walking in the direction of the apartment block. A second or so later the front door bell sounded. Alex pushed the buzzer that opened the street door and left her own door ajar.

She heard Chris bound up the stairs and burst into the room. 'What the hell are you up to?'

She shrugged her shoulders at him. 'It's probably better you don't know.'

'It's something to do with this knife? Yes?'

Alex shrugged her shoulders.

'Have you tried to contact this drug supplier?'

'Yes. I'm waiting for him to call back.'

'Christ, Alex, are you mad?'

'Probably, but I'm in it up to here.' She drew a line across her throat with her forefinger and then said, 'O'Connor is hopping mad. Forensics have to do more work enhancing the blood from the knife before they can get a profile from it. I'm sure this drug dealer is the killer. He's called Duff by the way, Hugo Duff. That kid standing trial isn't the right man.'

Chris asked her why she was so sure he was the killer. She gave him the evidence she had unearthed so far.

'That's not much. Drugs found in a pizza box, a similarity in the descriptions and some old bag who saw a man on a cycle soon after the murder. Oh and the victim ate a pizza three times the week she was killed. Great. The lawyers would throw the file back at you. It's pretty flimsy compared with a positive ID. And what are you going to do if this Duff character rings?'

'I'm going to meet him, and see if I can get him to offer me drugs, and then arrest him. Once we have him back at the station we can take samples for DNA. The girl had skin under her nails. Scratched the man, I guess. If I'm right it should match.'

The timer on the oven went off and she got up to go into the kitchen. Before she got through the door, the telephone rang, she picked it up and said 'Hello.'

'Is that Alex?'

'Yep.' She pushed the loud button so that Chris could hear what was said.

'This is Hugo. You rang about a packet. Who gave you my number?'

'Annie Devine, she said she'd had stuff from you.' She had hoped he wouldn't ask who had given her the number, she knew giving Annie's name was a risk, but she couldn't exactly say she had got it from Shelley Paulson's mobile.

'Annie, sure. Do you want the same?'

'Yes. That's fine.'

'I'm sure I can find you some, I can deliver.'

Chris shook his head. Alex nodded at him and then said, 'No, I have a problem here. What about a caff somewhere?'

'There's a coffee place on Notting Hill Gate. Fancies. Do you know it?'

'Yes, yes.'

'Meet me there in half an hour.'

The phone went dead.

Alex took a deep breath. 'Christ, the bread,' she exclaimed and ran towards the kitchen.

'I didn't know you could cook,' said Chris following her.

She pulled the baguette out of the oven, opened the refuse bin and tipped the burnt stick into it. 'Clearly I can't.'

Alex went to her bedroom and began rifling through her wardrobe until she found a well cut jacket she hadn't worn for some considerable time. 'What's with the jacket?' Chris asked.

'Police officers don't usually wear Armani.'

'Alex, this is stupid, I don't think you should go.'

She put her jacket on, 'Are you going to stop me?'

'No, I'm coming with you. I don't want to miss the fun.'

'You drive and go in first. I'll go on foot. He may be watching to see if I arrive alone. He may not make the contact if I'm with someone else.'

'He may not anyway. If he's as clever as you say, and he smells trouble.'

Quarter of an hour later Alex pushed open the door of Fancies, bought a large latte, and walked to the rear of the coffee shop where she took off her jacket, placed it on a chair, and sat down facing the entrance. She could see Chris sitting nearer to the window. He had a

316

newspaper open, behind which he was watching both the entrance to the shop and the customers already inside.

Alex looked round at the other people scattered around the oblong room. A group of four girls all under sixteen were sitting round a table, one of them produced some brightly coloured underwear, still bearing sales tags, from a plastic bag, and they began to giggle. A young couple sitting at another table were arguing, trying to keep their voices low, the woman's arms folded across the front of her grey coat, hugging herself. There was a man in his fifties, wearing a business suit, drinking a cup of black coffee. He turned to look at Alex and smiled at her. For a moment she thought perhaps he was Hugo Duff, and she had been wrong, but he made no move towards her. She looked back towards Chris, suddenly grateful for his bulky presence. She noticed her hand was shaking slightly as she lifted the cup to her lips and sipped her coffee slowly. She tried to keep her body relaxed, but could feel the muscles in her legs and arms tensing, as if she was getting ready to run. Her eyes flickered round the room like a cat on the hunt, watching and waiting to pounce.

She noticed Chris had shifted slightly in his chair, she saw him fold his newspaper and nod slightly at her. Just as she turned her full attention on the front of the shop, the young woman who had been arguing got up and walked swiftly towards the door, her long grey coat billowing out, blocking the view. Alex could hear the hiss of the coffee machines, and as if a long way away, the chatter of the teenagers.

The young woman reached the door, and, over her shoulder, Alex could see a tall young man, waiting for

317

the woman in the grey coat to leave the coffee shop. Alex stiffened as the man let the woman in grey pass, and then, as he hesitated at the entrance, she saw the large birthmark on his left cheek. Elated, she averted her gaze and looked at the four teenagers as they babbled on.

She felt she was waiting for minutes before someone said, 'Alex.'

She turned to look at the man, forcing a smile to her face.

'It is you, how nice to see you again.' He spoke with pleasant drawl, the words like a caress.

'Hugo. What a coincidence,' she replied going along with the pretence of friendship.

Hugo Duff sat down next to her and placed a brown paper sack on the table.

'How did you know I was Alex?'

'You're the only woman on her own. It had to be you.' He looked at her appreciatively. 'You asked about a packet.' He nodded towards the bag.

'Yes. The usual, is it?' Alex leaned forward to touch it. Duff took her hand and stroked it, pulling her away from the bag, his eyes flirting with her, but the pressure of his fingers increasing. She looked down, so that he would not see the fear in her eyes and pulled her hand away from his grip.

'What's your hurry? Got a date?'

'Sort of. I'm on my way to dinner with some friends,' she looked at her watch, 'I'm late already.'

He leant back in his chair and put one foot on his knee. 'Do you work round here?'

'No, I'm not working at the moment.'

'You like nice things, I can see.' He turned her jacket over and read the label. 'Expensive. I assume you can afford it.'

'Just about. One never has enough, does one?' She forced a laugh, telling herself to remain calm. 'I will have to go in a few minutes,' she said as she opened her handbag, and took out her wallet, then placed two twenty pound notes on the table between them. Duff nodded, opened the paper bag and took out a small plastic wrapped parcel. He placed it on the table. 'They're the real thing,' he said.

Alex looked him full in the face, holding his gaze as she saw Chris Dundy approaching. She put her hand in her pocket and pulled out her warrant card, but kept it concealed. When Chris was stood next to their table, she pushed it towards Duff, then stood up as Chris put his hand on Duff's shoulder. 'You're under arrest,' said Chris.

Hugo Duff looked up at Chris and then at Alex. 'Christ, what's a charmer like you doing in that firm?'

'It pays the bills. Hugo Duff, I'm arresting you for supplying classified drugs. You don't have to say anything but it may harm your defence if you do not mention when questioned something which you later rely on in court. Anything you do say may be given in evidence.'

Duff shrugged his shoulders as Chris snapped the plastic cuffs on his wrists and Alex picked up the brown paper sack and the small plastic bag.

Once he was back at the station, he asked to see his solicitor. 'Sure,' said Alex, 'and while you wait here we'll search your flat.' He didn't respond.

Hugo Duff's basement flat was a few minutes' drive from the police station. Alex let herself and Chris in with the keys she had taken from Duff's property. On the key fob was an additional key, which looked as though it would fit the gate to the gardens in Cotburn Square. While Chris searched the sitting room, Alex took out a pair of latex gloves and began to search the bedroom.

There was a fitted wardrobe, a chest of drawers and two small bedside tables, the double bed was unmade. Alex began with the chest of drawers, opening them up and taking out T-shirts, an assortment of underpants, socks and some worn swimming trunks. In the wardrobe she found a collection of designer jeans, a couple of pairs of chinos, a Paul Smith suit and a dozen neatly pressed shirts. She went through the pockets of all the garments as she took them from the cupboard. She pulled a variety of sweaters from the shelves, mainly cashmere. There was a bag of sportswear pushed onto the floor along with a collection of trainers and leather shoes. She pulled them out and felt into the toes of each. The track suit and top she emptied out onto the bed.

'Found anything?' Chris said from the doorway of the bedroom.

'No. Have you?'

'Not a thing. The place is as clean as a whistle. He doesn't keep his stuff here.'

Alex stood in the bedroom looking round, a frustrated expression on her face. 'Help me pull this off,' she said as she began tugging at the edge of the mattress. Chris came into the room and the two of them pulled it from the bed, but there was nothing between it and the divan.

'That's it. We'll have to do him for the supply of four tabs of E and wait for the lab to come back with the DNA results. Damn.' Alex sank back on the edge of the bed. 'I hope the custody sergeant doesn't release him on bail, or we'll lose him.'

Chapter 42

Marcus had informed Cassie he was beginning another trial, and he would be leaving her on her own after he had made his speech. She wasn't surprised, most silks started one trial before the last one had finished; it was one of the ways they kept their earnings up. She went to see Lenny in the cells before court began, and told him Marcus would not be there, and reassured him that if there were any problems he could be brought very quickly. Lenny nodded at her. During the couple of weeks he had spent in custody his cheeks had thinned and his nose seemed more prominent. His hair was shorter and the curls had been tamed to a wave, although it was still dark and thick. He was much paler and, today, his eyes were dull, as if he had lost the will to fight.

Cassie remained sitting with him although there was nothing left to say. His hands were on the table between them, and she reached over and took his left hand in hers. He looked up at her, 'I didn't kill her. Do you believe me?' She couldn't tell him it didn't matter what she thought, what mattered was what the jury concluded, so she said what he wanted to hear, then told him it was time she went back upstairs. He nodded, got up and walked out into the corridor that led back to the cells. Cassie followed him as he dragged his feet along the concrete floor.

She took the lift to the third floor and dashed along the broad corridor outside the court. Howard Alsopp and David Jennings were already in their seats as she came through the door. She had no sooner sat down than the jury were led into court, by Mrs Beswick.

Cassie watched as they took their seats. Anna Fry pushed a straw shopping basket under the bench in front of her, sat back in her seat and looked round the room. Amanda Conrad put a black handbag down, took off her coat and, once she was seated, pulled the exhibit files towards her and placed them in a neat row. Colin Heap took his seat, looked towards Cassie and grinned at her. She smiled back. She so wanted him to be the foreman. Brian Claxton slumped down and with an exasperated look on his face pulled a copy of a tabloid newspaper from his pocket and began to read. Deepa Nadswallah took out a pair of glasses, then, like Amanda Conrad, sorted out the exhibit bundles, before putting a notepad and pencil within easy reach.

There was tap on the judges' door, announcing Judge Crabtree was about to come in. Mrs Beswick shouted, 'Be upstanding in court.' Everyone rose as the door opened and a man in a velvet frock coat, britches and tights, carrying a golden mace over his shoulder, strode three long paces onto the dais, stopped and stood still facing the assembled court. Judge Crabtree followed. He ambled to his chair, stopped, bowed to the mace bearer, who turned and left the room, then to everyone else in the courtroom before sitting down and opening his red notebook. This was one of those ceremonies that reminded Cassie of a pantomime, bringing a sense of the ridiculous to the courtroom – the mace bearer dressed like a character in Dick Whittington, the black gowns and wigs from an earlier century – yet they were dealing with a serious crime that had been committed within the last few months.

'Members of the jury,' the judge started, as he turned to face them. 'Let me begin by describing our respective roles in this trial. I am the judge of the law and you are the judges of the facts. We try this case together. You will consider all the evidence and decide on the basis of those facts, what occurred on the night of the eighteenth of September. You will then apply the law as I direct you to the facts as you have determined them to be, and that way you will arrive at your verdict.

'So what are the directions of law that you must apply? The first is this. The burden of proving the case rests with the prosecution from first to last. The defendant, Mr Barker, doesn't have to prove anything. In this case he has given evidence and called an alibi witness, but it is for the Crown to disprove that alibi, not for him to prove it.'

Deepa Nadswallah was trying to watch the judge and write down what he was saying, as was Amanda Conrad. All of them appeared to be concentrating on his words; Cassie assumed they were looking for clues that might assist them with their verdict. Sometimes it wasn't the words a judge used which were important but the way he said it, his facial expressions and his body language.

'To what standard must the prosecution prove their case? Well, they must prove it to a high standard. They must make you sure the defendant is guilty, anything less will not do.'

While Cassie listened attentively to the judge, she continued to watch the jury, scrutinising their expressions in the hope they would reveal their responses to the judge's directions.

'Murder is the unlawful killing of another person with intent to kill, or to cause grievous bodily harm. In this case you will have no difficulty in coming to the conclusion that Shelley Paulson was unlawfully killed

324

by someone, that is, the blow was not in self-defence. The issue for you is who killed her.'

Amanda Conrad stopped writing and put the end of her pen in her mouth, her lips turned down, a slightly bemused look on her face, puzzled, Cassie assumed, by the mention, for the first time, of self-defence.

'The real issue for you to decide in this case is, was Mr Compton right when he identified Mr Barker as the man he saw killing Miss Paulson? Identification issues are ones the courts have to deal with frequently, and experience has shown that even the best witnesses can make an incorrect identification. A witness can be very convincing, but still be wrong.'

He continued by reminding them of the evidence given by Mr Compton; he stressed that what conclusions they came to were matters for them. Cassie relaxed a little. So far the judge was being even handed. She would have preferred him to say James Compton might have been mistaken rather than suggesting the delay in selecting Lenny was because he was over-anxious, but so far, his review of the evidence was fair.

'Mr Alsopp, on behalf of the prosecution, has pointed out three pieces of evidence that he says supports that identification. The coincidence that Mr Barker knew Miss Paulson, the fibres on her cardigan that come from a sweatshirt similar to one owned by the defendant, and the admission by Mr Barker that he was in Holland Park on the night of the murder. You must decide if they do indeed support the identification. You can convict without any supporting evidence, but you may think it is not wise to do so.'

Amanda Conrad and Deepa Nadswallah both stopped writing and looked up at the judge, their faces creased, as if they did not understand what he had just said about supporting evidence.

'The Crown say Mr Barker knew Miss Paulson, or perhaps it is fairer to say could recognise her as a customer in the shop where he worked, indeed may have served her a day or so before her death. Does that really support the identification by Mr Compton? It appears likely that in a collection of young men taken from the streets around Notting Hill and the Portobello Market a number of them would have known her by sight, as he did.'

Colin Heap grinned at that comment. Cassie assumed he was thinking that he too would have remembered the living Shelley Paulson, as he would never forget the dead woman.

'However, the match of fibres may be supporting evidence although there are very many similar garments, so I would urge you to treat that with some caution, but together with other evidence it may be of assistance.'

Cassie looked up at the jury and saw Deepa Nadswallah nodding at the judge's comments. Brian Claxton's eyes were half closed, but he had opened them as the judge mentioned the fibres.

'Mr Barker did tell the police that he was in Holland Park on the night of the murder. An admission he now retracts. You may want to look at his explanation for saying that, and I shall refer to that again in a moment.'

From the gallery a women's voice shouted, 'He wasn't there,' followed by the noise of a scuffle as the attendants rushed towards the speaker. Cassie looked up as Mrs Barker was pushed back into her seat. Judge Crabtree waited until it was quiet again.

'But that now brings me to the alibi evidence. Mr Barker now says he was at a football match at Stamford Bridge on the Fulham Road with his friend Edwin Walker, Hinds. No doubt some of you know where the ground is. The Crown argues that he could still have got to Holland Walk and killed Miss Paulson. You may think that is very unlikely. If he was at the football match then he could not have been in Holland Walk. He says he told the police he was there because he believed there was a video recording of him in the Walk. Is that true or is it a lie? People lie for many reasons including to bolster a defence. Only if you come to the conclusion that the only reason he has lied, and he has got Mr Walker to lie, is to cover his guilt, can you convict.

'So what is the evidence about the alibi? First it came to light in the most unusual way. An undercover policewoman was sent to befriend Mr Barker who was, very unusually, on bail. She failed to obtain any information from him that may have supported the Crown's case. Instead he talked about his love of football and his support of Chelsea, disclosing that he had been to the football match between them and Everton, at their home ground. That game was the same night as the murder. Mr Barker did not give the policewoman that information in anticipation of these proceedings. It was entirely spontaneous. On the other hand his explanation for saying he was in Holland Park is questionable.'

Cassie kept a straight face but inwardly winced at the judge's comment. Brian Claxton nodded at the judge's words.

'His solicitor, Mr Durrant, was told by Sergeant Dean that the recording did not show Barker at all.

There is no doubt that was conveyed to him. He says, and the officer conceded, he was distressed. Is that sufficient explanation for the admission? He is a keen Chelsea supporter, would he really have forgotten the date of the match, even after six weeks? In addition he learnt of the murder the day after he was at the game and it was reported in the same newspaper, a link between the two, which may have imprinted it on his mind. It is entirely a matter for you.

'And what of Edwin Walker, Hinds? He has a string of criminal convictions and admits he has been dishonest under oath before. He was at the game on the eighteenth of September. Was his friend, not his best buddy, Lenny Barker with him or not?'

That was a bit tough on Lenny, Cassie thought. Judge Crabtree could have said it was difficult to remember where you were on any particular day, but he had come down against the defence at this late stage in his summing up.

'Finally, two more directions of law. You have heard that Mr Barker is of good character, he has no previous convictions. Well, it doesn't mean he didn't commit the offence. All offenders are of good character at some stage. But it is something you can take into account when considering whether it is more or less likely that he murdered Miss Paulson and put it in the scales on his side.

'The other concerns majority verdicts. You may have heard of majority verdicts but for now you must strive to reach a verdict on which you all agree. The time may come when you can reach a majority verdict, but before that time arrives I will have you back and give further directions. Now when the jury bailiff has

328

been sworn, go with her, take all your papers with you, and try to reach a unanimous verdict.'

Mrs Beswick stood up, took the bible in her right hand and took the oath, promising to keep the jury in a private and convenient place and not to allow anyone to approach them without the judge's authority, until they had arrived at their verdict, and then asked them to follow her. She waited by the judges' door, as they collected their belongings, the files of exhibits and their notes. Cassie watched them anxiously, none of them turned to look at either her or Lenny as they were ushered out of the room.

Judge Crabtree nodded at the barristers and followed them out. Cassie made a pile out of her files and pushed them to one side. The court would reconvene soon, and another trial would start, while she waited for the verdict.

Chapter 43

On her way into the Old Bailey, on the second day of the jury's deliberations, Cassie met Lenny's mother and sister.

'Miss Hardman,' Mrs Barker said, 'Will the jury be long?' Her voice sounded tired and her eyes were red-rimmed, either from too little sleep or from crying or both.

'I really don't know.' Cassie searched for something to say to give the woman some comfort. 'We never know what goes on in the jury room, but perhaps they are taking their time because they aren't sure.'

Mrs Barker looked at her dolefully. 'How is he?'

'I'll go down and see him before court starts then, when the jury retire, I'll come and meet you here.' She pointed to the waiting area at the entrance. 'Let you know how he's coping.'

Once she was robed, she made her way down to the cells and waited for Lenny to arrive in the interview cell. He stumbled into the room his face pale, his left cheek twitching. He brought a crumpled cigarette out of his pocket and lit it.

'I didn't know you smoked,' Cassie said.

'It gives you something to do.' He laughed harshly. 'I'm not very good at rolling my own,' he added as he picked tobacco from his tongue, before lighting the cigarette.

'How are you feeling?' Cassie asked.

'Sick. Why are they taking so long?'

'I don't know, but it suggests that someone at least thinks you're not guilty.' She didn't like to use the word innocent. 'They have to reach a unanimous verdict for now. I think the judge will give a majority direction around the midday adjournment.'

'A majority verdict? What's a majority?'

'At least ten of them must agree.'

'And if they don't?'

'They will be discharged and there will be a retrial.'

'The whole thing again?' he exclaimed.

'Yes. But we're not there yet. What shall I tell your mother about you? She's very concerned.'

'Tell her I'm OK.' Lenny looked down and then directly at Cassie. His eyes were glistening but he went on, struggling over the words, 'Tell her I love her, and Jane.'

Cassie nodded at him, stood up and momentarily put a hand on his shoulder. They walked together along the low harshly-lit corridor, he on his way to the holding cells and Cassie out past the old door from the Newgate prison and into the public halls.

Once Judge Crabtree had reminded the jury they were to try to reach a unanimous verdict, and sent them back to their room, he said, 'Miss Hardman, Mr Jennings. If there is no verdict by twelve noon, I propose giving them a majority direction as soon as possible after that, unless either of you have anything to say on the matter.' They both said they had not.

Once out of the court Cassie returned to the waiting room and found Mrs Barker and Jane sat side by side on a low bench. 'He's being brave, and...' she paused searching for the right words, 'he wants you to know he loves you both.' Jane sniffed and then blew hard into a white tissue. His mother smiled weakly at her.

'That's my boy,' she said trying to look brave herself.

331

'Has Tim been to see you this morning? I haven't seen him.' Cassie asked Mrs Barker.

'He's trying to arrange for us to wait in the canteen, rather than sit in the public gallery.'

'Fine. At least you can get a coffee there.' She tried to find something else to say, some way of reassuring them that everything would be all right, but she couldn't lie to them, and she didn't know what the outcome of the trial would be.

She was about to say she had some paperwork to do, when Tim came up to them and said to Mrs Barker and Jane, 'Right, I've said I'd look after you two in the canteen. Come on, let's get a coffee or something.' And then to Cassie, 'We'll see you later.'

Cassie was grateful to him for letting her escape upstairs. She hated this point in a trial; she never knew what to do. She had brought some work with her, but she knew she would not be able to concentrate on it, and didn't even get the papers out of her bag. She sat down in one of the easy chairs at the library end of the Bar Mess picked up a newspaper and tried reading the articles in it, but didn't find the antics of celebrities interesting enough to hold her attention. A group of barristers from another trial came and bought coffees. She knew two of the group and went over to sit with them. They were waiting for the judge trying their case to finish a bail application, and soon they were called back to court. Every time a noise came from the loud speakers, she waited for the tannoy to call for all parties in the case of Barker to go to court, but each time it was for a different case

She hoped the jury were deeply divided and not just one or two people holding out for a not guilty plea. Cassie looked at her watch, another hour had elapsed and soon it would be noon and time for the majority direction. She continued to check the time, counting the minutes as they ticked by, until, just after twelve, she was summoned to court.

'He's going to give the majority direction,' Mrs Beswick told her and David Jennings, who had joined her outside the door of the courtroom. They walked in together and took their seats while the jury filed in, and Lenny was brought up from the cells to take his place in the dock. Cassie was dismayed when she saw that Deepa Nadswallah was sitting in the foreman's place, and next to her was Brian Claxton. As soon as Lenny appeared, white and anxious, Cassie slipped back to tell him that the jury had not reached a verdict. Judge Crabtree waited until she was back in her seat and then nodded at the court clerk, a blonde haired young woman, who asked first Lenny to stand and then the foreman of the jury. Deepa Nadswallah stood up with her hands clasped in front of her. The clerk continued, 'Madame Foreman, just answer my first question, yes or no. Have you reached a verdict upon which you are all agreed?'

Deepa Nadswallah took a deep breath and said, 'No, My Lord.'

'Thank you,' said Judge Crabtree, 'Now the time has come when I can give you a majority verdict, that means I can take a verdict on which at least ten of you are agreed. Now, please leave the court, return to the jury room and try to reach a unanimous verdict if you can, but if you cannot and at least ten of you are agreed, then I can accept that.'

While he was talking the jury members were looking at each other. Cassie saw Amanda Fry shaking her head and Colin Heap put a hand to his mouth.

333

Some of the others looked disappointed, and some just resigned. They picked up their papers, shuffled out of the jury box and left the court.

'I'll adjourn, while the next case is assembled,' Judge Crabtree said, and, nodding at counsel's row, he left the bench. Cassie walked to the dock and told Lenny she would come down to see him and then left the court, with David Jennings not far behind her.

'Looks like we might have a hung jury,' David said.

'Mm, possibly. I suppose you'd go again?'

'I can't see any reason why not, unless there is a match with the knife. I suppose we might reconsider then.'

Cassie turned swiftly away and walked towards the lobby, as David strolled along behind her. He caught up with her by the lifts, but she was too anxious for any small talk so she ignored him as they waited. Two lifts arrived at the same time and Cassie got into the one that would take her down to the basement, but before the doors closed a voice behind said, 'Mr Jennings.' From inside the lift Cassie saw Sergeant Dean.

'Mr Jennings, can I have a word, Sir,' the officer said.

As the doors to the lift Cassie was in closed she heard Colin Dean say, 'It's urgent, Sir.'

Chapter 44

There was very little Cassie could say to Lenny once she had explained the direction about taking majority verdicts again. Nevertheless she stayed with him, chatting about nothing in particular to help him pass the time. He didn't want to talk and they soon lapsed into silence. She waited for a few minutes in the hope he would say something, or ask her questions, but he was sunk in his own misery and she was superfluous.

'Lenny, I'm going back upstairs. I have some telephone calls to make. Is there anything you want?'

He shook his head and stood up to go back to his cell. Cassie followed him. Once out of the custody suite, she took the lift back to the Bar Mess, took out her mobile and phoned her clerks to tell them the state of play in Lenny's trial.

She looked up to see who else was in the Bar Mess, and saw Eleanor at the far end of the room, waving at her. Eleanor was the last person she wanted to talk to, but she couldn't ignore her senior colleague.

'I'm pleased to see you, has Richard spoken to you about Alison?' Eleanor asked.

Cassie shook her head, 'No, should he have done?'

'He's spoken to everyone else and we've all agreed she should be offered a tenancy. I understand he's already spoken to her and she will be joining us at the beginning of next month.'

'Fine,' said Cassie, suddenly weary of fighting, 'At least it is another woman.'

'Cassie, I don't give advice very often, but I suggest you accept this graciously. Alison's husband will be sending a lot of work to us in the future, and you'll benefit if you don't continue your opposition to her. It's the sort of work that puts you in front of the right judges, particularly if you want to apply for silk.'

Cassie didn't reply. Eleanor thought she might want to apply for silk in the future; she found that rather flattering. As she turned away to go back to the robing room, she saw David Jennings coming up the stairs, he looked round, and when he spotted her, made a beeline towards her.

'I've been looking for you,' he said.

'I've been in the cells. Is there a verdict?'

'No, but something has happened that you and Marcus should know about. I've told Howard and he said to tell you immediately, and then the judge. I've asked the usher to get Crabtree to rise and see us in chambers immediately.'

'What is it?'

'The police have arrested another man, who may be the killer.'

Before Cassie could speak, they were called back to court. As they rushed down the stairs, David told her about the arrest of Hugo Duff and the result of the forensic tests.

'You're saying the DNA profile from this man Duff matches the DNA of the skin under her fingernails. He's clearly the killer.'

'He's not been interviewed yet, and he may have an explanation for the match.'

'Come on, Compton said she scratched the man.'

'It's a matter for the judge. I'm just telling you what's happened.'

Judge Crabtree had already adjourned to his chambers, when Cassie and David arrived in the

336

courtroom, and a number of barristers were lounging around, chatting amongst themselves. Mrs Beswick led them through to the judges' corridor and into Judge Crabtree's room.

'Now what's this all about, David?' the judge asked.

'The police have arrested a man for drug dealing, and as usual, they took a saliva specimen. The DNA was compared with the DNA from the skin under Miss Paulson's nails. They matched. The man, his name is Duff, is a drug supplier, and that may be the link to Shelley Paulson. In addition he has a mobile phone registered in her name, he fits the description of the killer and there is other evidence that may tie him to Campden Hill Road on the night of the murder.'

'Are you saying this man is the murderer?' Judge Crabtree asked.

'He hasn't been interviewed yet. He may have an explanation for the matching profiles. If they had been intimate for example, or shared drugs. It's probable that he supplied her with drugs.'

'Mm. What are you suggesting, I do? I don't see how I can adjourn the case now the jury have retired. I could discharge them, but I think the Crown would have to indicate they no longer wish to proceed against Barker.'

'I'm not in a position to take that course at the moment. Mr O'Connor is adamant Barker is the killer and we are trying to get the solicitor from the CPS to come to the Bailey for a case conference.'

Judge Crabtree got up and strode to the window, looking down on the featureless square below. 'What have you got to say, Miss Hardman? Cassie, is it?'

'Cassie, yes. You should discharge the jury. It would be unfair not to do so,' Cassie replied.

'There is a positive identification of your client and his admission he was in the park that night. I know Dr Pretty's report was not put before the jury, because she couldn't be certain it was Barker's fingerprint, but...' He stopped for a few seconds before continuing, 'The evidence against this other man is limited to the DNA match, something he may be able to explain. You're right, Compton's evidence is that he saw Miss Paulson raise her hand as if scratching like a cat, that's if he is a reliable witness. After all. if this other man is the killer, his identification of your man is wrong and if he's wrong about one thing then...' He paused before saying, 'Have you both spoken to your leaders?'

'I haven't had the opportunity,' said Cassie. David said he had told Howard briefly what had happened but nothing else.

'I think you should both have some time to consider what action you wish to take, or rather wish me to take. Of course the jury may pre-empt you.' He ushered them out of his room and they both made their way back along the corridor.

'I hope we get the right door,' David said, 'I'm always terrified of walking into the wrong courtroom. You'd think they could afford to put numbers on them.'

Cassie wasn't in the mood for humour; she felt the judge should have discharged the jury from reaching a verdict. It was obvious that this other guy was responsible for Shelley Paulson's death. David held the door to the court open for her. Everyone in the room leapt to their feet as Cassie came onto the judge's bench, followed by David, who said, 'It's all right, you don't have to be upstanding for me, yet.'

The barristers in court laughed and someone threw a ball of paper at him. David was now leading the way across the courtroom. At the door he paused and put two fingers up at the men inside. They could still hear the laughter as the door closed behind them.

Colin Dean was outside the courtroom with, to Cassie's surprise, Alex Seymour.

'Sir,' said Sergeant Dean, 'This is DC Seymour, who arrested Duff.' He then added, 'Mr Jennings is prosecuting Barker. I think you know Miss Hardman.'

Alex nodded at the two barristers, but said nothing.

'Well, DC Seymour. You've put the cat amongst the pigeons, linking Duff with Miss Paulson. The judge won't do anything unless we throw our hand in, and we need to discuss that with the CPS and Mr O'Connor. I hope they'll arrive before too long.' Jennings said.

Marcus Pike was in the middle of cross-examining a witness when Cassie located him. She walked round the back of the court and sat behind him. At first he didn't notice her, but when he turned round to speak to his current junior, he raised his eyebrows, as if to ask why she was there. She wrote on a piece of paper, 'Help! The police have arrested a man who may be the murderer.' Leaning over she placed the note on his lectern, Marcus stopped mid-sentence, staring at the words.

'Yes, Mr Pike, is there a problem?' the judge asked.

'My Lord, a difficulty has arisen in a case in which I am instructed in another court.'

'I think we can finish this witness before we need adjourn, Mr Pike. You have nearly completed cross-examination, have you not?' The tone adopted by the judge made it clear that he thought Marcus should finish whether he had or not.

Marcus asked another few questions and then sat down.

'Right, I'll adjourn now. Do you have any idea how long you will be, Mr Pike?'

'No, My Lord. I hope half an hour?' Marcus said.

'Half an hour. Members of the jury, we will reconvene then.'

Marcus was half way round the courtroom by the time the judge had left the bench. He told his junior to hold the fort and asked Cassie what was going on. She repeated what David Jennings had told Judge Crabtree about the forensic evidence and the proposed conference.

The discussions with the police and the representative from the Crown Prosecution Service took longer than Howard and David had anticipated, leaving Cassie and Marcus waiting. Marcus was anxious about his other case, and went back into court to ask the judge to wait a little longer. It was a further twenty-five minutes before the prosecuting team appeared outside Court 12. 'Have you seen O'Connor about dropping the case against Barker?' Marcus asked.

'We've had a conference and we want to proceed. If the forensics had been able to show that the blood on the knife was Shelley's, then the position might have been different, but without that they think the case against Duff is weak, particularly with the positive ID of your client,' Howard said.

'Come on, the further tests on that sample may take ages. I think the jury should be discharged now,' Marcus replied.

'I have instructions to proceed. The CPS view is that if the verdict is guilty, then your lad sits it out, and if the result of the DNA analysis confirms the blood is Shelley's, then they will agree to an appeal and bail pending the hearing.' Howard was being very firm.

Cassie looked at the two men facing each other defiantly, and said calmly, 'It's not just the forensics, surely if the jury knew Shelley had a pimp, a man who is a drug dealer, who fits the description of the killer, and who hid a blood-stained knife in the gardens close to where she lived, don't you think that might just affect their verdict? Shouldn't the jury be discharged whatever the forensics so that on the retrial we can call that evidence? That would be fair and just, wouldn't it?'

'Just what I was going to say,' said Marcus as he pushed through the door into the courtroom, and then asked Mrs Beswick to inform the judge that counsel wished to see him.

'In court or in Chambers?' she asked.

'In court, I think. Do you agree, Howard?'

Howard said he did, and she bustled off, grumbling under her breath at the highhanded behaviour of some people.

While they waited for Judge Crabtree to come into court, Marcus was summoned back to his other case. 'You'll have to explain what's happened, and ask for the jury to be discharged. Just repeat what you said to Howard,' he told her.

Cassie told herself she was perfectly capable of making the application. She looked up at the public gallery, where Mrs Barker and Jane were leaning over in anticipation, no doubt, of a verdict. Mrs Paulson had returned to her seat near the exhibit table, hoping that

341

at least this part of her ordeal was nearly over, her face as immobile as it had been throughout the trial. Cassie wondered what she was thinking, and how she would react to the news about the arrest of Duff.

When Judge Crabtree was back on the bench, Cassie apologised for Marcus's absence and told him she was applying for a discharge of the jury. She suggested that Howard might want to give the court the details of the investigations that had led to the arrest of Duff. Judge Crabtree agreed, and Howard explained about how the knife was found in the gardens of Cotburn Square, together with a box containing drugs, both bearing Duff's fingerprints. He told the court of the similarity between the initial description given by Mr Compton and Duff, including the birthmark, which he conceded could give the impression of a beard. Then he outlined the result of the DNA analysis so far and the tests that were still continuing.

There was a gasp from the public gallery and Mrs Barker was on her feet, yelling 'Let my son go. He didn't kill her,' before the attendant asked her to sit down again. She began to sob. Cassie looked round at Lenny, who looked bemused, clearly he couldn't understand what was happening.

When Howard had finished, Cassie repeated that they were applying to have the jury discharged, because this further evidence supported the defence case that someone else was the killer of Shelley Paulson.

Judge Crabtree thought for a moment and then said, 'I am inclined to agree with you. You should have the opportunity of calling whatever evidence is admissible on your client's behalf. I'm not sure it is all relevant, but the DNA evidence in relation to the fingernail

342

scrapings is compelling. It would throw doubt on the reliability of Mr Compton's identification. Miss Hardman, unless Mr Alsopp has anything else to say, I will have the jury brought back and discharge them from reaching a verdict.'

Before Howard could respond, there was a knock on the judges' entrance and Mrs Beswick popped her head round the door. 'We have a verdict, My Lord,' she said.

Cassie closed her eyes in disbelief. The discharge of the jury was now impossible.

'Miss Hardman, I'll give you fifteen minutes to check the law, but as I understand it I must take this verdict.'

'Thank you, My Lord,' mumbled Cassie. She began to rifle through Archbold, looking for the passages on juries and verdicts. When she found the paragraphs, they confirmed her understanding of the law. She could find no exceptions. 'He must take the verdict,' she said to Howard and David. They agreed, and Howard asked Mrs Beswick to tell the judge they were of the same opinion and the jury could be brought into court.

While they waited, the court began to fill up with police officers, probation officers, crime reporters, solicitors and barristers, as if summoned to witness the moment of drama that was about to unfold. Cassie was never sure how word spread around the courthouse, it was as if the very stones of the Old Bailey whispered of suspense.

The jury filed into the jury box, Deepa Nadswallah taking the front seat nearest to the judge. She held a large piece of paper in her hands, which she was turning over and over. She looked towards the judge throughout the time the other jurors took to sit down and rearrange their belongings. Would any of them look at Lenny? Cassie wasn't sure it was true that they would direct their attention towards the defendant if they were going to acquit, but nevertheless she scanned the two rows of faces. Amanda Conrad was pushing her bag under the bench, Brian Claxton was looking up at the public gallery. Anna Fry and Colin Heap did turn towards the dock, raising Cassie's hopes.

Marcus slipped back into court and resumed his seat in front of Cassie. When she told him the jury had a verdict he leant back, his left elbow on the front of her bench, his head propped on his hand, and said, 'Actually it's academic. If they convict we have a cast-iron appeal. We couldn't lose.' He grinned at the thought. The room became very quiet as the clerk turned to the dock and said, 'Prisoner at the Bar, will you please stand.' Lenny stood slowly leaning on the front of the dock to support himself, his knuckles white as he tensed against the ledge.

The clerk then faced the jury, 'Will the foreman of the jury please stand.' Deepa Nadswallah got up, the piece of paper still clutched in her hand. The clerk continued, 'Madame Foreman, please answer my first question, yes or no. Have you reached a verdict on which you are all agreed?'

'No.'

'Can you answer my next question simply, yes or no. Have you reached a verdict on which at least ten of you are agreed?'

'Yes, we have.'

'Madame Foreman, do you find the defendant, Leonard Barker, guilty or not guilty of the murder of Shelley Paulson?'

For a moment the court was still, as if everyone in the room was posing for a photograph. Cassie's breathing stalled and, in the audible silence, she thought her heart missed a beat, and then Deepa Nadswallah said, 'Not Guilty, My Lord.'

Cassie looked down clenched her fists under the bench, and suppressed the word yes that came to her lips. Marcus rose to his feet and asked for Lenny to be discharged. When Judge Crabtree confirmed Lenny was free, she spun round and saw him wave at his mother, his life restored to him. He looked towards Cassie, a broad smile across his face, his eyes alight again, and then he was led back to the cells to have his property returned.

She began to gather her papers together, tying them with pink tape. Out of the corner of her eye she saw Alex and DCI O'Connor talking to David Jennings, and Sergeant Dean guiding Mrs Paulson from the courtroom. Cassie wondered how she felt; Mrs Paulson would have been told by the police that they had her daughter's killer, yet he was walking free and she was no nearer knowing who had killed Shelley, or why.

She caught Alex's eye and mouthed the words 'Thank you.' Alex nodded in acknowledgement before following DCI O'Connor out. She hoped Alex wouldn't be in any trouble.

Cassie realized Marcus was saying he had to get back to his other case and asked her to bundle up his papers and leave them at the back of the court for his clerk to collect. 'Congratulations,' he said. 'You've been very resourceful. Have you got a red bag?' Cassie told him she hadn't.

'I'll get you one, you deserve it. I'll be in touch.'

A red bag, the replacement for the blue brocade one Cassie had bought when she first qualified, was a symbol of success, a gift from a silk to a junior barrister whose work had been exceptional. Now she would ring Ben and arrange to celebrate her victory with him, but first she needed to speak to the clerks. She turned on her mobile, Jack, the senior clerk answered. She told him the verdict, and that Marcus had said he would give her a red bag.

'Very good, Miss Hardman, and a red bag from Mr Pike. Now tomorrow, there's a trial at Snaresbrook, just a shoplifter, that's OK isn't it?'

Lightning Source UK Ltd.
Milton Keynes UK
UKOW04f0208080115

244127UK00002B/22/P